CAGE OF GLASS

Cage of Glass Series Book 1

GENEVIEVE CROWNSON

Dreamspire Publishing

Dreamspire Publishing

www.genevievecrownson.com

Publisher's Note: This is a work of fiction. Names, characters, places, and incidents are a product of the author's imagination. Locales and public names are sometimes used for atmospheric purposes. Any resemblance to actual people, living or dead, or to businesses, companies, events, institutions, or locales is completely coincidental.

Cover Art by Rebecca Frank

Cage of Glass/ Genevieve Crownson—1st edition

ISBN: 978-1736171103

For more information on this novel or Genevieve Crownson's other books please visit www.genevievecrownson.com

For anyone who felt like they never fit in. This one's for you.

CHAPTER 1

My entire life had been determined by an intricate eye scan, sealing me into a Pandora's box of terrifying nightmares.

I was sixteen years old and already knew my place in this world. There were no dreams, no hopes for the future. That die had been cast before my first birthday.

I suppose that is how I found myself with a hollow belly and a terrible thirst as I strolled through the marketplace of W1 Nova, my hometown.

I scanned the crowd. Today's errand had become routine, but it still left me with sweaty palms and a roaring in my eardrums. Despite the tight knot in my stomach, the raging storm that ripped through my veins spurred me on, empowering me to keep going. I thought of my brothers and sisters, their sunken faces raw with hunger; I couldn't come home empty-handed.

The government ruling implemented years ago claimed the threads in the eye revealed personality, ideal occupation, and social standing. When born, you were taken from your birth parents to a temporary facility where a scan divulged your appropriate placement in this world. That way, those of like kind would stay together. Apparently, our eyes betrayed us, and my siblings and I found ourselves at the bottom of the fishbowl, scrambling to survive. The so-called windows to the soul left me with only burdens and heartache. I gritted my teeth and squared my shoulders, determined to see this through. Wallowing in self-pity would accomplish nothing.

Standing in the shadows cast by the late day sun, my over-sized, green-hooded sweatshirt hid my raven black hair and pale skin. I'd done this so many times before—observing the masses—seeking out the foolish and the rich. And I was always faster and smarter.

I spotted my first victim almost immediately, pushing his way through the crowded square. He was a tall man with a slicked back blonde mop revealing a sharp widow's peak. He wore a tailored tight-fitting suit you just knew was designed especially for him, and a solid gold ring glinted on his pinky finger. He oozed wealth—a definite oddity in this God forsaken place.

I narrowed in on him, moving silently alongside the periphery of the old brick building. It housed the now non-existent bank, which folded a few years back when cash became an outdated form of currency. The new system used microchips implanted in your hand, much more efficient. At least, that is what the government had assured the people. They told everyone they would never again be caught in a situation where they would be without funds. That is, assuming you had any to begin with.

I gripped the stone cold brick in anticipation, waiting for the perfect moment, receding even further back under the crumbling archway. Nobody would notice me here, and it was the ideal place to scope out the playing field.

As the gentleman grew near, the smell of food from his takeout made my mouth water. I stepped out, enveloping myself in the most congested part of the horde, never taking my eyes off the expensively dressed man. The jostling of warm bodies and the odd bodily smells were familiar, and I granted my muscles permission to relax, as I stepped closer to my target. I opened my palms, letting my arms hang limp, giving the appearance nothing was amiss, and then I brushed by him, just one of many in this pushy throng, and silently lifted a single container from his bag. I allowed the tide of people to take me down toward Main Street, but slowed my steps allowing space between me and my mark. The guy hadn't spotted me. Not that he ever would. I'd learned to blend in years ago. It was necessary for survival.

As the monied man got further and further away, unaware he was missing half his dinner, I peeked inside the box. Chinese noodles. I forced myself not to steal even one noodle, abruptly closing the container. My siblings needed this first. They were younger.

I continued to wind my way through town, past a lone café and a seedy bar where a few men who couldn't afford to drink milled around outside. They leered through the window at the patrons who had ample cash credits to purchase their wine and whiskey. Which, to be honest, weren't many.

I reached the end of the stalls just as the vendors began to close up shop, evening rolling in, their tired shoulders slumped over and weary. Every day was a battle, a hope that that they'd sold enough to keep their families going and would not be cast out into the street. They were so preoccupied they didn't even notice when I pinched some produce—a couple of apples here, a potato or two there.

It was too easy.

As it turned to dusk, I came to the edge of the main drag of town. It parted into two roads, one leading back home and the other to the nicer side of the borough where the mayor lived in all his finery. My mouth grew metallic just thinking about it. But my mind never left the game, remaining hidden in the now dwindling group of people.

It only took a few more paces to find myself at the entrance of the local grocer that stood smack in the middle of the fork in the road. It was a government owned building run by a man named Harold. He was an easy target; always too busy flirting with Amara, the pretty checkout girl, to notice anything. He never even realized I was inside his shop; I was that quick. Grabbing a small box of chocolates, a loaf of bread and medicine, I slipped past them like a whisper on the wind and grinned, proud of my haul. My siblings would have plenty to eat tonight.

Laden down with as much as I could carry, I headed home, my pockets bulging with my prizes. To comfort myself, and keep my attention off my numb toes in my threadbare shoes, I counted the number of trees I passed, the way I often did. It kept my thoughts from going haywire with worry about everything else going on in my life.

The aroma of the fresh bread I'd hidden under my hoodie made my stomach growl. Instead of caving to my hunger, I grabbed some semi-clean snow from a low hanging branch and stuffed it in my mouth, to attempt to appease my aching belly.

But it only drove my teeth to chatter.

I picked up the pace, noting the sun setting over the horizon. If I was out after dark, I would get mugged. Or maybe something worse.

Poverty and hunger brought out the worst in people.

It was my job to keep my family safe. Nothing could happen to me. Their lives depended on it.

CHAPTER 2

Despite the moon rising in the night sky and the shadows edging their way in, I decided to take the risk and stop in at Mrs. Peters'. She was one of the oldest people living in Nova, since most here died long before old age set in—usually much too young, claimed by sickness or starvation.

But Mrs. Peters was sick, barely surviving in fact, due to a heart condition. To make things worse, her medicine was ridiculously expensive. I'd known Mrs. Peters my whole life, and she'd always showed me kindness. That's why I didn't think twice about stealing a few doses of her meds while in town—enough to last until next week. I was all she had. Her only living relative had died in a smallpox epidemic the previous winter.

I knocked on the door. *One. Two. Three. Four.* It was an even number. I couldn't stand an uneven sum of knocks. I waited a beat, then heard the slow familiar shuffle of Mrs. Peter's worn slippers as she made her way across the rough stone floor.

"Who's there?" A tired old voice croaked from the other side of the battered door.

"It's only me, Mrs. Peters. Luna? From down the road?"

The bolt released, and there she stood, draped in a threadbare gown, her hair hanging damp and limp around her now sallow face. Her green eyes were alert today, much less cloudy than yesterday; I breathed a sigh of relief.

"I brought you more medicine. This should last you for a little while."

She took the bottle of pills from my outstretched hand and ushered me in. "Thank you, my dear. You're too good to me. Now come in out of the cold, child. You'll catch your death."

I stepped inside, pushing my hoodie down off my head, but soon realized I'd acted too hastily, the place wasn't much warmer than outside. The little house reeked of rotting wet wood, and mold clung to the thin timbered walls. I worried how that would affect her health. The freezing floor penetrated through my threadbare shoes to the soles of my feet, and I shivered. I crossed the sparse but clean living room and bent over to poke the flames dwindling in the hearth. "It sure is cold in here, Mrs. Peters."

"I told you to call me Dara," she said irritably.

I hid a grin, my back still turned to the fire. Glad to see she hadn't lost her snarky spirit. "Sorry, Dara. Force of habit. I've called you that so long, it's kind of stuck in my brain." I picked a log from the basket and tossed it into the flames, making a mental note to cut her more wood tomorrow. She barely had enough to get her through the night.

Mrs. Peters tsk tsk'd under her breath and shuffled to the kitchen which only occupied a small corner of her one-room living space. Her mattress, in the opposite recess, lay rumpled and unmade. "We've been through too much together to have you calling me Mrs. Peters. Makes me sound like an old schoolmarm."

Satisfied with the now blazing fire, I turned to adjust her bed, ignoring her slew of complaints. Mrs. Peters always made a mountain out of a molehill. But I loved her just the same.

"What in God's name do you think you're doing Luna?" she warned.

"Helping you tidy up a bit."

"Lord knows your Mama has you doing enough of that. Come sit at the table and have some soup; you're probably run through with cold."

"No, Dara, I don't—"

"Sit!"

I dropped the tattered sheets mid-tuck and obeyed, not wanting to upset her. The truth was, Mrs. Peters didn't have enough food for herself, let alone me. I didn't want to take it from her. Still, I risked her wrath once more, and gave the bed one last smooth down with my hand, unable to stand the mussed quilting.

"I managed to get some bread today; let me share it with you, Dara," I said, distracting her.

Mrs. Peters shook her head vehemently. "Absolutely not. I'm not taking sustenance from your young babes' mouths. I know that's for your siblings. Now sit down while it's hot." She fussed, agitated as she ladled the steaming liquid into cracked earthenware bowls—two of the few dishes in the little shack.

I sank down on the floor beside an archaic wood crate she used for a table. She set the soup in front of me and I inhaled its fragrance. It didn't smell like much of anything, except maybe dirty old socks. I waited for Dara to ease herself down and then straightened the dish so it lined up with the edge of the makeshift table, burning myself on the bowl in the process. I quickly put my thumb to my mouth to cool the stinging and to stop myself from cursing in Mrs. Peters' presence.

I picked up the chipped wooden spoon and dipped it into the hot broth. There wasn't much to this soup. I plucked out the lone carrot from the thin greyish liquid and brought it to my lips. The water had some flavor, a sort of feeble chicken taste. I couldn't complain; it filled a small void, and I could pretend I was full. Besides, it was more palatable than snow. I devoured the meager offering, ignoring the permanent stomach rumbles inside me.

Satisfied I was eating, Mrs. Peters started in on her own

meal. After only one bite she dropped her spoon in disgust and scowled. "You can't call this soup, Luna. I'm sorry I even made you eat it. To tell you the truth, I'm looking forward to my death; I hope to forget this place."

I put a hand over hers. It felt cold as ice. "It's perfectly fine Mrs. Peters. It stops the ache a little. And you shouldn't talk like that. Don't give in to them; that's what they want. We have to be strong."

Dara wiped her tears with a shaking finger. "It's just not good enough. Ever since that rebel leader Roy Ball Red came into power no one has cared about our agriculture. How are we going to survive if we can't even grow food in this God-forsaken place? His keep what you kill motto is meaningless. All it will do is straight up kill us. Literally."

"I know. But what can we do, Dara? Our lives were mapped out for us before we even spoke our first words. Sometimes, I wish I could just rip my eyes out and replace them with ones that wouldn't leave me and my family with such empty bellies. But since that isn't an option, we do what we can."

Mrs. Peters snorted. "It's all a farce. I remember Roy Ball Red said he would free our society. But in reality, we've gone back to the old Viking motto. Be fearless or be conquered. It doesn't help the poor and downtrodden." She paused, her tired green eyes looking kindly at me. "You're fearless, Luna. That's how I know you'll be okay. Just don't let them take you, all right?" she whispered.

I was startled by Dara's quick turn from outrage to concern for me—worried she might be going a bit senile. That was the third warning she'd given me about someone taking me in a matter of days. But what information could Dara possibly obtain in her remote corner of the world? She rarely left her house now. Perhaps it was only her fears affecting her good sense. God knows this place was full of everyone's trepidation.

"Of course I won't, Dara. I'll always be here for you and make sure you're okay." I knotted my hands together so tightly my knuckles turned white. My blood boiled in anger over all the innocent souls suffering. People like Dara deserved the best care, not to be cast off to die. Hell, we all deserved better. How dare they decide based on our eyes who we should be and how we should be treated?

Mrs. Peters, blind to my inner turmoil, smiled and picked up her spoon again as if satisfied. "Good, I'm glad you agree. I can feel better about going when it's my time, knowing you can take care of yourself. Just promise me one thing."

"What's that Dara?"

"Promise me that no matter what happens, you'll always seek the truth. Nothing is as it seems, Luna. Remember that."

Puzzled and not knowing what else to say, I replied, "I promise."

Mrs. Peters gave me a nod, and I pushed my empty bowl aside, her ominous words hanging in the air between us.

CHAPTER 3

By the time I left Dara's, the menacing shadows of the evening had turned into a blanket of darkness. The acrid odor of burning fires in the shacks I passed on the way home filled my nostrils, and I coughed as the hazy smoke traveled down to my lungs.

There had been no electricity in this neighborhood for over ten years, leaving the run-down town without light, save for a few candles glowing in the windows. So when I turned the corner to my street and saw my home lit up like a Christmas tree, my heart leapt in my throat.

Something was wrong.

My hunger pangs were instantly replaced with acid bile. Every hair on my body pricked up. I picked up the pace and rushed the few yards home.

We'd lived here as long as I could remember. Mama complained incessantly about our old run-down cottage, but in truth, it was the only home I'd ever known.

It was bigger than Mrs. Peters' place—we actually had a couple of rooms—but it was drafty and cold. And no matter how much you cleaned up—the dirt and the dust always found its way back in through the broken slats. I pushed hard against the warped door. It required an exact amount of pressure to open due to the swelling wood.

As I passed through the entryway, I grabbed a burning candle sitting on the sideboard and crossed the misshapen floorboards to follow the bright light permeating from the living room. I discovered all five of my siblings huddled together on the rickety couch. Their faces, reflected in the soft glow of the lantern, looked pale and drawn, their eyes big as saucers. I made a mental note to steal more food next trip to town; they obviously weren't eating enough.

Something else itched at me though; this whole scenario wasn't right. They were dressed in their shabby coats and shoes rather than their bedclothes when it was well past the little one's bedtime. I glanced down and discovered our family's only small suitcase tucked away in the corner. *What the hell?* My gaze jumped back to my siblings, examining them further. A few tell-tale, blotchy red marks had bloomed on their necks and faces, indicating Mama had scrubbed the grime off their now shiny cheeks. My heart lurched. Mama never paid any attention to them, ever.

"What's going on?" I demanded moving closer to my brothers and sisters. "Where's Mama?"

No one answered. "Look. I got us some bread, and I even scored some takeout noodles. And as a special treat, a small box of chocolates. But no fighting over the candy," I warned pulling my bundles out from under my hoodie and placing them on the overturned crate we used as a coffee table.

They stared at me like Zombies for a moment longer, before my littlest sister, Trinity, suddenly burst into tears and ran over to me, hugging my legs.

I disengaged her tiny arms and knelt down beside her. "What is it Trinity, what's happened—"

I was cut off by the stomp of heavy boots on the staircase; the stink of too strong cologne filled the small space. No one in this house wore cologne. I quickly stood up and pushed Trinity behind me. I glanced at my siblings, the blood drained from their faces—and they were quiet. Too quiet.

"Good, you're home," a familiar voice said.

I pivoted toward the sound and saw Mama in the doorway, her crystal blue eyes ice cold.

"What is it, Mama? Why are the children so scared? I thought I heard boots on the stairs. Is someone else in the house?"

"You're being returned as government property, Luna. I'm sorry; you've left me no choice."

She stepped aside and a government agent came briskly into the room. He was a massive man, at least six foot four, with blond hair and piercing brown eyes that looked almost black. His face was a mask of indifference; forbidding lines etched his mouth, causing a permanent frown, bulging muscles rippled under his crisp shirt. His uniform was the usual Government Issue, grey and blue, with the hideous pin of our nation pinned to his lapel—a single gold eye—that stared at me as hard as Mama and this agent.

I swallowed nervously and lifted my chin. "Mama, you know you can't do this without me. What's this all about? Who will look after the children?" I could feel Trinity shaking behind me, pulling my jeans into a vice grip.

The scent of this odious man's tart pear cologne threatened to suffocate me. And I struggled to keep my breathing even.

"Trinity, come away from Luna. She's going on a little trip. We packed a suitcase for her, remember?" she nodded toward the worn luggage.

Trinity didn't move. And I gripped her small hand in mine.

"She's not going anywhere, Mama."

"Talin. Get your sister now."

I watched as my oldest brother, barely twelve, already developing a cruel countenance, stared at me with steely contempt. He leapt off the couch and ripped Trinity away from me. He'd always been completely ungrateful and unwilling to help with the little ones. He was selfish, and I knew he wouldn't come to my aid now.

Trinity's scream pierced the air, as she reached for me. But Talin simply pulled her to him and made her sit beside him, his features unmoving. She squirmed, trying to escape, but his hold was steadfast.

"This is a chance for a better future for me, Luna," Mama said stonily. "In trading you, we can all get out of this forsaken hell hole of a home. It's just the way it has to be." She crossed her arms and glared at me smugly. "Agent Simms, cuff her."

He stepped forward, handcuffs in hand. I backed away, but in a single stride, he was on top of me, yanking my hands behind my back and locking my wrists. "You can't do this to me," I yelled. "I've kept you all alive. Risked everything for you. Please, Mama."

"Well then, consider this your one last sacrifice, Luna."

Everyone was aware social standing could be improved upon if given permission by the government, but you had to give them something in return. I never thought in a million years that Mama would trade me for it. I knew she didn't love me—she tolerated me at best. But I was naïve. I believed since I kept food in their bellies and a fire in the hearth, she needed me. And it would never happen.

But I was wrong.

Dara's words echoed in my head. *Don't let them take you.*

How had she known?

I struggled against my restraints as the agent shoved me down hard on my knees. "Under the law, article 1046, I hereby pronounce you property of the United States government. You must revoke all rights and connection to this family. This purchase contract may not be rescinded as by consent of all parties..."

As the agent rambled on, my brain scrambled for a plan. I needed to act like I was going along with this scheme so they'd let their guard down and I could escape. Luckily, I was still wearing the hoodie I used for pick-pocketing.

Trinity had stopped screaming, but tears poured down her face in big droplets, her lips trembling. My heart lurched. She would be the hardest to leave. She was only five. Too little to rely solely on the likes of Mama.

I glanced over at the rest of them, there was Monty, Farrah, Dafina, and of course, Talin. They ranged in age from seven to twelve years. I hoped they would look after each other. They'd never helped me much, relying on me for everything. But perhaps without my assistance, they would bond together, support each other. I had to believe they would or I would never be able to walk away.

Agent Simms, now done with reading me my so-called rights, hauled me up from the floor and slammed me onto the broken wooden chair in the corner. I felt a sharp splinter of jagged pine slice through the skin of my back and I winced.

He turned to Mama. "Come, Mrs. Redwood, there are papers to be signed. The property is secured."

Mama's face flushed with excitement. "Yes, of course. I'm so thrilled to get things started. Children, run upstairs and gather the rest of your belongings. We're leaving this hovel tonight!"

I watched as my siblings obediently filed out, like emotionless robots. Only Trinity glanced back, stifling a sob before hastily turning away, padding silently behind Talin.

Satisfied they were out of the way, Mama ushered the agent to the kitchen. "Let's sign those documents, Agent Simms!" she chirped cheerily, her big blonde curls bouncing with anticipation. She'd applied too much makeup, and she looked almost racoonish with her overshadowed eyes. Her thin body, wrapped in her best dress, a worn-out black floral print, gave off the image of a scrawny scarecrow. I scowled in disgust as she practically threw herself at him. He brushed her off, eager to get on with the job at hand.

As soon as they left, I got to work. I tugged on my sleeve and the emergency kit I kept rolled up in it slid down into my palm. I made it for such an occasion as this. Though I never expected to be handcuffed for being traded; rather, I'd assumed it would be for stealing.

I sighed; at least today, my planning had paid off.

I pulled the small pin from the pack, letting the rest fall to the floor and inserted it into the cuffs. They fell away easily. I'd designed the pin especially for the government-issued restraints. I'd never seen the cuffs up close, but based on the propaganda they spewed around, I'd studied enough pictures. I'd made a sketch of them and used what I had to make my tool. I grinned, pleased at how well they'd worked.

I bent down and undid my ankles, also bound, and hastily picked up my emergency pack, stuffing it back into my sweater.

I tiptoed to the nearest window, careful to avoid the squeaky, broken floorboards. I dared not risk the door; I'd have to pass through the kitchen to get to it, where Mama and the agent were still talking.

I slid the cracked glass pane open, then angled my body deftly through the small opening, leaping panther-like to the ground.

I ran, not caring where I went, as long as it was far away from Mama and that awful man.

Tears burned my cheeks. My own mother had sold me for a better life. How could she do that? Anger surged through me, spurring me onwards. No one would ever own me again. I would take care of myself.

My heart lurched as, somewhere behind me, I heard Mama's screams and the pounding of footsteps on the hard, cold ground.

They knew I'd escaped.

CHAPTER 4

The frigid air burned my lungs as I pumped my legs harder. Agent Simms was closing in. He was so tall and fit; it was only a matter of time before he caught up with me. No amount of camouflage would help me now.

Still, I wasn't going down without a fight. The moon behind the clouds cast everything in complete darkness, but I knew every inch of this place and I could use that to my advantage.

I rushed into the woods and wove silently amongst the trees. I'd learned a long time ago how to move through the snow quietly. The only sounds were that of an owl hooting in the tree canopy above and the north wind whistling through the oaks, maples, and beech. Their branches creaked, buried under the weight of the last snowfall as I drove my way deeper into the forest.

I veered left, hoping to disorient Simms, but before I made any headway in that direction, long strong fingers reached out and grabbed my wrist.

I yelped and came to an abrupt halt, as I felt my arm practically yanked out of its socket.

Agent Simms wasn't even breathing hard, he looked cool as a

cucumber. Only his angry flashing eyes revealed his true displeasure.

"It's a felony to run from a government-issued order, Ms. Redwood."

I kicked at him, trying to get away. But he stood immobile, completely unfazed by my efforts. "I'm not going anywhere with you. I was traded against my will. I have rights! Get your hands off me!"

"If you do not cooperate, I'll be forced to physically restrain you. You belonged to Rheya Redwood, and it was within her jurisdiction to trade you in. You should feel privileged. It is not often the government trades individuals; they are quite picky. You must have some value or skill." He raised a skeptical eyebrow at me, as if he didn't really believe that.

What was with this guy, anyway? He sounded like an android, completely monotone and deadpan.

"Get your government paws off me!" I yelled. Somewhere in the distance, I heard a coyote howl as if in agreement. I hoped it came along and scared the crap out of him. Personally, I would enjoy the show.

"I'm sorry Miss Redwood, you've given me no choice." Picking me up as if I were nothing more than a feather, he threw me over his shoulder and carried me, kicking and yelling, out of the woods.

I pounded on his back, begging him to let me go, but he ignored me. By the time we got to his non-descript blue van parked in the rear of my house, my voice was raspy and raw. The only thing that gave this vehicle away as government issue was the small golden eye delicately painted above each door handle. Subtle, but sickening all the same.

He shoved me into the back seat and grabbed a second set of cuffs from inside his jacket, securing my wrists. Almost as an afterthought, he pulled a handkerchief out of his pocket and stuffed it into my mouth.

"Since you can't seem to keep your trap shut, let's add a little security, shall we?" he said smiling.

I tried to bite him, but Agent Simms was quick and soon had my lips completely covered in tape.

I steamed with rage. I would never forgive my mother for doing this to me. I would figure out how to escape, even if I died trying. I refused to be anyone's property.

I'd seen these so-called trade-ins on the news a few times over the years, but for some reason, I never thought it would happen to me. I'd been a fool.

"Luna! Luna!" I whirled around in my seat. It was Mrs. Peters. I wanted to yell at her to go back inside, warn her to stay away, but the more I willed her to flee, the closer she came. I could hear her clearly now through the glass window of the transport vehicle. "I'm so sorry. I was too late... It's all a lie, Luna..." Her voice trailed off as Agent Simms pushed her, she stumbled back and fell to the ground. He grabbed hold of her, hauling her away from the van. "You don't know about the cage of glass," she cried out, "Cage of glass. Cage of glass. Cage of glass," she repeated again and again, all the while struggling uselessly with all her might against Simms. He didn't budge despite her best efforts. I choked back a sob. Mute and unable to respond. What did she mean? What cage of glass? What was a lie? I was confused.

"Cage of g—" Dara said one last time before her words were cut short. The air went silent, as Simms plunged something into her neck. I choked on a scream. My covered mouth burning as my lips tried to move and break free. I felt tears slide down my cheeks, unchecked.

What had he done? Frantic, I glanced around, willing someone to come out and help her, as he dragged her back out of the way, leaving her on the side of the road like a piece of trash.

No one came. Everyone must have heard the screams, but no one came.

How had she known? She tried to warn me before. But I still couldn't figure out how she may have foreseen this. Was it possible my mother had bragged to her? It seemed unlikely. Rheya was selfish and a loner, never bothering to befriend her neighbors. I worried about how Mrs. Peters was going to get her medicine without me. How in the world would she survive? Honestly though, as I looked at her slumped form, I wasn't sure if there was any life in her to save. Had Simms killed her? A sharp pain flooded my chest as I struggled to breathe, just thinking of it.

I kept my eyes glued to Mrs. Peters as we pulled away, not letting go until we turned the corner and I no longer had her in my line of vision.

She didn't move.

A numbness seeped into my body, shutting away the pain. The betrayal and guilt I felt over what I just witnessed was too much. My tears dried and I grew cold as I morphed into survival mode.

This was not the time for weakness. Dara would want me to fight. It was imperative I get out of this for her, and if she was still alive when I returned, I'd help her escape and find out what she desperately wanted to tell me.

Her words echoed in my ears. *It's all a lie.*

I looked out the window to distract myself from my morbid thoughts, all the while trying not to gag on the cotton material in my mouth, noticing we were headed south into the city.

The slums of Nova were a thing of the past as we entered into the sparkling clean community of Hadon. High rises towered over us, and the bright lights, only afforded by the capital, practically blinded me. I'd seen pictures before, but they did not do it justice. The glaring beams of light exposed the opulence of the metropolis. This was the place of dreams, where full bellies and warm houses were everyone's right. The place you wanted to be if you were lucky enough to have eyes that did not betray you, and hadn't cast you into a life of hunger and depravity.

The buildings here, even on the outskirts of town, were made of brick and stone, and looked as if they could endure forever, unlike my family's own ramshackle dwelling, which would likely collapse in the slightest wind. I stared at the doors on each house, with the gold and glittered symbol of the capital reflected under the porch lights.

The golden eye.

Here, the retina scan was celebrated. Most homes flew the flag of W_1 proudly, black with one single golden eye in the middle. They waved in the breeze as if to mock me.

The van ascended a steep hill and the heart of Hadon stretched out before us, high rises, dotting the landscape as far as I could see. I imagined in the light of day, the streets would be crowded with bodies, all in a rush to get somewhere. Each of the buildings here boasted gold walls, that glinted bright as midday in the moonlight. More eyes were plastered to each of the concrete sides—making me feel as if millions of people were spying on me simultaneously—and I cringed. We wound our way down the narrow lanes, drawing closer to the harbor and the cold, choppy river. The smell of the fish market hit me as we neared the docks; even though I couldn't see the marina, the fishy odor gave it away.

After several turns, we rumbled toward an enormous gated outcropping of buildings on the east side of the city. The compound dominated this quarter, its sleek glittering diamond walls expertly crafted for beauty, but also for fortification. The large windows gleamed, clean and pristine, each one lit vibrantly from within. I couldn't help but wonder how much electricity it took to light this section of the borough alone. My mind scrambled, unable to comprehend such wealth. Agent Simms slowed the vehicle to a stop in front of a wide fenced barrier bearing a huge sign. I gripped my bound hands together tighter as I stared ahead at the black lettering reflected in the van's headlights.

Government Facility Keep Out. Authorized Personnel Only.

Simms reached into the upper pocket of his stiff military blue-grey shirt and pulled out a small device no bigger than his palm. It was ink black with a strange gold button in the center. He pressed it and the gadget beeped, opening the gate. I had to admit to being a bit disappointed in the technology. One would think in this high tech city they would have come up with something cooler than a push switch.

Simms wasted no time and barreled through the chasm, taking us to a tall building on the far side of the lot. I thought about picking the lock on my cuffs again and jumping Simms when he moved to pull me out of the vehicle. But he was stronger than me and would probably catch me within minutes, if not seconds. I needed a better strategy if I were ever to escape this place.

Simms stepped out of the van and came around to open the door; the gust of cold winter wind hit me full force, causing my eyes to instantly tear. He ripped the tape from my lips and unshackled my ankles. "If you scream or try to run again, I'll make sure your life isn't worth living. Understood?"

I quickly nodded in agreement. Normally, I would have liked to spit in his face and tell him to go to hell, but the cotton handkerchief stuffed in my mouth had left my tongue so dry I could barely swallow and my lips stung mercilessly where he'd removed the tape. Besides, I had no idea if he had any more special injections in his pocket. I could be his next victim. And then what? How could I help Dara then? I had to believe she was still alive.

He expunged the offending object, and I coughed and spluttered, relieved. Before I could question my own foolishness, I rasped, "What did you do to Mrs. Peters? Is she still alive? Did you kill her?"

Simms snarled at me, yanking so painfully on my arm I yelped. "Shut up. You don't have the privilege of asking questions. Ask any more stupid questions and I'll stuff this back in your mouth." He held the gag right up to my face in warning. I said nothing. Waves of pain shot through my clenched jaw as I bit back a snide retort.

"That's what I thought," he smirked. "Now come on kid. Let's get this over with. My shift is almost over."

He hauled me along the sidewalk, my hands still secured tightly together in front of me. We marched through a revolving door into a beautifully furnished main lobby. My feet sank into a plush periwinkle blue carpet. I looked around. Gilded couches with overstuffed cushions, as comfortable as soft clouds dotted the area and beautiful paintings of various happy scenes adorned the walls. *So this is where all the money went.*

Agent Simms pushed me forward toward an elevator on the far side of the room and shoved me inside. He pressed the button for the twenty-ninth level. Warm air, smelling of cinnamon and spice wafted through the vents above us. I inhaled deeply; it smelled so good. As we ascended, each floor ticked by on the digital screen of the menu panel, and my mind scrambled. If the only way to leave this building was through the elevator, how would I ever be able to escape? I tried to control the rising panic that clawed up the back of my neck, threatening to strangle me. No. I couldn't go there. There had to be a set of stairs somewhere. I clung to that small ray of hope.

When we reached the twenty-ninth floor, the lift dinged, and the doors opened. I found myself in another reception area, similar to the one before, except this lobby had floor to ceiling windows that offered a stunning view of the city. I gazed out, fascinated to see so many towering buildings dazzling against the dark winter night sky.

I'd stopped walking to take a closer look, but Simms thrust me forward so hard I almost fell on my face. "Stop gawking, kid. It's time for your close up."

"Close up?" I rasped, my throat still raw from the stuffed cotton handkerchief.

"Yeah. Your debriefing. It's standard procedure. My advice? Don't mess it up. And don't try any of your tricks. My boss won't be as accommodating." He grinned derisively, almost as if he loved the idea of me getting into even more trouble.

I snorted back a laugh. Accommodating? He'd stabbed my friend with some drug and left her on the street. Still, I was smart enough to keep my comments to myself. I'd pushed him far enough.

At the end of the long hall, we came to a door marked with the insignia D5, and a sign that read *High-Security Area—Use Caution.* Agent Simms scanned his badge on the secure electronic lock and strode inside, dragging me with him.

Adrenaline surged through my veins and roared in my ears. The urge to run was potent. But as we turned the corner it became apparent we weren't alone, a massive man sat behind a cold metal desk in the center of a white, sterile room. His forced smile and rigid posture filled me with a dark, unfathomable foreboding. I'd never make it out of here, pitted against these two.

"What is this?" I demanded hoarsely. "Why are you doing this? Please let me go."

"Simms, fetch the girl some water, then leave," the brutish man said dismissively.

Simms dropped my arm like it was a hot potato and stood to attention. "Yes, sir. Right away, sir."

He disappeared around the corner, and within seconds had returned with a paper cup full to the brim with water. He pushed the drink into my bound hands and gave me a warning look.

My toes curled in my shoes as I tried to resist the urge to throw the water in his face. In the end, I decided not to part with the precious liquid. My throat burned, and I wouldn't waste the deliciously cold refreshment on this pond scum. I gulped it back greedily.

"That will be all, Simms. See you at fourteen hundred hours."

"Yes sir," he said, raising his hand in salute.

I wasn't surprised to find I was glad to see the last of Agent Simms. I detested him and what he'd done to Dara. On the surface he appeared considerably friendlier than the officer sitting before me, but we all knew the truth. This gentleman looked to be in his early fifties, with greased salt and pepper hair slicked back in a weird, old-fashioned style that came to a point in the middle of his forehead. The harsh lighting of the chilly room only accentuated the sharp planes and angles of his features. His large belly protruded over his navy uniform pants and dark spectacles hid the masked eyes of a hunter. Definitely a man that commanded authority, and clearly always had a price for every deal he made.

I shivered, but not from the cold temperature of the room. Then I heard Mama's voice echoing in my head.

Never let them see your weakness.

I shook off my trepidation and stood tall, my eyes blazing furiously at the odious man. As much as it annoyed me to say so in this moment, Mama had taught me well.

The anger fueled me as I squared my shoulders and flung my hair back in a gesture of defiance.

He ignored me and continued shuffling papers on his desk. He'd probably seen it all before.

"Sit down Miss Redwood. I've been expecting you," he said, not looking up.

I lifted my chin. His indifference didn't bother me. I'd dealt with worse. I could freeze him out, but my curiosity was stronger, so I broke first.

"How long have you and my mother been in cahoots?" I blurted, trying to cover my discomfort. "Am I just a piece of meat to you?"

The man regarded me, raising his bushy eyebrows in surprise. He rose to his feet, hands splayed out on the desk and leaned forward, towering over me.

"I suggest you sit, Miss Redwood, if you know what's good for you," he said in a low tone. "While I admire your fire, there is a time and place for it. Don't be stupid and be quiet."

My heart pounded in my chest as I stared into his eyes. He wasn't bluffing. I needed to stay alive—so I sat.

"Excellent choice. Let's get down to business, shall we?" he said, lowering himself back down behind the metal desk.

I clenched my teeth to prevent myself from saying something I'd regret and surveyed the frigid office. It was a study in desolation. The room, a stark contrast to the warm reception areas, was cold and uninviting and housed only a desk, and an examination table. Strange instruments hung nearby, and a computer sat in the rear corner.

The ugly man's voice returned me to my senses. "Now, you may be wondering who I am."

"Not really," I said, rolling my eyes.

He frowned, the lines in his face deepening, his cheeks mottled red with rage. "I've had about enough of your insolence Miss Redwood," he bellowed.

I raised my chin and looked at him head on. This guy didn't intimidate me. He had no idea who he was dealing with.

"My name is Officer Arden, the operating director in charge of the placement of all returned government property. You should deem yourself privileged that you were considered for such a trade in. It's not as common as you might think."

He steepled his fingers together and peered at me intently, as if waiting for me to thank him for his so-called virtuous deed.

I burst out of my chair and glared down at him, ready with an insult. But I found it died on my lips. Something he'd said had sparked my curiosity. I narrowed my eyes. "Why was I such a good trade in?"

Arden smirked. "I knew you would come around," he said. He rose and skirted the desk, with a dangerous, predatory grace. He leaned forward his hot breath on my cheek. "You're a fighter, girl. You kept your family alive practically single-handed. We like that kind of tenacity here at headquarters."

The paper cup I was holding crushed under my fingertips. "You were spying on me?" I shouted enraged.

Arden pulled back and returned to his desk. His sagging jowls twitched in agitation as he spoke. "I would prefer if you kept your tone civil, Miss Redwood. And no, spying is not how we conduct business here. We simply checked into your background. We do that on all our offered trade-ins. To see who will be suitable."

"Suitable? How dare you? I am not your property Officer Arden," I said seething, jaw clenched. I leaned in as close as I dared.

"Ah. But I'm afraid you are, Luna."

Hearing him say my name like that ran a chill down my spine.

As if sensing my unease, his mouth quirked up at the corner. "Miss Redwood. I'm pleased to inform you, that as property of the United States government we are bestowing upon you the highest honor. You, my dear girl, are going to be sent to an alternate universe. You have the skills I believe to really make a go of things. Though I would try to control your temper. No one likes a hothead now do they?"

My breath came raw in my throat as a cold fist closed over my heart. I'd heard the rumors, understood what happened to those who got sent away. They would wipe my memories. I wouldn't remember my sister Trinity or Dara, or anything for that matter. All that would be left of me was my name.

The Luna Redwood that everyone knew would cease to exist.

CHAPTER 5

Officer Arden left me alone.

He'd gone to process my paperwork for transfer and threatened bodily harm if I so much as moved an inch. Upon exiting, he'd slammed the door shut so hard the walls shook, then locked it with a flourish from the other side, as if to say; *you're not going anywhere.*

He certainly didn't know me that well. I thrived on a challenge.

Alone, the room seemed smaller now; the walls closing in on my confined prison, the stale, antiseptic air suffocating. The trifle of water I'd had earlier had done nothing to satisfy my thirst, and I licked my dry lips.

Right. It was time to pull myself out of this hellhole and get Dara help. She *was not* dead. I refused to believe that. First things first. I needed to remove these handcuffs. Arden had also shackled my ankles before leaving, thinking that would stop me, but he didn't know about my hidden pin.

I stared at the ceiling, counting the tiles to calm my jangled nerves. All the while slowly using my sweater to pull down the apparatus I'd hidden in my sleeve.

One. Two. Three. Four...

By the time I counted to ten, the little tool rested in my palm. Beads of sweat formed on my forehead, despite the coolness of the room. I had minutes. This may be my only shot. When he came back, he would take my memories for sure.

With shaking hands, I maneuvered the pin into the hole of the handcuffs. With a satisfactory click, the restraints popped open, and I quickly moved to my ankles to free my feet. With that done, I stood and looked around; I needed to figure a way out of this mess. I bit my lip, noticing the lack of windows; that meant no fire escape, so that option was out. The only light came from a fluorescent bulb hanging above the desk. The incessant buzzing from it rattled me, but I tampered down my jitters and concentrated.

Think. Luna. Think. The electronic lock on the door indicated there had to be some kind of security system in place. My eyes flew to the small laptop in the corner of the room.

Without making a sound, I rushed over and opened the lid, pleased to find it already booted up. The government defense emblem flashed onto the screen, asking for my thumbprint scan or authorized user name and password. My heart pounded. The only way around this was to hack into it.

I'd never actually used a computer before, but I'd stolen a book about them and had learned everything in it cover to cover. Besides, I'd mastered how to extricate people's information from their wrist ID's to steal money, hadn't I? How different could this be? I set to work. According to what I'd read, a login may be bypassed using hardware vulnerabilities such as an open port. From there I could get into the mainframe and hack the security, including the lock on this room.

Every minute that ticked by felt excruciating as I searched for a back door to outsmart the system. After what seemed like an eternity, I finally cracked it. But once inside the network there were a lot of firewalls; the government had certainly done their homework, but I was determined to take every barrier down.

This system was wireless; radio frequency signals were being sent from every door and window sensor to a massive control center housed somewhere on the premises. The signal would deploy if any of the doors or windows were breached. The signals were encrypted, but by some mercy, I managed to get around that.

With a shaking finger, I hit enter on the keyboard and shut my eyes, willing it to work. Within seconds a distinct click echoed in the room as the door unlocked.

No alarm.

I grinned. I'd done it. I quickly exited the program and closed the computer lid, leaving it exactly the way I'd found it.

Unable to believe my good fortune, I sagged against the wall for a moment. Now to get out of here without being spotted. This wasn't Nova anymore; my skills at blending in would be put to the test—dodging security men I'm sure were hiding in the shadows, just waiting to pounce.

My eyes lighted on Officer Arden's jacket that he'd tossed on the back of the desk chair. I darted over to it and plucked it up, quickly pulling it on. Then I pulled my dark hair up into a bun using my pin. Nobody would consider looking for it there if I was caught.

I glanced at the clock. It had taken me ten minutes. I probably didn't have much time to escape. Possibly only seconds once someone discovered the security system was down. I sped to the door and opened it, wincing as it hissed in protest. I froze for half a beat, but no one jumped out at me. I placed a hand on my heart to steady myself before peeking out to look both ways down the corridor. Coast clear, I stepped out cautiously, then tiptoed past the elevator before breaking into a full run, stopping short when I reached the end of the long hallway. Which way now? The sign for the stairwell indicated left. With the system down, I would have easy access. Taking one cursory glance around, I made a beeline for the stairs, wrenching open the door. I breathed a sigh of relief, so far so good. Without a second thought, I headed down the steps, almost tasting my freedom.

I leaned against the wall for support. Suddenly, the familiar tenor of voices came from behind the exit I'd just left and I froze. Officer Arden and another man were talking—but I was unable to make out what they were saying. But it didn't take an idiot to figure out I was in grave danger. My stomach knotted even as I launched myself down the steps. I had to get out of here, fast. Only twenty-eight more floors to go. Sure. No problem.

Exhausted and sweating, I finally made it to the ground floor. And then the lights went out.

I turned every which way in the pitch-black, reaching out to find the door, fumbling for the knob I had seen only seconds before. I grabbed it in relief. Surely, this would lead me to the lobby.

I was right, I'd found the lobby, also shrouded in darkness, save for the emergency exit light above the doorframe that provided a tiny sliver of illumination in the large expanse. From my vantage point, the coast was clear, but my line of vision was minimal. I strained to listen, but heard nothing but the sound of my own breath, seemingly too loud in the eerie silence. Could I really be alone?

A horrible feeling of dread caused me to stop short. This was too easy. Where were all the guards? Were they that confident, to leave this area unattended? No. Something didn't add up. I paused; straining against the blackness. All I made out was the furniture, looming like black globs against the walls. I gulped hard. Somebody might be out there. Still, I had to risk it. What choice did I have? If I didn't move now, every second that ticked by gave me more chances of being caught. I took one cautious step forward and let out a yelp of surprise as very large hands descended out of the gloom and clamped down on my shoulders.

"Going somewhere, Miss Redwood?"

CHAPTER 6

I was moments away from losing all my memories.

They had taken us to an undisclosed underground facility, the place where we would leave W1 and head to our so-called new home. It had been two days since that awful meeting with Officer Arden and I was exhausted. My world had become full of debriefings, and propaganda about what happiness and freedom awaited me.

There was a hole in my stomach bigger than an ocean that didn't come from hunger, but from knowing that none of this was right. However, there was nothing I could do to stop it now; time marched forward whether I liked it or not. My breath came raw in my throat, my dread palpable, as our small group of "trade-ins" walked like obedient toy soldiers toward our fate. I felt sick wondering what had happened to Dara. The agonizing torture of not knowing if she was alive or dead twisted my gut to shreds.

The air lay heavy with a heady floral perfume, giving me a horrible headache as we headed into the crowded terminal. The taste of sweet cinnamon lingered on my lips from the breakfast pastries they'd provided for our last meal. It had been the most opulent food I'd ever eaten, but it crumbled like sawdust in my mouth.

The main guard ordered us to a halt and I had a chance to observe my surroundings. We appeared to be on the platform of P8, one of the so-called alternative universes. Earlier, we had been told that this single terminal accommodated eighteen gates, each leading to a discovered cosmos. The place sparkled with immaculate, white-tiled floors and walls. Colorful photographs of people laughing, playing and living their best lives lined the bulwarks, sending a message that "transfer" equaled happiness.

Sweat trickled between my shoulder blades. It seemed as if every single one of my nerve endings was on alert. The government wanted to make you complacent, make you believe you were going on holiday for fun to a warm tropical destination. But I wasn't buying it. Nobody played me for a fool.

The skylights in the ceiling had been specially designed to take advantage of the vast amounts of natural sunlight pouring in. Even on cloudy days, the building would be well lit from hidden artificial light lamps up in the rafters. Apparently, officials believed no gloomy vibes belonged in a place like this. Being relocated was supposed to be the thing of dreams. But there was no evidence of joy in this raggle taggle group. There were six of us going to P8 today. Another teenager about my age stood to my right. She could've been a model, towering over me, her sleek blonde hair falling smoothly around her beautiful face. I squirmed uncomfortably, feeling like a garden gnome next to this lovely creature. I longed to have her looks, and wondered if her Mom had sold her for a better life, too. But for what reason, I couldn't fathom. Poverty made people do strange things.

She smiled at me, but I lacked the zeal to muster up any effort to smile back. I turned away to consider the others. They didn't bother to make eye contact. Probably caught in their own worries. It surprised me to find adults in our gathering. I'd never seen any evidence that they traded them as they did children. But the terminal oozed with them, my group included. Either way, they had to bring something valuable to the government or they wouldn't be here. Or was that another lie? If trade ins were so rare why was there so many people in this terminal? It simply didn't add up.

Three nondescript, middle-aged men stood to my right, and an attractive young woman in her twenties, all dolled up in a striking gold gown, remained to my left, along with a little girl of about five who reminded me of my sister Trinity. Her eyes, wide as saucers stared up at me, the same shade of brown as Trinny's. Her bottom lip wobbled and I patted her shoulder gently in sympathy. They had dressed her to the nines in a baby blue dress and white tights. Ruby red slippers donned her feet. The government had suited us all up. Exchanged our rags for the finest designer clothes money could buy, promising that our lives would be different once we passed through the glowing golden arch before us.

I smoothed down my own dress. Not because my appearance concerned me but because I didn't want anyone to see my trembling hands. They had decked me out in an exquisite red satin number that fell to my ankles in liquid pools. My toes pinched in the too-small sequined silver sandals. I longed for the threadbare shoes my feet were accustomed to. I touched one hand to my head, remembering the woman who had styled my hair into this complicated braid. Her fingers had worked diligently, shaping flowers to weave into my tresses, talking nonstop all the while. Her final words to me as I left were; *All your dreams are about to come true.*

How wrong she was.

I wanted to scream against the noise in my ears as the overhead PA barked out orders and announcements. Every gate had a large television filled with President Roy Ball Red's face. He was a shrewd-looking man with pale waxen skin and silky titan red hair that fell to his shoulders—he wasn't someone I preferred to meet. His macabre green eyes darted back and forth, as if calculating his next move. I didn't trust the guy at all. There was way too much "selling" of this P8 place. The screen flashed from him to clips of people that had made the transfer successfully and left all their worries behind. Above the monitors a gold banner read; *Be fearless or be conquered.* One of Roy Ball Red's favorite mottos. Well, it seemed a bit late for that, as I was being taken somewhere against my will.

The little girl clutched at my hand startling me from my reverie. "Miss? Do you know where we're going?" she whispered, her voice trembling. "I'm scared."

I knelt down and straightened her dress. "You're going on a new adventure, someplace beautiful and fun." I couldn't believe I was spouting Roy Ball Red's propaganda to her. But I daren't tell her the truth. How would you explain to a young child that in a few minutes she wouldn't even remember who she was before this moment? Who was I to promise her such riches when I had no idea what lay on the other side?

"What's your name?" I asked the brown-haired girl.

"I'm Ever."

"That's a beautiful name," I replied. "Just like you."

Ever smiled at that. "What's yours?"

"Luna," I said squeezing her hand.

"Luna. Promise you won't leave me."

I didn't have time to answer as one of the officers came along, ordering us into a straight line. I heard Ever whimpering as the officer separated our hands and pushed her behind me. I felt the tug of her small fingers on my dress as she latched on to me.

I didn't dare turn around; not wanting the agents to separate us, especially with Ever scared out of her mind.

The first transfer was about to begin.

I thought the tall, middle-aged man in the front of the line would be the initial target. But instead a stern, thin uniformed woman stepped into the gated area. Tight lines framed her mouth, and the leaden color blue skirt and jacket did nothing to hide the sharp contours of her body. She headed straight for Ever and grabbed her arm.

"Ever Hopkins. I will escort you to P8. My name is Agent One. Do not be afraid. You will have lots of friends in your new home."

Her voice sounded digital; I took another look at her face. Then I realized—she wasn't human, but an android. The sharp lines of her silhouette I'd noticed before were actually bonded metal.

Outrage boiled in me. "You can't let her go with a robot. She needs somebody real," I yelled to anyone that would listen. I tried to pull Ever toward me. "I'll take her with me."

The robot's cold hand came out and firmly plucked Ever from my grasp. "You are interfering with government protocol fifty-nine. Please step aside so we may proceed."

Another human officer seized me while Agent One carried Ever to the lighted arch. Her screams echoed down the terminal but the robot didn't stop.

I kicked and yelled at the officer, but his grip held me firmly in place. "If you're in such a hurry, Luna Redwood, you can go next," he sneered.

So much for the tranquil environment. I watched as Agent One placed Ever before the arch. The T.V screen overhead flashed again to Roy Ball Red. "Safe travels on your journey to P8 Ever Hopkins, please enjoy the movie of your best memories to keep you happy and entertained during your transfer."

Ever, still screaming, held out her little arms, reaching for me, as she stepped through the arch with Agent One. A flash of brilliant gold light blinded me, and I blinked.

When the light snuffed out, I looked again. Both Agent One and Ever were gone.

Before I could even process what happened, another agent gripped me around the shoulders and dragged me to the front of the line. "Try anything and your transfer will be made very unpleasant," he spat in my ear before releasing me.

He pointed to the white boundary under the arch and I obediently stood behind it. There was nowhere to run now. I had to accept the fate my mother had dealt me. A buzzer sounded, and the agent motioned a deft finger to where Ever had just disappeared.

I swallowed hard. My turn. I took small steps up the incline until I was in what almost looked like a clear glass photo booth, only the two front and back panels were devoid of glass. Above me, the slight glow of the arch cast a golden prism of light all around me, creating rainbows against the side walls. I jumped as the pane behind me locked into place. Tears pricked my eyes, thinking of my family and Dara. I would never know them again. I angrily swiped them away and took a shaking breath. No way I would give those stupid agents the satisfaction of seeing my pain.

I started at the sound of a demanding computerized voice. *Ready for transfer. Luna Redwood. Step forward beyond the green line.* We had gone through this in training. I was supposed to walk right through and not dawdle, but I appeared stuck to this spot, unable to move my toes past that inevitable barrier.

They must have accounted for this, as a sudden inexplicable force propelled me through. I yelped in surprise.

As I stepped beyond the line to the other side, the arch's blinding bright light seemed to explode in what seemed like a thousand watts around me, but something was wrong. This wasn't as we practiced. I heard Roy Ball Red's welcome somewhere in the back of my mind, but the happy memories he promised never came.

The light of the arch flickered and sputtered, and I wondered if anyone else noticed. Had I imagined it? I tried to hold on to my last memories, desperate to retain at least a shred of who I was.

As I descended into darkness, I screamed into the infinite void that surrounded me before glimpsing the looming light of P8 somewhere in the distance.

CHAPTER 7

When I awoke, the memories came.

I hovered somewhere between sleep and wakefulness, the air cold on my skin. The recollections hit fast, and sharp. Flashes of people, places, and sounds invaded my mind—until one dream in particular lingered, triggered by a glorious fragrance that filled my senses. I inhaled deeply, the smoky sweetness of maple syrup and bacon tickling my nose.

I didn't open my eyes as I tried to grasp onto the rushing images and focus on what I was being shown. My heart pounded with a sudden horrible realization, and a cold chill raised goosebumps on my arms.

These weren't my memories. So whose were they?

Fear and panic clawed at me, bringing me out of my hazy stupor. I sat bolt upright, instantly awake.

I remembered everything. I recalled what happened to me. Where I'd come from. My entire life on Nova. But how was that possible?

I looked down and found myself no longer clad in my red satin skirt, rather in a set of pajama shorts decorated with little clouds and a matching blue t-shirt. Where was my dress? I had hidden my emergency kit under its folds. My hand flew to my hair, my fingers frantically searching through it. The braids the woman had painstakingly styled for me had vanished—along with the pin.

I took some calming breaths to get a hold of myself. I had to think. I regarded my surroundings and gaped in awe at this opulent bedroom. I sat on a canopy bed with a silky azure duvet. Mirrored dressing tables flanked each side and a French style desk and chair rested in the corner on a plush green rug.

I'd never been anywhere so grand. Yet, I found myself frozen, unable to move—torn between wanting to run and stay inside this small bubble of paradise. I had to be imagining all this. It couldn't be P8. It must be something I conjured up in my imagination. Surely.

I startled out of my reverie when a strange woman I didn't recognize came barreling into the room. I pulled the covers up closer to me, trying to create a sheaf of protection for myself. I felt exposed in these ridiculous pajamas.

"Luna! What are you still doing in bed? You'll be late for school! Get up at once. I have breakfast on the table, ready to go." The woman had a tall, slim frame and blond bouncy curls that swished every time she bent to clear the clothes I apparently left on the floor. Only I'd never seen the dress that now dangled from her fingers.

"Earth to Luna?"

Something in the woman's voice rang true. And another foreign memory sliced through me with such force it overtook me.

The sunlight beams through the large French doors and casts a glow on the feast before us. Mom and I have been baking all day. My mouth waters at the thought of eating the golden turkey in the center of the table. I smell the butter from the mashed potatoes and I rub my hands together in anticipation. I look at Mom and Dad who are smiling at me so proud. "Merry Christmas sweetheart," Mom says squeezing my hand.

"Merry Christmas Mom," I say. In that moment, I'm perfectly content. I couldn't have asked for a better holiday.

Someone shook me. "Luna?" Are you all right?"

As the world came back into focus, I noticed the woman sitting on the edge of the bed, concern etched in her blue eyes. Then a sudden realization hit me. This was supposed to be my mother.

My mind scrambled. I had to play the part. If anyone became suspicious and figured out I had my memories, would they send me back? Arrest me? I licked my dry lips and looked at this stranger head on. "I'm fine, Mom. Sorry, still half asleep I guess." I gave her my best sheepish grin.

She seemed satisfied with that and stood up. "Well, let's get a move on. If you don't hurry, you'll be late."

After she disappeared down the stairs, I slipped out of bed, my bare feet hitting the luxurious carpet. I wiggled my toes in it for a minute, reveling in its splendor. My feet looked the same as they always did, except now they appeared perfectly manicured in delicate petal pink. Not exactly my style but I'd roll with it. Curious, I held up my hands. The scar I'd acquired at the age of five, a circular moon shape located between my thumb and forefinger was gone. And my fingernails, usually packed with dirt were spotlessly clean and painted the same petal pink. I marveled at my soft palms, no longer callused and rough.

A terrifying thought occurred to me and I raced to the mirror. I put my hands to my face and breathed a sigh of relief when my familiar countenance stared back. The same old freckles peppered my cheeks and my unmistakable green eyes peered out from my pale skin. I touched my full lips, ensuring it was truly my reflection. It seemed only my hair looked a little different—shorter—just brushing the tops of my shoulders, but the same midnight black. Gone were the dull tones and split ends; it now shone in glorious waves.

My mind flashed to the debriefing training we'd had right before transfer. They'd said we would undergo a complete transformation and be wiped clean. We would be free from our "blemishes" and start life fresh and unspoiled. At the time, I believed it to be a way to sugarcoat the memory loss, but perhaps they really had meant they would renovate every aspect of us. How else might I explain my soft skin and missing scars? I pushed the thoughts of W1 Nova aside. I had a role to play, and I needed to concentrate.

I crossed to the closet and opened it. I'd never seen so many new clothes in my life—none appeared ripped, torn, or threadbare. I let my fingers slide over the garments, all hung up neatly on their hangers, organized by color and category. A delicious thrill of satisfaction swept through me just gazing at them. Finally, something familiar.

"Luna! Are you dressed yet? Breakfast is getting cold!" The woman called.

I started at the sound of my name. If I didn't want to draw any attention to myself I'd better hurry. I made a mental note to snoop around later. I grabbed some khaki pants and one of the many white t-shirts from the closet and threw them on as quickly as possible. Though I did pause for a moment, checking my appearance in the mirror, to make sure my shirt was wrinkle free and perfectly tidy. It was the first impression, after all.

I ran to the door before realizing I hadn't brushed my hair. I looked back and saw a brush on the small French vanity. I quickly sprinted over and picked it up, sweeping it through my already smooth locks. I spotted a tie and hurriedly pulled it into a ponytail. I smoothed down any loose strands and ran my fingers up each side of my head, making sure my work was perfectly centered, all the while trying to still my shaking hands. There. Well, at least this style helped me feel a little more like me.

Turning, I raced down the hall, somehow having the intel of knowing exactly where I was headed. I reached the bottom of the stairs and found my new parents, if you could call them that, sitting at the kitchen table. My dad sat reading a newspaper while Mom glared at me, exasperated.

"Well, come on then. Don't just stand there. Eat your breakfast," Mom said, pointing to an empty chair.

A plate of scrambled eggs, bacon, and pancakes rested on the table; my stomach growled loudly. I'd never seen such an abundance of food in my life.

I quickly slid into the offered seat and raised my fork, tidying up the corners making sure the different foods didn't touch. *Much better*, I thought to myself. No matter how hard my belly complained, I refused to start eating if the plate appeared messy. Without looking up, I started in on the food. I packed it in, practically inhaling it. The sweetness of the syrup rolled over my tongue as I devoured the pancakes. I almost moaned as my taste-buds savored all the new, overwhelming flavors. I was in heaven.

It wasn't until I'd nearly finished, that I realized my parents were staring at me.

"What? I was hungry," I said mumbling as I swallowed my last bite of food.

Dad raised his eyebrows and grinned. "It appears so."

I regarded him carefully for the first time. He had kind, soft silver-blue eyes, and short salt and pepper colored hair. It looked like he worked out, based on his toned muscles. I noticed he had the whitest teeth. I ran my tongue over mine, wondering what they would think of them. Dentists weren't exactly for the riffraff of W1 Nova.

Maybe they had changed, too. I made a mental note to check.

Mom took my empty plate and scooted me out of the kitchen. "Hurry up now, Luna. Go get your things."

I climbed the stairs, grabbed my backpack and jacket, and said goodbye to my fill in parents.

As I headed out, I realized I had an unexplained knowing about so many details. I knew this girl's route to school, the loca-

tion of her belongings in the bedroom, and other small specifics
—but not an entire lifetime of memories, only pieces. Yet—my
own personal recollections appeared intact. As I walked the
familiar, albeit strange road to school, I checked on my memories. Yes. My brothers and sisters, Nova, my life there—none of
it had disappeared.

I gazed around the quiet neighborhood. A lot of the homes
were identical to each other, with white picket fences and manicured lawns that looked like carpet. Perky marigolds and pansies
peeked out from wooden window boxes. I breathed in the warm
air gratefully; tired of the bone-chilling cold.

There was a sameness here though, that left me a little on
edge. Even the trees were identical—too perfect with their same
height and width. I counted them as I walked, trying to ease my
mind with the soothing monotony, but it weirded me out, so I
switched to counting the concrete slabs of the sidewalk.

I couldn't believe I was going to high school. In W1 Nova, if
your retina scan put you in the bottom of the pile, your education was finished for you by the age of ten. The ability to read
and write was considered more than adequate—because nothing
would come of you, anyway. I'd been sent to Rheya as no more
than a piece of trash.

But here in P8, I was in a different class altogether. These
new memories had shown me that the retina scan didn't exist
here. At birth, you stayed with your biological parents. And
everybody attended school; in fact, the law stated it was a
requirement until you were eighteen. To my delight, they
encouraged even more learning after that. The motto of this
place was "everyone helping everyone." Despite the joy of the
thought of advancing my studies, a gloomy cloud descended
over me.

This all seemed too good to be true. The government back in
W1 specifically stated that my faction couldn't afford proper
clothes, goods, and housing. Why would they change my circum-
stance so drastically? Did poverty not exist here?

My mind whirled with all these unanswered questions until I reached the school—a red brick building, warm and inviting with blooming flower bushes and more perfectly symmetrical trees. I found the symmetry comforting and off-putting all at the same time. There was something unnatural about it. But a part of me loved the tamed identical shapes as well.

Kids milled about the lawns before the bell rang indicating the start of classes, all dressed in similar clothes to mine, khaki pants, and white shirts. This had to be the required uniform. I must have had that memory implanted and not realized it to be able to get that detail right. Thank goodness for that. If I'd come in the wrong outfit, they would have singled me out for sure. These people looked happy. Everyone smiled and greeted each other kindly. I sensed no hatred here.

I steeled myself and forced my legs to move forward toward the double doors. Once inside, my feet seem to know where to go, even though I didn't. I found myself in front of a locker and instinctively recognized it as mine.

I grabbed my needed materials and headed to class, the blueprint of the school already in my mind like I'd been here millions of times before. I sat down and realized I was in AP Calculus.

I looked up to see the teacher, a small man with a quirky mustache and a distinct cupid's bow facing the class. He too, wore the customary white and khaki, his shirtsleeves rolled up to the elbows, and a pencil nestled behind his ear. He held up his hand to silence everyone without saying a word, and to my astonishment, within seconds you could hear a pin drop.

"Please get out your e-tablets from your desks, I've loaded your examination there. When done, electronically forward your test to me and leave your devices in their designated areas. Good luck, students. You've worked hard for this." He smiled and I got the feeling that he really did care about us doing well. He paused just a moment to gaze warmly at us from behind his dark-framed spectacles before returning to his desk.

Unfortunately, no amount of kindness would get me out of this mess.

I gulped hard, desperately peering around. Nobody looked up. Their tablets were already out, intensely concentrating on the test. I glanced at the clock and groaned inwardly. It was only nine a.m. How would I survive this day? There was no way I'd pull this off. Would they see through me when I didn't know any of the material? Then what would they do to me?

I pushed those dark thoughts aside and pulled out the tablet hidden in my desk. The screen came to life under my fingertips and I saw the first page of the test staring back at me. My skin grew clammy and my breath quickened in a momentary panic until I realized something.

I understood these equations. More than that, they looked easy. I wracked my brain, trying to recall any new memories that would explain why I comprehended this so easily, but no answers came to mind.

My stomach contracted into a tight ball, and I fidgeted in my seat, unsure what was happening to me. The lines between my world and this one were frighteningly different. I had to get to the bottom of this.

But my first priority was to stay under the radar and that meant taking this test. I straightened my tablet, lining it up with the desk exactly; then set to work.

After only a few minutes, an anonymous text message showed up at the top of the screen. "ARE YOU OKAY? YOU'RE ACTING WEIRD."

I jerked up. Sure the teacher had found me out and realized I was a fraud. But he sat at his desk, just where he'd been before, typing away on his laptop, not even looking at me. Cautiously, heart pounding, I scanned the room. Everyone had their head down except for one boy near the middle of the classroom. His piercing blue eyes locked on mine and he raised his eyebrows in question.

At that moment, I recognized exactly who he was. This

handsome boy with the perfect golden skin lay in the forefront of my mind. His voice was familiar to my ears before he spoke, the fragrance of his cologne burned into my senses before getting near enough to touch him. I knew him almost as well as I knew myself. Yet, I was hearing his name for the first time.

"Orion," I whispered. The thought wasn't mine. But the name filled me with a deep desire I had never experienced before.

Orion could be my downfall.

CHAPTER 8

Orion Duncan was my boyfriend. And I had no idea what to do with that information.

I'd avoided him all day, dodging him at every opportunity. But when the last bell rang, he'd caught up with me, grabbing my hand to walk me home. I groaned inwardly, knowing my face had turned beet red. I wasn't used to this kind of attention. His cool smooth hand grasped my sweaty palm, and I wondered if he noticed how clammy it was. Even if he did, he would probably be too polite to say anything. At least, that is what I hoped. But honestly, who could blame me for my nerves? It wasn't every day you gained a boyfriend you knew virtually nothing about. Sure, some snapshots of us flashed across my mind, but it wasn't real. Not really. The memories weren't mine.

A couple of kids came out of the school and ran over to join Orion and I, laughing and joking around. From what I could gather, the four of us were fast friends.

I'd never had friends before, and I wondered how I should act. But it appeared my brain had turned into scrambled eggs at Orion's touch. Not because I personally had an attraction to him but because the memories told me I should. Apparently, I loved this boy, even though I didn't trust him. Talk about confusing. When I'd first seen him I realized immediately that my feelings were implanted. To survive in this little picture paradise I would need to find a means to separate fact from fiction.

As we made our way down the perfectly symmetrical tree-lined streets toward home, I snuck a closer look at this Orion boy. He was tall, at least six feet, with the shiniest blonde hair I'd ever seen. His letter jacket failed to hide strong, rippling arm muscles.

"Earth to Luna. Are you sure you're okay?" Orion asked in a deep baritone voice.

I wanted to scream. *Of course I'm not okay! I have a pretend boyfriend when I've never even had a real one! Hell, none of this is real!*

But instead I simply smiled, the corners of my mouth teasing up at the edges. "I'm fine, Orion. Stop worrying. I'm just nervous about this morning's Calculus test. I didn't get much sleep last night thinking about it."

He raised an eyebrow. "Since when do you worry about school? You're a genius. I don't remember you ever studying a day in your life. What's really going on? You're acting weird."

"Leave her alone, Orion," the tall, willowy blonde, I instinctively knew as Mara, said.

I turned to face her and realized I'd seen her somewhere—but where? I stared at her openly, not caring what she thought. Even dressed in our boring regulation school outfit she looked pretty. Her flaxen hair hung past her shoulders in long spirals, and her coral colored lipstick accentuated soft, pouty lips. Definitely model material.

That's when it hit me. Of course. Who else had looked like a model?

I came to a screeching halt.

I'd met this girl before. Back home, at the gateway to P8. She had smiled at me, just as she was smiling at me now. A few things had changed. She appeared less harrowed, and her cheeks had filled out, no doubt the result of a few good meals, or they had "rejuvenated" her as they'd promised us in our departure debriefing.

Without thinking, I reached up and placed my hand on her arm, wondering if she was purely a figment of my imagination.

But she was definitely real.

I wanted to ask her a million questions. Did she remember anything about her life on WI? Or did she just wake up in this place like me? All of these thoughts were tumbling through my mind when her voice brought me back to my senses.

"Are you all right?" Mara asked. "You're kind of pale."

I jerked away instantly, realizing I was making a fool of myself.

Mara's boyfriend, which my memories told me was Jonah, squinted at me through the late afternoon sun. "Dude. You seriously look like you're about to choke. What gives?"

He was a bit shorter than Orion, but still very attractive with dark curly hair, and skin the color of chocolate. He made a good match for Mara, they seemed to fit perfectly together like two jigsaw puzzle pieces. Too bad their whole relationship was a lie.

"Um...nothing, just a little light-headed is all," I whispered hoarsely licking my dry lips. "I better get home. I probably just need some rest."

"You are home, silly," Mara said pointing to my house. Had we really come that far? I hadn't realized, I'd been so caught up with everything. Besides, all the houses looked identical to me.

"Oh yeah." I gave her a wan smile and laughed a little to ease the tension—but it didn't work.

"Hey, why don't you guys go on, I'll walk Luna to her door," Orion said placing an arm around my shoulders.

My heart fluttered wildly in panic. The last thing I wanted was alone time with Orion. I fought the urge to shrug him off.

But before I could protest he guided me to my front stoop and turned me to face him. He traced a finger gently down my cheek. "Are you sure you're all right?"

I nodded silently, not daring to speak. Who knew what would come out of my mouth to incriminate me if I did?

He hesitated, then rubbed my arms, as if trying to comfort me. But honestly it only made things worse. He leaned close, and at first I worried he would kiss me, but relief washed through me when he bypassed my lips and spoke softly in my ear instead. "Well, call me if you need anything okay?"

"I will," I whispered, lying. Did I even have a phone? I must. I noticed everyone at school today with them, but never assumed I'd have one of my own. I'd never had such a fancy device on W1. That was for the rich.

Orion adjusted his stance, his lips now hovering over mine. I realized he was going in for a kiss after all. I did not want my first kiss to be with a virtual stranger. Plus, his hot breath smelled like popcorn. *Ugh, no thanks.* I turned my head so his lips only grazed my cheek. A part of me warred with my decision, the foreign memories tugging at my mind telling me I wanted this— him. I pushed them down.

"I might be coming down with something," I muttered, quickly coming up with an excuse. "You better go, see you tomorrow." I hurriedly whisked inside, leaving him staring after me, mouth agape.

I quickly shut the door behind me and leaned back against its sturdy frame, closing my eyes. *Whew. That was close.* I inhaled deeply. The next step was facing my parents. If I was lucky, only one of them would be around. Patricia, a.k.a. Mom was a nurse so there was a good chance she'd be at the hospital. But Martin's schedule as a professor was more flexible. As if on cue, I heard him call my name.

"Is that you, Luna?" Dad yelled from the living room.

It felt odd to be calling these people Mom and Dad, yet it seemed to flow naturally from my lips, even though I'd only met them hours before. My mind spun wildly. What was happening to me?

"Luna?" Dad called again, shaking me from my stupor.

"Yes. Coming!" I replied. Realizing I had to face the music sometime I forced my wobbly legs to move out of the entryway and down the hall to greet my "dad". He sat in his recliner, television blaring, watching the news.

"How was your day, Luna Bell?" Dad asked, his kind eyes full of interest.

"Fine. I'm pretty sure I did really well on my math test," I mumbled, stumbling over my words, taken aback someone cared enough about me to give me a nickname. I shook my head, reminding myself again that none of this was real.

But what if I wanted it to be? Would that be so bad? A sliver of guilt raced down my spine as I thought of Mrs. Peters and my siblings back in WI. I allowed myself a moment to think of Trinity's smile when I brought her home a treat, and Dara's small cottage and the many hours we'd spent together giving each other the hope to go on. But now they were just a memory. And there wasn't much I could do for them from here.

Dad's voice shattered the musings from my past and brought me back to our conversation.

Dad beamed proudly. "That's my girl."

"What are you watching?" I asked, even though it was obvious. I needed to gather as much information as possible on this strange new world.

"Just catching up on the broadcast. There's been a recent bill put forth for more federal funding for schools of learning and agriculture. I really love how the President is supporting these initiatives to help as many people as he can. With everyone's support, we'll have virtually no one who goes without. It's a brilliant proposition."

I perched on the edge of the couch next to Dad's recliner and watched a clip of a tall, thickset man of about sixty standing behind a podium. His snow white hair lay flattened neatly against his head and deep lines etched his face, revealing a lifetime of service. The caption at the bottom of the screen read *President Falkov gives a speech to the masses in the capital.*

Every member of the audience appeared captivated. I frowned, puzzled. How could the government here be so different compared to the one I came from? Back home, the motto was survival of the fittest—a horrible race to survive. Here, they offered you a helping hand, education, healthcare. Opportunities abounded. The governments were so contradictory. Roy Ball Red said he had authority over everyone, and that we were his conquests. Why had he lied? Clearly, President Falkov and Roy Ball Red had opposing ideals.

"Dad?"

He turned to glance at me, "Yes, Luna?"

As if that was all the permission I needed to ask the many questions whirling around my head I blurted, "Who founded the government? How did President Falkov come to power? Has he been in residence long?"

Dad laughed. "Aren't you learning about this at school? I'm sure they broadcast his inauguration in all the classrooms in the country. I remember you coming home and talking about it. Has that boy Orion made you forget all your studies?"

I bit my lip in frustration. "No, of course not," I replied, momentarily annoyed. As if a guy would ever be more important than what's happening to the people. I took another deep breath to steady myself.

Hold your tongue, Luna. I admonished myself. *This is a different world. Relax, or they will find out immediately you are a fraud.*

I forced myself to smile and even gave a slight giggle. "Well, maybe a little," I lied sheepishly. Hating every word.

My father seemed satisfied with that answer. I breathed a sigh of relief.

"Luna, it would be a more beneficial learning experience if you went to the library to have your questions answered. You won't remember if I just tell you. There's a lot to be learned from books. Besides, I'm sure your research will be much more informative than what I can offer you." He rose from his recliner and stretched. "Well Luna Bell, time for me to get a little more work done before I knock off for the day. My students have a pop quiz in their future." He chuckled, a bit pleased with his idea. Then, without waiting for a reply he patted my head and left, heading for his office.

I sat there for a minute, considering. My fake Dad may be onto something. Perhaps the library would give me some clues about this new world. Mind made up, I climbed the stairs to my room to study. Already hatching a plan for tomorrow.

☙❧

After I'd finished my homework, which to my relief was really easy; I went downstairs to make dinner.

But when I got to the kitchen I saw the nice woman, my mother of P8, rubbing herbs and butter down a small plump chicken. My stomach growled. Would it ever be satisfied? After years of deprivation and malnourishment, I doubted it. Though here, I did appear less skinny, as if they had somehow camouflaged my protruding bones.

"Luna!" Mom said looking up. "I wasn't expecting to see you down here so early. You should be doing your homework."

"I planned to make dinner," I said confused. "I assumed you were working." I consistently made supper back on W1, or at least tried to conjure something to fill my siblings' bellies. God knows Rheya would never do it.

Mom laughed, its comforting sound soothing my frayed nerves.

"I'll prepare dinner, sweetie; you know you don't have to worry about that. I prefer to be home in time to cook and be with you and your dad. Besides, you have enough going on with school and everything else." Mom crossed to the sink and washed her hands, then dried them on the towel hanging on the stove. She picked up the tray of chicken and put it in the oven before turning back to me, still staring at her in disbelief.

She came over and gave me a hug. "There, Luna. You know I

love when you help. Just not during homework time. Now, go study and make your mom proud."

Her eyes shone with pride and I swallowed the big lump forming in my throat. What a different world I lived in. I actually felt special and wanted by two parents. I had no idea what to do with the feelings it stirred within me. But I didn't want it to ever end.

Still, hours later, I tossed and turned in my bed. The government's contradictory message—and hell, my contradictory existence—plagued my mind.

Why was I here? Had this happened before?

I was determined to uncover the truth.

CHAPTER 9

The next afternoon after school, I headed back into town toward the library, determined to get the answers I needed. I'd looked up its location today during computer lab, not wanting to tip anybody off by asking its whereabouts. Fortunately, it wasn't far from the school.

I picked up my pace as I passed through P8's city center, and pulled my coat tighter around me grateful for its warmth in the cool late afternoon air. The quiet streets cast an eerie pallor on the pre-twilight avenues. I turned the corner onto Renault Avenue, keeping my head down, not wanting to bring attention to myself. Not that there was anyone lurking about. Yet, I shivered, and not from the cold. I felt exposed, almost as though someone was watching me. Of course, I was just being paranoid, so I forced myself to focus on my feet, putting one foot in front of the other, counting the cracks in the pavement.

One. Two. Three. Four...

An unexplained, urgent need to hurry burst from somewhere inside me, propelling me forward. As I walked, I pondered my new situation and realized I preferred it in many ways. Or at least I thought I did. Didn't I? With a belly always satiated and two loving parents, what more could I want? Yet somehow it didn't feel right—like I didn't belong. Did that mean I shouldn't be in P8? Perhaps they'd made a mistake. I couldn't think of any other answer.

Five. Six. Seven... I allowed the soothing rhythm of the sums to calm my scattered thoughts. I wasn't sure when I became so OCD, every year it seemed to get stronger. I liked things in their place, and numerology because of its precise order—it just made sense. And unlike people, the numbers never lied. There was a comfort in having control and I craved it, having little in my own life.

I checked the map on the phone I'd discovered in my bedroom last night. I verified the location I scouted out earlier in the day. Apparently implanting the locality of the library into my brain lay low on the list of priorities—to whoever had been in charge of these things. Perhaps being studious didn't matter as much as I believed it to.

For goodness' sake, I thought angrily, taking a right turn before stomping down Peris Street toward the library entrance. I had to stop acting like any of this was legit. My new memories were interfering with the old and creating havoc in my mind.

I stuffed my phone back into the pocket of my khakis and contemplated what had been weighing on me since I'd arrived. These new memories they had given me—whose were they? At the debriefing before departing W1 Nova, the officers had said our memories would be wiped clean so we'd leave our haunting pasts behind and begin anew. Being implanted with completely new memories was not mentioned. I'd been so caught up in trying to escape my fate, I never took the time to think about all the implications of that. I suppose if they stole original thoughts and impressions from you, you would have to have some baseline life facts to start over.

Was it possible to exist in more than one place? Or had they stolen someone else's identity completely so I could come here? I shivered again and counted the steps that led up to the imposing brick building in front of me. It appeared almost identical to the school except for the big sign overhead that read—P8 Public Library.

The sameness of this place really wigged me out.

I pushed one of the heavy wooden doors open and it squeaked loudly. I winced as the sound pierced my eardrums.

I gazed in awe at my magnificent surroundings. I'd never seen so many books—not like this. They loomed above and around me, stack upon stack, all different colors and sizes resting on shelves that reached the ceiling. Ladders attached to the walls ran along the ledges for access to the high reaching publications.

I cautiously stepped forward into one of the isles. The smell of old volumes filled the atmosphere, and I inhaled their musty odor.

I dropped my backpack and slid a finger down the spines. I perused the titles—realizing this must be the classics area. *Moby Dick, The Tale of Two Cities, and Pride and Prejudice* peaked out and I itched to pluck them from the shelves. I wanted to read them all.

I jumped when someone behind me cleared their throat. I whirled around to find a boy about my age, staring inquisitively at me. He had crystal clear blue eyes, the color of a mountain stream.

"Are you looking for a particular book, Miss? I'm happy to help." The smile in his voice made me relax a little.

The soft library lighting shone down on his short chestnut brown hair and he wore a button-down pink shirt that showed off his golden tan skin. He wasn't quite as tall as Orion, but still he towered over my petite frame. The fact he wasn't wearing the school-issued colors indicated that he was beyond school age, but he appeared young; probably a recent graduate.

"Can you tell me where the section on government is located?" I asked.

The boy flashed me a surprised look, but quickly schooled his features, giving me a curt nod.

"Of course. Please come this way."

He led me through a maze of isles until we reached a dimly lit back corner of the library. The first place I'd seen since arriving in P8 that didn't seem to have that perfect polish.

"Here we are. These last two rows are all that we have on government and politics. If you are looking for a particular title, I would be happy to help you find it."

I rushed forward eager to get started. "Oh no. This is fine. I don't have a particular book in mind. Thank you. You've been really helpful."

He smiled, but a hint of sadness shadowed his crystal blue eyes. "Any time, Miss. By the way, my name is Zander. Give me a holler if you need anything."

With that, he turned on his heel and disappeared. I stood there for a minute, looking after him. Zander, yet another stranger that seemed somehow familiar. But unlike Mara, there was no memories of him—new or old. I shook my head, certain I was being ridiculous. Of course I wouldn't recognize this boy, I just met him.

Get a grip, Redwood, I admonished myself. Time to get down to business. I needed to find some answers. I turned to face the books before me; I decided to start my search in the last row closest to the wall. My gaze flitted over the titles and I picked out a few volumes that looked promising and took them over to a cluster of circular tables in the center of the room. The lighting was a lot better over here, thanks to the warm glow coming from the stained glass dome overhead. One couldn't help but admire the rich diamond configuration of the opalescent glass set into a framework of brass. The paisley-patterned maroon carpet under-foot probably cost a year's wages back home. I'd never seen anything so plush. I resisted the urge to bend down and touch it and instead settled down to read.

I spent the next hour pulling books from the shelves, skim-ming through them, and then returning them for more. All the records seemed vague. The only useful information I'd gleaned was that the president came into office ten years ago and had no limit on how long he stayed in term. Based on these accounts, everyone seemed to be happy with the system and didn't want to change anything.

I was flipping through the last hardcover when Zander suddenly appeared. "Are you sure there's nothing I can help you with, Miss?"

I smiled up at him, grateful for any distraction from these tedious records. "Call me Luna. Miss seems so formal." I squished up my nose and he laughed a little.

"Well, Luna. Is there anything you need?"

I shut the final book in frustration. "I'm looking for information on political structure, and how this, I mean—our government all got started. But I can't seem to find much on the history."

Zander frowned. "There really aren't any volumes on that topic, I'm afraid. Perhaps you should call it a day. We are about to close soon, anyway."

I nodded, surprised at his dismissive tone. Something I'd said had apparently ruffled his feathers. I wanted to ask him what his deal was, but bit my tongue. I needed to stay under the radar.

So instead I stood up to go. "You're probably right. I better get home."

"Here, let me take the rest of those for you, I can re-shelf them. Have a good night, Luna."

Quick as a flash, he had all the books scooped up and hurriedly made his way back to the stacks.

"You too," I replied belatedly, but he'd already gone. I shrugged and left him to it.

It was twilight by the time I stepped out of the building. The electric lamps cast a warm glow onto the concrete pavement, and again I marveled at the cleanliness of everything. Even the roads were swept spotless. What I wouldn't have given to have all this on Nova. But on second thought, debris and lack of electricity made it easier to hide in the shadows and steal, so perhaps it had been for the best. On my brief sojourn home, my mind mulled over the information I'd read at the library, and I began to wonder why, for a place so adamant about education, there was so little on how the very framework of this country was built. Zander's strange behavior also niggled at me. Why did he look so nervous when I asked for information on government structure? Nothing added up.

Before I knew it, I'd arrived at the house. I lifted my fist, giving four even raps on the door, when it dawned on me this was supposed to be my home. I gave a quick cursory glance around to check no one had seen my *faux pas*. I placed a hand to my heart, relieved to find the street behind me devoid of people. I had to be more careful.

I twisted the doorknob and discovered the door was unlocked. I stepped inside. Both parents were in the kitchen waiting for me, their faces pale and concerned.

A chill shot up my spine. They'd found out. That had to be it. I dropped my backpack on the floor with a thud and stared at them both. "What's happened?" I whispered.

My mother ran to me and squeezed me so hard, it took my breath away. "We were so worried. Where have you been all this time? We called you multiple times and you didn't answer. Your father and I were about to send out a search party," she said, her voice muffled in my sweater.

I furrowed my brow in confusion. "Sorry I missed your calls; I had my phone on silent. I was at the library. It's not that late, is it?" I pulled back from Mom and grabbed my cell from my back pocket. The screen read 6:30 p.m.

I was used to coming and going as I pleased. Rheya had never cared. Besides, what would she say? Most of the time I was out getting food for her and her children. Perhaps I missed something, miscalculated. In this world, I must have a curfew. But what sixteen-year-old kid had a curfew before seven p.m.?

My father came over and looked down on me sternly. He put a firm but shaking hand on my shoulder. "You're grounded through the weekend, Luna. We were worried sick. You shouldn't have spent that long at the library. There might be consequences. You know that."

"Grounded?" I asked perplexed. "You were really that upset about me being gone?" It seemed hard to believe. Did these people truly love me that much, that not knowing my location for even a few hours rattled them to their core?

For the second time in a matter of days, I found tears pooling in my eyes. The need in me to be wanted and loved had always been a pipe dream that would never happen, but now here it was, staring me in the face and I didn't quite know how to react.

I wiped away the tears, but my parents saw them, and mistook them for frustration over being punished.

"We're sorry, Luna, but this is just the way it has to be. These are the rules. You shouldn't upset your mother," Dad said gruffly, but he gave me a comforting pat on the back.

Somewhere in the recesses of my mind, my father's words about not spending a considerable time at the library issued warning bells. Hadn't he been the one to tell me to go in the first place? It didn't make sense. But I couldn't worry about that now.

All my suspicions were buried and muffled in the warmth of my parents' arms. The power of how much they cared over-whelmed me.

All I dared do was breathe it in. Never knowing how long it would be mine.

CHAPTER 10

I'd avoided Orion since that night he'd tried to kiss me on my front porch. But there was no getting around him now. He, Mara, and Jonah were heading straight for me as I opened my locker and stuffed my backpack inside.

"Hey Luna," Mara said. "Where have you been the last few days? Every time we try to come talk to you, it seems like you duck out of the way. What gives?"

"Sorry, guys. My parents grounded me, and I'm not allowed to do anything but go to school and return straight home." I felt better knowing it wasn't a total lie.

Jonah looked at me questioningly. "Sure, but that doesn't stop you from talking to us at school."

I nodded, as if considering. "That's true, I suppose. I'm just worried about getting into more trouble than I already am, I guess."

Now it was Orion's turn to stare at me funny. "Yeah, right. Since when do you care about the rules? You're my little party animal," he teased, putting a possessive arm around my shoulders, squeezing me close. It made me uncomfortable and I resisted the urge to shrug him off.

Fortunately, Mara saved the day. "Speaking of which, that's why we came over."

I furrowed my eyebrows confused. "What do you mean?"

She leaned in conspiratorially. "Well, Jonah's parents are out of town this weekend, so we're throwing a party." She giggled excitedly. "It will be a huge blowout with tons of people. And that's where you come in, Luna. Everyone knows you're the queen of parties, I thought you could help us plan. We only have a couple of days to pull it all together."

"Me? I'm sure you'd be fine without my help, I'm not—"

Jonah cut me off. "You have to, Luna. It's my first big shindig and I want to make a good impression. Please say yes," he put his hands into a prayer position and bent down on one knee, practically begging.

"But I'm grounded, Jonah. How am I supposed to plan your party? I won't even be allowed to go to it."

Jonah's dark chocolate eyes clouded over. "It's never stopped you before. Sneak out like you always do. It's not like your parents will ever figure it out. Remember the escape hatch episode of last year?"

They all laughed, and I giggled along with them, trying to fit in. All the while, my mind scrambled for the memory. *Damn it.* I didn't have that one. I bit my lip, hoping none of them would ask me about it.

"So what do you say?" Orion said, giving me another side squeeze. He smelled of apple spice and a small part of me enjoyed being near him, the part that held the memories of us together. But those memories were a fabrication—and not mine. Furthermore, I found I didn't really like Orion that much. He was pushy. The last thing I needed was someone else telling me what I should be doing. But I had no choice. If I broke up with him, wouldn't that be a big red flag? That would definitely draw unwanted attention.

"Hello? Earth to Luna," Mara said waving a hand in front of my face, snapping me out of my thoughts.

"Sorry guys, I can't do it. Maybe next time. I don't want to be grounded for another forty years. I think I need to follow my parent's rules this once. Anyway, I better head to class," I said, eager to escape. "I'll see you at lunch." I stepped out from under Orion's arm and turned to go, but Orion grabbed my shoulder and spun me around to face him. His normally blue eyes had transformed into a stormy grey; his mouth twisted into a firm line.

"What's going on with you, Luna?" Orion growled. I glanced in both directions down the hallway, hoping no one was watching. Relieved to find most people had scattered. The bell was about to ring any minute.

I shrugged off his hand, my hackles rising. "There is nothing going on with me. I'm fine," I said through gritted teeth.

"Oh yeah?" he countered. "What about all that crap about studying? Since when did you become such a book nerd? You never needed to study before. And the Luna I know would never balk at a party."

"Why do you care if I study or go to a stupid party?" I yelled back.

An audible gasp echoed through the group. "How dare you say Jonah's party will be stupid! What kind of friend are you?" Mara exclaimed. "If this party isn't one hundred percent fun, it could be social suicide, you know that."

I narrowed my eyes fed up. "I'm sure you guys can come up with a perfectly nice party without me. How hard could it be?"

Mara's mouth fell open in shock. "Well, just forget we ever asked you, Luna Redwood. Orion's right. You've changed, and not for the better. Friends don't treat each other the way you do," she said snootily, sticking her petite nose high in the air. "Come on Jonah, let's go to class." Without another word, she grabbed his hand and they sailed down the hall, disappearing around the corner.

I wondered as I watched them leave, if I would've been that way too if I'd lost all my memories. Would parties and my reputation be all I cared about? I thought to the girl I'd seen on plat-form P8 back on W1. She seemed so kind, not the type to get hung up on trivial stuff. Anger welled up inside me and made my chest burn for what they'd taken from Mara. I had to find answers, not only for me, but for people like Mara too, who had forgotten their true identities, and lived off some contrived new world visions that weren't even their own.

Orion was staring at me. My morose thoughts must have been reflected in my eyes.

"Don't be sad, Luna. I realize you must be going through something right now that you're not willing to share, but does that mean you can't be there for your friends? For me?"

I tightened my hands into fists and dug my nails into my palms to keep from screaming. It was just a party, for goodness' sake. Didn't they understand there were people out in the universe starving and suffering? That parties were no big deal? I paused. Well, perhaps not. I'd gotten somewhat lucky. Without my memories, I would presumably act this ditsy, too. I tried to cut Orion some slack.

"I can't help this time. You have to understand, I wouldn't say no unless it was important."

Orion slammed my still open locker shut in frustration. "You just don't get it, Luna." He breathed out heavily. "We should probably take a break. You've changed. I saw how you stared at me when I went to kiss you the other night. So don't do me any favors and lie and tell me everything is the way it used to be. Because it's not." He pushed his fingers through his blond hair and looked at me one last time, but I couldn't think of anything to say.

Finally, with the silence hanging between us like a noose, he turned away and picked up the backpack he'd dropped on the floor. "I have to get to class," he said without turning around. "You'd better too, if you're still so insistent on this goody two shoes act. Look me up when you return to normal. Bye, Luna."

And just like that, I stood alone in the hallway. Without a boyfriend. Without friends.

Honestly, I felt nothing but relieved. Being a loner I understood. This I could do.

❧

The day's transgressions seemed to be a faraway thing as I sat at home, enjoying the roaring fire in the hearth, belly full. My parents and I had just finished another amazing dinner cooked by Mom, and I was still kind of half dreaming about her chicken potpie and apple crisp.

Dad and I played a game of checkers under the glow of the evening lamps before heading up to bed, while Mom sewed. I'd learned that people didn't watch much T.V. here. They mainly used it to get news about the happenings in the world, not for entertainment. It was considered better for the brain to do more stimulating things in the evenings, such as spend quality time with family. A nice gesture, but the rules appeared a bit oppressive. Under the veneer of happiness, I began to discover that many individuals were afraid of the consequences of not following orders.

My reasons for conforming were highly personal—not wanting to get caught, and have the authorities find out I remembered my life from before. But what was everyone else's excuse? Sure, my ex friends didn't seem to mind breaking the rules. But what normal teenager didn't? Perhaps the consequences rested solely on the parents. I still had much to learn about this new world I found myself in.

"Your turn, Luna," Dad said gently.

"Sorry Dad," I replied, annoyed he had caught me lost in my reverie. I picked up one of my black checker pieces and contemplated my next move on the board.

"You looked so far away. Everything all right, Luna Bell?" Dad asked.

Smiling at him, I nodded and he sat back, satisfied with my response. I breathed a sigh of relief, about to make my play when the buzz of the house phone startled me. I didn't even realize my parents had one. Nobody had called them on it since I arrived. Everyone seemed to use cell phones.

Mom's eyes filled with instant concern and I looked to Dad. He rose quickly and picked up the receiver on the credenza mid ring.

"Hello?" he asked in a gruff voice. "Yes, this is Martin Redwood." Dad's silence permeated the room for another minute or two. Listening to the other person on the line.

It was weird hearing this man, my so-called father, speak my surname out loud. How did he have the same last name as me? That had been my Nova W1 identity. How did that work? But I pushed the thoughts aside, intent on Dad's turned back, his shoulders hunched in defeat. Something was wrong. And it had nothing to do with a surname.

"Of course," he continued, glancing over at me. "I understand how important these matters are and will keep a close eye on things. Have a good evening, sir. Goodbye."

My heart hammered in my chest; pulse roaring and I found my hand instinctively clutching my neck as my father turned around, thick frown lines contorting his face.

"Well it seems Luna, word has gone out that you have had a fallout with your friends. Is that true?"

I swallowed hard and stared at him with huge eyes. "How did you know about that? Who were you speaking to?"

He waved my questions away dismissively. "No need to worry about that. Just someone who has your best interests at heart. You should have told us; we can help you get through these kinds of emotional upheavals. Expressive outbursts are not the way to go. There's always a peaceful solution."

I dared not speak. Did I have spies? What did Dad mean by "expressive outbursts"? It took everything in me not to stand up and stamp my foot and demand he identify who he'd spoken to.

I bit down on my tongue to stop myself.

Mom got up from her spot on the couch and knelt next to me. "You understand you can come to us about anything, right, Luna?"

I gave her a false smile and tried to act normal. "Of course, Mom. It was no big deal, my friends were mad I couldn't go to the party they're throwing because I'm grounded. They'll get over it."

My parents exchanged glances over my head and I realized I said something I shouldn't have. Damn it. For someone who prided herself on being stealthy, I certainly did a poor job of blending in. I would have to study these new memories more carefully. I should have done that in the first place, but a part of me didn't want to face it. I wanted to believe that these parents, whoever they were, loved me for me, not some memory of me that didn't really exist.

"Well, to be honest," Dad said sitting back down in front of the checkerboard, "I never cared for your friends. A bit of a bad influence, I'd say. Perhaps it's time to make some new ones, eh?"

He tried to act casual, but even he couldn't hide the trepidation in his voice.

"Yes, I agree with your father," Mom said petting my hair. "You can always start afresh tomorrow." Her brown eyes glistened in the firelight, fear etched into the lines of her face.

They were afraid for me. They thought I was acting strange, just like everyone else did.

The desire to figure out what the government was doing reignited with a fiery passion.

I had to find out what was happening to me, even if it meant shattering a world where I had found myself loved and cared for.

Some sacrifices were worth the truth.

CHAPTER 11

I had to learn all I could about P8 regulations and understand what kind of place I was dealing with if I didn't want to get caught out.

Because if I did—who knew what would happen to me?

After the weekend I'd just had with my parents, I was grateful for the quiet confines of the library book stacks. Mom and Dad had hovered over me the whole time, following my every move. I thought I might suffocate from the attention.

But here, alone, I breathed easy again; the hushed atmosphere soothing my shattered nerves. Cool air brushed my skin, and I inhaled the familiar scent of old books as I walked deeper into the library archives. There were no librarians milling about, so I headed back to the government section Zander had shown me earlier. There had to be information recorded about their regulations; every place had rules governing their society, especially one as tight-laced as this. I ran my fingers over the spines, admiring the guild lettering of each title. My hand paused when I reached a small paperback tucked against the wall—pale blue and much plainer than the others. I pulled it from the shelf and studied it.

The Rules and Regulations for P8 Society, issue number four. "Bingo," I whispered. With trembling hands I opened to the first page.

"Luna."

I jumped and whirled around, the small volume falling from my grasp. "Zander, you scared me half to death," I yelped, annoyed with myself for being caught off guard. Was I losing my touch?

"Sorry, didn't mean to startle you," he said. "I spotted you come in and thought I would see if you needed help finding anything. Although I think you've pretty much read everything in this section," he added with a smile that didn't entirely reach his eyes. I detected a sad weariness but I couldn't quite pinpoint the source. I sighed. Probably me just being overdramatic. Still, I was unable to shake the weird vibe coming off him.

"No, um... well I actually found what I was looking for," I responded, stumbling over my words, as I stooped to retrieve the book. Why was I so nervous?

Zander read over my shoulder as I stood up. "*The Rules and Regulations for*—" he cut off. His mouth set in a firm line.

He stepped closer, so close that I felt his warm breath on my cheek. "They've already called your parents, haven't they?" he whispered.

I furrowed my brow, perplexed. "What are you talking about?" I hissed. "Why are you standing so close? You're freaking me out." I wanted to run, but I couldn't ignore the desperation etched on his face.

Every nerve ending in my body screamed, but I stayed put.

"If the authorities have already called, you shouldn't be here. Especially getting caught looking at that." He pointed at the book as if it might jump and bite him.

"Why not? I'm free to do what I want, Zander," I said, my voice rising. How dare he tell me what I should read? He had a lot of nerve. I moved to go, annoyed, but it didn't stop my stomach from contracting into a tight ball.

He knew about the phone call.

Zander appeared unfazed by my reaction and took a step forward. This time I had nowhere to go, and I bumped up against the back wall. "Listen Zander, I'm stronger than I look, you might want to—" Before I finished my threat he cut me off, raising his hands in surrender. He spoke so low I barely made out the words.

"They're constantly watching Luna, and if you're not careful, they'll come to your house."

I threw my hands up in the air, exasperated, "Do you always speak in riddles?"

He placed a finger over my lips and glanced around as if checking to see if anyone had noticed us.

Could someone really be keeping tabs on me? But who? And why? My mind fuzzed over as I tried to sort everything out. Nothing made sense. I looked directly into Zander's eyes. They were kind and compassionate. My instincts told me he just might be telling the truth.

As if he sensed my weakening resolve he said casually, "So, have you and your family lived here long? I haven't seen you around the library before the other day. How do you like it?"

He was probing me, seeking information. I had no intention of answering any of these questions, especially since he hovered merely inches away from my face. Talk about an awkward conversation. What would I say, anyway? *Life here is great, Zander, I remember everything—I think there was a mixup and I've got some memories that aren't mine.*

Yeah right, I'd love to see his expression then. So instead I raised my chin haughtily and replied. "I don't have to answer your questions."

Zander shoulders slumped a little. "Fine, suit yourself. But please allow me to re-shelf that text for you." He plucked the small book out of my hands and neatly placed it back on the shelf. "I'll check in with you later," he said smiling, before casually sauntering away.

I crossed my arms over my chest, feeling exposed. What the

hell was Zander up to? Why was he acting so weird? One minute, he appeared panicked and the next he seemed to not have a care in the world.

I scanned the room, but noted nothing odd. Everyone had their own agenda, none appeared interested in me. There were only a couple of people in here, anyway. One—an old man in the corner pretending to read a newspaper with his eyes closed, taking a nap. The other was a woman of about thirty. She wore a perky, rose-colored pantsuit and was busily skimming the books in the cooking aisle.

I drew a deep breath and steadied myself. Obviously, Zander was paranoid. Still, the fact he knew about the phone call didn't sit well. I needed to discover what was in that rule book. Checking that Zander hadn't returned, I picked the text back off the shelf and tucked it under my arm. I made a beeline for my waiting table and quickly got out my homework to cover it up.

But before I even cracked open the manuscript, I heard somebody behind me clearing their throat. I spun to give Zander a piece of my mind, only to find it wasn't him, but an older gentleman of about seventy, with a sharp, angled face and impeccably groomed, snow white hair. He wore a muddy brown sweater as drab as himself, and his perfectly pressed slacks gave the impression of a man of rules. My cheeks flushed hot under his impenetrable scrutiny.

"Miss, it has come to my attention that you are in possession of a reference book. One must sign out these types of volumes, if one wishes to read them." His voice sounded monotone and prehistoric; I cringed at the coldness.

"Book? Um... I'm just doing my homework sir."

"Last I checked the title—*The rules and regulations for P8*—was not required reading at the school. The book please, Miss." He held out his large hand, waiting.

I swallowed hard. Should I give it up? Did I have a choice? I groaned inwardly as I plucked the paperback from under my papers and handed it to him.

"Thank you. If you want to sign for it, you can come to the circulation desk. Enjoy your study time," he said tilting his head at me in acknowledgement. His thin lips upturned into a forced smile before turning to leave.

"What a creep," I muttered under my breath.

How had he known I had it? He must have seen me take the volume. But I knew I would have noticed him. I'd been so careful. He'd literally come out of nowhere. I gripped the table, trying to get some control. Why hadn't Zander told me it needed to be signed out? Besides, what kind of library didn't let you read reference books, as long as you stayed within the confines of its walls? There had to be a reason they wanted the names of everyone that looked at it. Zander had tried to warn me; they were examining my every move.

I shook my head. I was being ridiculous, letting my imagination get the better of me. It was just a reference book. I wasn't in Nova anymore. Not everything was life or death. I stood to leave —this place was starting to make my skin crawl. Besides, nothing else would get done today.

I shivered as goosebumps crawled up my arm. The sooner I left the better. I quickly organized my homework and placed it into their respective folders. Satisfied the papers were all in alphabetical order and accounted for, I slid them into my backpack and zipped it shut.

As I made my way to the exit, I realized leaving was probably for the best. The last thing I needed was to be home late and have my parents on my tail.

I slipped out into the cool afternoon, breathing in the fresh air. Suddenly a rigid hand landed on my shoulder. I froze.

Zander's desperate voice whispered low in my ear. "Don't worry about anything but surviving, Luna. Please."

I turned to face him, but he had already gone, his dire warning ringing in my ears.

CHAPTER 12

"Good evening," a voice boomed as Dad opened the door. "Mr. Martin Redwood, I presume?"

"That's me. Can I help you?" Dad gripped his hands tightly behind his back, knuckles white. Something about this man made him uneasy.

"As a matter of fact, yes." The agent flashed a badge, the gold shield glinting in the moonlight. "I'm Agent Morrow, here to do a general sweep of this area. May I please have a moment of your time?"

A general sweep? What the hell was that about? It had only been a few days since I'd been at the library—had they come because I tried to read that book of regulations? No. That would be insane. But still, I couldn't rid myself of a bad feeling deep in my bones.

Whatever the agent's mission, something was off.

I stood on tiptoe and peered over Dad's shoulder to get a better look at this guy. A well-built man I guessed to be some-where in his late twenties was decked out in a crisp white uniform. He towered over Dad with a threatening demeanor. His dark, gel-slicked hair peeked out from a matching stiff cap. Even his fingernails, neat and trim, were rounded to perfection.

Dad stepped back, and I moved out of the way. "Please come in. Would you like anything to drink? It must be a long night for you, having to check the whole neighborhood and all."

Agent Morrow smiled politely, but it seemed to pain him to do so. His eyes leveled on me and I averted my gaze, staring at the floor uncomfortably. Zander's warning echoed in my brain.

They're always watching Luna, and if you're not careful, they'll come to your house.

The stern-looking government official took off his hat and clutched it to his chest as he crossed the threshold as if unsure what unkemptness he would find. In a word, he was a snob.

"I don't believe refreshment will be required, Mr. Redwood, but I appreciate the offer just the same. What I do need, however, is a space to conduct my testing."

I couldn't hold my tongue any longer. "Testing? What kind of testing? What's it for?" My heart pounded. Ever since Zander's warning on the library steps the other day, I'd kept a low profile —done nothing wrong, or so I thought.

The agent quirked a dark eyebrow at me and stood silent for a beat. "You live in P8 and you are unaware of the general sweep process?" he inquired dubiously.

I shut my mouth and frowned. Was I supposed to have a memory of this? Crap. I quickly covered myself.

"Oh, of course, I do. I simply wanted to hear it explained from someone who has experience doing these sweeps first hand."

Agent Morrow's frown deepened. "I don't have time to explain these things to a child." He turned back to Dad dismissing me. "Now, where should I do the testing Mr. Redwood?"

Dad looked nervous, there was a small sheen of sweat on his forehead, and his eyes darted about like a timid deer in the woods. Just in that moment, Mom bustled in, looking as if someone had just announced a death in the family.

"Welcome Agent, I'm Patricia Redwood, Martin's wife," she said extending her hand in greeting.

Agent Morrow frowned and ignored the gesture and she awkwardly withdrew the offered appendage.

"I realize who you are. There's no need for formalities Mrs. Redwood. It's my job to know everything. Now, where should I start my testing?" His eyes twitched impatiently, as he disdainfully glanced around.

"Of course. Come into the living room," Mom said, ignoring his rudeness. "I'm sure this will be an adequate space for you."

"Thank you." He turned to follow Mom, but abruptly paused, pivoting in Dad's direction. "Give me a few minutes to set up, Mr. Redwood and then bring your daughter in."

Dad nodded in understanding and the agent disappeared with Mom into the other room. I opened my mouth to protest but nothing came out. Blood rushed to my head, *what was happening?* I swung round to face Dad, and managed to croak, "What did he mean? Why does he want to test me?"

Dad looked at me quizzically. "Luna, you've been doing these tests since you were old enough to talk. They check all the children during the general sweeps to determine potential risks. Why are you acting so strange about it now?" He placed a cool hand on my forehead as if checking for a fever.

I pushed him away. "If this is so routine, why are you and Mom so freaked out?" I hissed quietly, so Agent Morrow wouldn't overhear our conversation in the next room. "And what potential risks are they searching for exactly?"

Dad ignored my protests and placed an arm around my shoulders. "You're being too inquisitive, Luna Bell. Do as the agent asks and hold your tongue and you should be fine."

He gave me a reassuring smile, but I sensed his nervous energy.

Something didn't add up here. But what power did I have? It's not as if I had the option to run away. Where would I go? I wasn't as familiar with this place as W1 Nova. Besides, I wouldn't get the answers I needed if I scuttled off like a cowardly dog, tail between my legs. I let out a breath and straightened up. I came from tough stock. I'd clawed my way out of starvation, hadn't I? This should be a piece of cake to handle. The thought of home released a little pang in my heart. And for a moment, I allowed the image of my sister Trinity to filter through my mind. I prayed she was okay and not hungry. I bit my lip until I tasted blood on my tongue. I shook my head and told myself to stop acting stupid. There was nothing I could do for her. Maybe someday that would change, but not now.

Mom returned to the kitchen. "He's ready for you, Luna."

I glanced at Dad and he gave me a nod, so I did the only thing I could do and headed right into the lion's den. Mom stopped me in the doorway, placing a hand on my arm. "Be a good girl, Luna," she whispered.

I swallowed the large lump in my throat. "I will. Promise," I said. I pulled back my shoulders and schooled my features before stepping into the room. The last thing I needed was Agent Morrow to sense fear.

He sat on the couch, all his weird equipment in front of him on the coffee table. There was what appeared to be a recording device, a small gadget with a microphone, and an electronic tablet similar to the ones we had at school, except this one had a single red and black wire coming from its base, with electrode pads attached to the ends. There was also another smaller, hand-held unit he was typing into at a frantic pace.

My palms grew clammy and a sudden stab of anxiety hit my gut like a bullet as I stepped forward.

Morrow glanced up from his tablet. "Ah good, you're here. I've been recording the preliminary information before we get started. Please, have a seat. You know the drill. This won't take long."

I looked over to the doorway and glimpsed Mom pointing frantically to the couch, her eyes pleading with me to be cooperative.

I smiled weakly at her, then forced my stiff limbs over to the sofa and sat down.

"Right, let's get down to business, shall we?" He gave me a mercenary grin, and a shiver ran down my spine. I quickly began to tap my finger against my palm, counting, to calm myself.

One... Two... Three... Four...

Agent Morrow interrupted my count, as he selected something on his screen and forced the tablet into my hands.

"I need you to sign this consent waiver. It's the same as last year, nothing's changed. You just need to verify that we completed the testing on this date per law code seven-hundred and eighty-nine."

With shaking hands, I gripped the edges of the device and stared at the monitor display. There was no information here, just a simple consent form with a line for a signature. I had flash-backs to the paperwork I signed back on Nova giving away my life.

Another forced signature.

I regarded my parents, who stood nervously waiting in the doorway. I hesitated.

"Today, Miss Redwood," Agent Morrow said impatiently practically rolling his eyes. "I do have other clients this evening."

Before I talked myself out of it, I quickly signed using the tip of my finger.

Morrow snatched it back and tapped a few more times on the screen. Satisfied everything was in order, he closed the tablet and put it down, reaching for the other, slightly bigger device.

I stared with fascinated horror as the agent placed the circular sticky electrode pads to each side of my forehead.

"I appreciate you've done this before, Luna, but it's proce-dure to explain everything I'm doing so you don't feel uncom-fortable. We wouldn't want that, would we? Hmmm?" His mouth curled up in a sinister smirk, his steely eyes trained on me. "It's federal law to have periodic checks of all children up to the age of eighteen. So you have a couple more years of this."

I didn't say a word, not sure if my tongue was still hinged in the middle. Sweat trickled down from my armpits.

"Well, there's no point in fussing about. Let's get started. I'm going to use my apparatus," he held up the port screen attached to the probes, "to scan your face. It detects different physiological changes to determine potential risks."

There it was. The potential risks garbage again. I wanted to yell. What potential risks? But I didn't dare. The urge to rip the electrodes off my head grew more intense.

"If there are any abnormalities or detection of something irregular in the mind, we will then take measures to correct the problem. Be assured that you'll get the proper care, so you can become an exemplary member of society before you come of age. But don't worry, the test is very routine. Most pass with ease. Questions?"

He gazed at me, bored as if he'd given this speech a million times and he didn't give a flying fig whether or not I excelled. I had plenty of questions floating around in my head, but not any I could ask. I mean, they thought I did this test yearly since I was able to talk. Why would I have any questions? I'd give myself away immediately if I said anything.

In my mind, there was only one thing left to do.

Give the performance of a lifetime.

Good thing lying came naturally; this should be a cakewalk. Agent Morrow and his little tracking machine would never discern that I had kept old memories. I would shut down that part of myself and allow the Luna of P8 to rise to the surface.

I could do this. No, I *had to* do this. My life depended on it.

"Miss Redwood?" Agent Morrow interrupted my reverie with an annoyed tsk.

I realized suddenly they all had been waiting for me to answer. "No questions," I said hastily, forcing myself to sound confident.

"Good. Now, this won't hurt and will only take a minute. Keep your eyes wide and relax please."

I did as instructed and relaxed my muscles. Concentrating on the four lobes of my brain, I willed myself to embody all the new memories, letting them take me over.

There was a small hum, and a hint of vibration tickled against my temples as Agent Morrow held the device up to my face. The probes pinched a little, but I didn't dare move. I saw my reflection in the screen and a small yellow line passed from top to bottom scanning my mirrored image. When it was finished, Morrow's other machine beeped. It scanned me three more times from every angle possible. My eyes watered and I tried not to blink. After what seemed like an eternity, he finally laid the instrument down, and I let out a sigh of relief.

"All done," he said removing the electrodes from my skull. "Thank you for your cooperation."

I couldn't hold it in any longer. "That's it? You're not even going to tell me the results? How it went?" I asked exasperated.

Agent Morrow's snort conveyed his annoyance. "The results are none of your concern, Miss Redwood. I will discuss them with your parents. The rules have not changed since your last examination. Unless there is something you would like to share with us all?" he said projecting his voice authoritatively, making sure I knew who had the upper hand.

I opened my mouth, ready to give him a piece of my mind but Mom came over and interrupted me. "Of course she knows the rules. Don't you, Luna? She just likes to ask questions. She loves to learn."

I realized from the terror on Mom's face I'd really put my foot in it this time. I tried to backpedal.

"You're right, Mom. Sorry Agent Morrow, please continue." I gave my best contrite expression. I was an expert at giving people what they wished to see.

"Hmmm... well, keep your questions to yourself in the future. Children have no place in the sweeping procedure."

"Of course."

Agent Morrow didn't even consider me. Instead, he went

back to his tablet and began tapping away once more. I wanted to grab it from him and see what he was writing about me. But rather, I clasped my hands together waiting for him to finish. Finally, he folded up his device and scowled when he realized I was still sitting there.

"I believe I dismissed you, Miss Redwood."

"You did?" I asked, feigning confusion. I didn't want to leave. I shouldn't ask any more questions but there were so many riddles. I opened my mouth to speak, but my father's grip on my shoulder prevented me from saying anything else.

"Luna, you must be tired after your long day. Why don't you head upstairs and get ready for bed," Dad's tone sounded ominous.

The agent stood. "Yes, I believe that is the best course of action. I have all the data I require here. Goodnight, Miss Redwood," Agent Morrow said, giving me a dismissive nod. His jaw tightened, revealing his annoyance.

My feet remained glued to the spot. The pressure from Dad's hand intensified, telling me to leave. I don't know how I did it, but somehow I propelled myself up off the couch.

I said a polite goodbye to Agent Morrow, and kissed Mom and Dad goodnight, leaving the room without a backward glance.

I got about halfway up the stairs when their muffled voices floated up to me. No doubt they were discussing this evening's events. My curiosity took over, and I quietly retraced my steps and crept to the closed door, pressing my ear against the wood panel to eavesdrop. I just barely made out the conversation.

"What is going on, Mr. Redwood? Your daughter was confused with the proceeding tonight. And she certainly has no regard for authority. Can you explain that?"

Dad's voice sounded apologetic. "I'm sure she was only tired. She's had a lot of schoolwork lately. You can appreciate how teenagers are."

"Well, as long as you ensure she's following ALL the rules,

Mr. Redwood. Here's my business card. Call this number if Luna acts strangely, has any outbursts, or does anything that concerns you. I remind you it's your civic duty as a citizen of this region to report any abnormal behavior at once; it's for the greater good of the community. She passed her test this evening, so I will over-look any discrepancies I saw here tonight. But to be cautious, I've made a note of it, in case any other issues arise at a later date. Now, I must go."

I overheard a squeaky clank as he picked up his briefcase, then Mom's higher than normal octave. "We'll watch her, Agent Morrow. You can count on us. But as we said before, we're sure there's nothing to worry about here."

Mom's voice suddenly grew louder. Damn it. They were coming toward the stairs. I leapt back as silently as a cat and fled up to my room. Once inside, I soundlessly shut the door and flung myself on the bed, not even caring to see if the sheets were smoothed straight.

I gripped the quilt, squeezing it hard with my hands.

The government detected a rat. I'd made them suspicious, and it would only be a matter of time before they found me out.

I needed a plan. Fast.

I rolled over and punched the pillow in frustration. Me and my big mouth. I'd ruined everything.

CHAPTER 13

I'd lain awake all night contemplating my next move. It seemed there was only one option available to me. Lie low and do my utmost to blend in.

After all, that's what I did best. Back on Nova, it had fed my family and kept us alive.

But would it be enough to keep me alive here? The lack of sleep left me feeling a bit fuzzy. I was grateful for the crisp morning air, cooling my hot cheeks as I headed towards the school. I still hadn't heard hide nor hair from my so-called friends or my pretend boyfriend. Since I'd already burned that bridge, I decided to let it go. Besides, it was easier to blend in if fewer people were paying attention to you. That was rule number one.

As I turned the corner and the school came into view, I noticed a commotion on the quad. As I got nearer, I spotted a group of kids encircling a boy. I'd seen him before and remembered thinking he looked like a freshman. He still had the chubby cheeks of a child, but they were now sprouting the patchy, short stubble of impending manhood. His blonde hair flew wildly in all directions and blood gushed out his nose. The teens in the circle started kicking him and I recognized Orion, Jonah, and Mara amongst his tormenters.

I wanted to run over and pull them away, get them to stop. But I didn't want to bring attention to myself. Guilt edged in. I couldn't stand by and do nothing just to save my own neck. There had to be something I could do to help.

I glanced around; a group of girls by the door were talking on their cell phones. I paused and considered for a minute. What if I stole my former friend's phones? They were always on them, so it would be torture for them to suddenly "misplace" their precious devices. At least it would be a kind of punishment, to make up for my inability to assist this kid now. Hopefully, once they realized they were gone, they would be so panicked looking for the darn things they wouldn't pick on anyone else.

I casually sidled over. The bullies seemed to be getting bored —I didn't have a lot of time. I walked up behind Orion and Jonah and, with a quick sleight of hand, deftly removed the cells from their back pockets. I moved to the pile of backpacks and with careful precision unzipped the bright blue one in front, revealing the gaudy, blinged-out phone I recognized as Mara's. I quietly lifted it out and grinned. I hadn't lost my touch. You could tell so much about a person just from the way they acted— including what kind of backpack they were likely to have. If you watched how they talked and carried themselves, you began to pick up the signals. This was universal, no matter where you lived.

I retreated; my feet soundlessly treading across the grass toward the front entrance. Before I reached the door, I quickly stuffed all three of their phones in my bag, noting to my satisfaction that none of them had even realized I was ever there. Before I went inside, I turned and cast one last glance over my shoulder, and was just in time to see Orion reach for his phone and discover it was missing. Panic ensued, the tormented boy forgotten. The commotion caught the attention of a teacher who began to make his way over to the small group, his lips drawn into a pencil thin line. Most of the kids froze, realizing they'd been had. I smiled to myself and made a beeline for my locker.

Mission accomplished.

The day dragged on slowly after the incident that morning, but I found school work to be a lot easier to navigate with my new memories.

Or so I thought.

Mrs. Lorry destroyed that illusion in fifth period. She'd been rambling on about the city's forefathers, stuff I'd already learned, thanks to my library stint—so I had been sitting there contemplating how best to approach Zander. He was the only one who seemed to be aware something weird was happening in this town. I needed to ask him some questions, even if that meant my plan to lie low would be shattered. When I first came here, I told myself it might be possible for me to go along with this little charade, as long as I had a full belly and love from my parents. But the image of that boy with the bloody nose wouldn't leave my mind. And I now understood: None of this was reality. Underneath all this perfection, fear and confusion raged.

My friends and the rest of the tormenters had been placed in quarantine for twenty-four hours to assess their behaviors. Concerns that they lacked the qualities to become model citizens ran high. They were even paraded out in front of the entire school in a special assembly, as an example to show how anyone who bucked the system would be shunned.

I realized right then that my plan of invisibility would only work for a short while. Eventually, I would slip up, no matter how stealthy and clever I managed to be.

I'd just decided to return to the library after school and have a little chat with Zander, when Mrs. Lorry interrupted my musings.

"Luna? You will be late for your next class if you don't hurry.

As much as I love your company, I think you better get a move on." She smiled, and I stared at her, dumbfounded.

I blinked and looked around, realizing for the first time that everyone else had gone—we were alone in the classroom. Heat rose in my cheeks.

"Sorry Mrs. Lorry, I didn't hear the bell ring—" I stammered.

"No need to explain, Luna. I will allow you the indulgence of daydreaming during the lecture this once, but remember history class is not the place for it. In the future, I expect your full attention."

I stood up hastily, grabbing my book off the desk. "Of course, it won't happen again, I promise."

She placed her hand on my shoulder in a confidential gesture. "The truth is, Luna, these past two weeks you've been doing simply excellent work. I feel like I have a different student in my class. You answer questions; you're engaged and you actually apply the smarts I already knew were inside of you. You've had quite the transformation." She looked kindly at me through her spectacles, her white haloed hair accentuating her angelic features.

My heart pounded, and I swallowed hard, trying to stay calm. "I'm still the same old Luna. No changes to report here." I laughed, but it came out awkward and hollow.

Mrs. Lorry gave me a strange look. "Well, whatever the reason, you keep it up. All right?"

I nodded, wanting desperately to run out of the room. As if reading my mind, she moved aside to let me pass. "You better get on to your next class, Luna; I understand that Mr. Egan isn't so forgiving."

Not needing any further invitation, I hoisted my bag on my back and made a beeline for the door, the sound of Mrs. Lorry's soft chuckle floating behind me. Apparently, my weird behavior was amusing.

If only she knew how dire my predicament really was. I'd

become entangled in a web of deceit so thick I was unable to claw my way out.

But I would never give up.

No one could know about the real me.

Ever.

CHAPTER 14

No one knew where I'd gone. I got an awful tightening in my chest, just thinking about being caught.

That was not an option today.

I slid down further into my seat at the front of the library, as if that would help. I sat close to the big bay windows that provided a view of the park across the street. It was a highly unusual common, with the oddest gardens I'd ever seen. Rather than random trees dotting the landscape, the saplings had been placed symmetrically in these strange, square configurations, each identical to the other and perfectly spaced. Simple white daisies coated the perimeter of the area, all the same size and height, as if they dared not be different. You would expect I would find the clean lines pleasing. Instead, the whole thing creeped me out. The work of some gardener's hands had twisted and forced this odd garden into something it was never meant to be. Just like me.

Not wanting to look at it a moment longer, I turned away and glanced around the oversized room. Only a couple of people milled about—an elderly man hunched over his cane, and a young schoolgirl with a uniform similar to my own. She seemed intent on her task of reorganizing the bookshelves in the far corner and hadn't noticed my penetrating gaze. There was no sign of Zander from this viewpoint. I'd already waited about fifteen minutes and didn't dare push my luck much further. I considered asking the girl if Zander was working today, but decided against it. No reason to bring unwarranted attention.

I'd better head home, I mused. But failed to make a move. I needed a bit longer to get my bearings before I headed back. I had to act a part, and I wanted somewhere to think for a minute without being examined like an amoeba. A stellar performance would be required, and I was willing to risk the extra time.

I pulled out my tablet, set to do some Calculus problems. I'd discovered Math was my favorite subject. I hoped solving a few of these equations might settle my nerves. Thanks to Luna of P8's smarts and memories, it was an enjoyable task.

Within minutes I was engrossed in my work, until someone sat down beside me, making me jolt. I looked up to see who it was.

"Zander."

"Hi Luna," he said smiling, his crystal blue eyes warm and friendly.

"Hi, I didn't realize you were working today."

I groaned inwardly. That had to be about the lamest thing I could have said.

"Yeah, I'm not on the schedule, but I was walking by and spotted you through the window." He gestured to the clear glass pane in front of us. "I don't think I've ever seen anyone come to the library as often as you."

My eyes widened in alarm and I gripped the underside of the table. "What do you mean Zander?" I whispered. "Does nobody else hang out here? Am I weird for—"

He placed a finger over my lips to shush me, and despite my trepidation, my heart skipped a beat at his touch. He dropped his hand, and cast a quick glance over his shoulder as if he was checking for someone. It gave me a moment to catch my breath.

I sat up straighter, his contact meant nothing. It was just a fluke. Adrenaline.

Zander turned back to me. Momentary relief flashed across his face. "It's all right. I won't say anything, I promise." Had he been worried we might be watched?

I nodded; appeased, but still confused. "So why is it bad?" I whispered, not daring to risk anyone overhearing me.

He ignored my query, jumping into a completely different topic, throwing me off guard. "So, are you new here?"

I looked at him, my mouth turning dry. What was he talking about? He'd asked me that last time we met. Had he forgotten? No, I doubted it. He didn't seem the type. True, I hadn't answered his question the first go round, but something else had to be going on, as if he wanted me to pay particular attention. But to what? The way he'd articulated it, seemed strange, as if he was trying to convey a message.

I rubbed my sweaty palms down my pant legs. I wasn't sure what to say. Dare I trust him? There were too many missing pieces. Yet I ached to tell him. The chemistry between us felt electric, but also murky and muddled.

Plus, I'd learned a long time ago, the only person to really rely on was yourself.

"Look, Luna, you don't have to answer that question. It's none of my business. I just wanted to get to know you better."

"Why?" I blurted out before I could stop myself.

He grinned then, his beautiful smile filling his face. "Because you're pretty and a nice girl. I can tell."

My cheeks flushed, and I looked away to hide my discomfort.

"I'm putting my foot in it today, aren't I? I didn't mean to embarrass you. I'm sorry."

He stared down at the floor for a moment, composing himself. After a minute, he surprised me and looked up, staring me straight in the eye as if begging me to read what was on his mind.

The intensity of his gaze almost willed me to uncover what lay hidden behind those deep blue pools.

I furrowed my eyebrows, studying him. I had no memories of him to go on, so everything had to be based on gut instinct.

"Luna, it's clear we have a lot in common. And I don't know about you, but I'd like a friend. What do you say we meet outside these library walls for a change? How about dinner tomorrow night?"

I wasn't sure I should answer yes. I mean, what intel did I have on this guy anyway? I was supposed to be flying under the radar. But perhaps Zander might be the perfect cover. The old Luna liked to party. So it would make sense for her to go on a date. How hard could it be? Besides, he hadn't even called it that. He wanted to be friends.

Either way. I needed answers, and I had a feeling this guy was privy to a lot more than he was admitting.

"I'll have to check with my parents, but I'm sure it will be fine," I breathed.

Zander smiled again. "Great. Here's my number. Call me later," he said, scribbling it down on my scrap of math paper. Then he got up and was out the door, before I had a chance to ask him anything.

I sat there, puzzled. It seemed obvious he wanted to tell me something, but was afraid someone might overhear. But if that was the case, wouldn't there be people in the restaurant who would listen to our conversation, too?

I sighed, packing up my things. There were too many secrets in this place. As I descended the steps out onto the street, I cast a look around, hoping to see Zander, but there was no sign of him anywhere.

Not knowing what else to do, I headed home. Ready to face the music.

I tried not to reflect on Zander during dinner. My parents might sense my unease—especially after the visit from the agent and the dire warning he'd given before he left.

Mom cooked lasagna, which I'd never tasted before. Talk about heaven, it served its purpose in helping me to forget my problems. All the pasta, cheese, and sauce melted on my tongue like liquid butter and I did my best not to inhale it all at once. I made sure I ate slowly and deliberately, even though part of me longed to lick my plate. After I'd devoured the last morsel I looked up to find Mom and Dad staring at me. "What?" I said my mouth still full. "Do I have sauce on my face?"

Mom grimaced. "Don't talk with your mouth full Luna, it isn't ladylike."

Heat burned my cheeks, the delicious flavors turning to sawdust in my mouth. I swallowed quickly. "Sorry," I mumbled.

Mom patted my hand across the table. "It's all right, dear, just remember in the future."

Embarrassed, I picked up my water glass and took a sip.

Dad cleared his throat. "Luna, we want to talk to you about something."

I put down my cup and stared at him. Oh my God. They'd found me out. The government agents were coming for me. I started to stand up, ready to run, but Dad's stern voice rocked me from my panic.

"Sit down, Luna."

Not having any real choice, I plopped back down on the seat, my legs two pieces of wobbling Jello.

Dad sighed. "You realize we want what's best for you, right, Luna Bell?"

"Yes," I said my words barely above a whisper.

"Well, last night you worried us with your strange behavior around the agent. You seemed convinced that we were hiding something from you. We managed to smooth it over, but Luna, you need to be more careful."

"Careful of what?" I demanded, temper flaring. It was time for Dad to tell me the truth.

Mom intervened. "Careful of how you conduct yourself. We just want the agents to see the same wonderful girl we do. However, we expect you to be on your best behavior. Those government checks are completely normal, nothing to be concerned about. They're scheduled. You know that. What your father and I found to be more alarming is that you appear to have no recollection of ever having one."

Mom and Dad stared at me intently, and the blood drained from my face. My stomach clenched into a knot. This wasn't happening. I had to get a grip on myself before I fell apart. I straightened up in the chair, determined to convince them I was fine.

"Luna Bell? Don't you have anything to say?" Dad prodded, his kind blue eyes gently encouraging me to speak.

I clasped my hands tightly under the table and dove in. "I remember the sweeps, I guess I just expected I was getting too old for that sort of thing. Besides, I believed I had a right to my own results. But I understand there are rules in place for a reason," I added hastily. "I'm sorry if I embarrassed you. I suppose I've been a little out of sorts since my breakup with Orion."

The fear in their eyes evaporated into instant understanding.

"Of course you are, dear," Mom crooned putting a hand on my hair. "Heartbreak is difficult to navigate. If you ever want to talk, I'm always here for you."

"That goes for me, too," Dad said gruffly, patting my shoulder.

I smiled at them. "Thanks."

"Now that's settled, how about some dessert?" Mom rose from the table, reaching for the dirty dishes as she did so. "I've made us all some apple pie. I picked the apples myself just this afternoon."

"It sounds great Mom."

She beamed at me as she carried the plates to the sink. "Would you like vanilla ice cream with that?" she asked brightly as she bustled over to the stove, all her fears erased. She pulled out the dessert warming in the oven.

"Yes please," Dad and I both chorused in unison and we laughed, breaking some of the tension.

"I'll get the ice cream, honey," Dad said still chortling. He rose from the table and headed for the freezer.

I sat there quietly for a minute. So far I'd been able to convince my parents everything was fine, but how long could I keep it up? Would anyone else believe my little charade? I hoped Zander would have some answers for me when I saw him. One thing had become strikingly clear.

Mom and Dad were lying to me.

CHAPTER 15

The doorbell rang, and I practically ran down the stairs to answer it. I didn't want my dad to get there before me and start peppering Zander with a million questions. The last thing I needed was Zander in my parents' crosshairs. There was no telling how long he would be interrogated if that happened. A bubble of excitement welled up in me. My first real date. I couldn't help but grin.

I opened the door and Zander stood there looking *really* hot in a black denim jacket, navy sweater, and dark jeans. He held a bouquet of violets in his hand. Our eyes met, and I noticed a new determination behind those crystal blue lenses.

"Hi Luna. These are for you. I saw them at the market today and they made me think of you. They're usually hard to find. I guess it's your lucky day. Well, if you like violets, that is," he said awkwardly, shuffling his feet.

I hesitated. I loved violets. How did he know? I took a deep breath, probably just a crazy coincidence. I had to stop being suspicious of everything or I would go bananas.

"Thank you, they're beautiful," I finally blurted taking them from his outstretched hands. They reminded me of the small purple blossoms that scattered the hillsides in spring back on

Nova. They were always a ray of hope after the long bleak winter. Every year, I would escape to the meadow near my house, and lie down amongst them. As I drank in their scent, I would try to imagine a world free from hunger and pain. It felt ironic to me I now lived in such a place and yet still didn't feel safe.

Before I could say anything else, Dad showed up like a bad penny. He wedged himself in the doorway between me and Zander, and I stepped aside to avoid being trampled on.

"You must be Zander," Dad boomed. "I'm Luna's father, Mr. Redwood." He extended his hand toward him. I noticed Zander didn't shy away from Dad's forceful introduction but stood straighter, meeting him in the eye. It was weird for me to have a parent be so protective. Half of me liked it, and the other half resented it. I wanted to remain independent; but I also enjoyed having the caring concern of a dad, a novel experience for me.

It didn't matter, anyway. I reminded myself that none of this role-playing was as it appeared on the surface. Zander's clear, strong voice interrupted my thoughts.

"It's lovely to meet you, sir. I've come to take Luna to dinner. With your permission, that is."

Dad nodded as if considering. "Yes, Luna mentioned it to us. And as long as you pass the introduction test that will be quite acceptable."

Zander paled. "Introduction test? I don't think..." His voice trailed off.

Dad roared with laughter, clapping him on the back. "Not to worry, son, I'm sure you'll do fine. Please, come in and meet Luna's mother. She's chomping at the bit to be introduced to you."

"Dad," I said, embarrassed.

Too late. Dad had practically hauled Zander inside. I sighed. Would we ever get out of here?

As if on cue, Mom bustled forward, her smile warm, but her demeanor cautious and assessing.

"Hello, you must be Zander. I'm Patricia; it's lovely to meet you. Don't mind Martin, he's a terrible tease." Mom's eyes were soft, not as overprotective as Dad's. Still, I could see beneath her easy going demeanor she was evaluating him. I'm sure Zander hadn't missed it either, but he didn't show it.

"The pleasure is mine," Zander replied smoothly, like he practiced sweet-talking parents all the time.

"Look," I blurted out impatiently. "We'd better go. I promise I'll be back before curfew."

That was another new concept I had to get used to. Having a curfew. It seemed ludicrous, considering I'd always taken care of myself. I didn't need a clock to tell me when I should arrive home. But still while I was here, I needed to play along.

"Well, you kids have a good time," Dad said gruffly. "Take care of my girl, Zander, or you'll be hearing from me."

My heart gave a little flutter at the warm sound of Dad calling me 'my girl', but I quickly admonished myself. None of this really rang true, it was imperative I remember that. He loved a daughter that didn't truly exist.

"Yes sir. I promise."

"Good. Well, I'll let you kids get a move on."

I handed my flowers to Mom. "Would you mind putting these in water for me?"

"Of course, my dear." She took the bouquet and smiled affectionately at me.

I had to get out of here. This whole fake scenario, suffocated me. I grabbed my coat off the peg and shoved it on as I kissed Mom and Dad on the cheek. After that, I practically sprinted for the door.

Zander followed at a more casual pace, making polite goodbyes to my parents. We met up at the end of the driveway.

"Sorry about them," I said.

"Nothing to be sorry about. It's nice they care so much for you."

"Yeah, something like that," I muttered.

"Come on, I bet you're hungry. I know I am. Let's go eat."

I agreed, and we set off, heading toward downtown. The full moon lit up our path and I looked up at the bright stars blanketing the night sky. I drew in a deep breath and counted as high as possible in an effort to quell my frayed nerves, stuffing my hands in my coat pocket at the same time, hoping Zander wouldn't notice how twitchy they were. It took all my resolve not to ask him all my questions right out of the gate. I didn't want to spook him. He might be the only person who could give me the answers I needed.

We walked along in silence, each lost in our own thoughts, but pretty soon Zander started talking. He seemed nervous too, like he needed to fill the void with endless chatter.

"So, do you want to go to Bob's Diner? Have you ever been there before?"

"I've never been anywhere before," I blurted out. Oh crap. What did I just say?

Zander raised his eyebrows. "You've never eaten out?"

I laughed it off casually. "Sure I have. That came out wrong. I meant to say I've never been to a diner before." Technically, I'd stolen other people's take out. That counted as dining out, right?

I wasn't sure he believed me, but he let it drop all the same.

"What about you? Have you been to this place before?"

Zander grinned, probably more to put me at ease, than anything else. "Tons of times. I'm practically a regular. Once you try their fries, you'll be addicted. I apologize in advance for that."

It wouldn't be hard to beat my past experience with French fries. If I managed to steal some from somebody's take-out bag, they were usually long cold. That is, if I got any at all after my siblings had their fill.

"What are you thinking about, Luna? You seem to be having some very serious reflections about French fries."

I pursed my lips, annoyed. "I wasn't thinking about the fries," I admonished.

Zander's grin widened, and he held up his hands. "Hey, I'm

not gonna judge," he said winking. "French fries are serious business."

I opened my mouth to retort, but before I could, he said, "Looks like your wait is over, we're here."

I looked up to find we were standing outside the entrance to a quaint little café. A brightly colored striped awning stretched the length of the roof's overhang, and the words Bob's Diner were painted in bold red across the front window glass. I'd passed this place on my way to school, but never really paid much attention. Eating out anywhere seemed such an extravagant luxury it never occurred to me to give it a second look.

"After you, my lady," Zander said eyes sparkling mischievously as he took hold of the big brass doorknob and opened the oversized door for me.

"Thanks." I swept past him and nearly tripped over the small step, but regained my equilibrium just in time. I groaned inwardly. I seriously rotted at all this social stuff. The interior was packed with people, most of them clustered around the old oak bar. A few customers sat at wooden tables, laughing and chatting as they ate their meals. A sign on the bar listed the daily specials. The perfectly handwritten menu promised everything from fresh chicken fried steak, to something called the lunch box burger with shoestring fries and coleslaw. To the left of that, a slightly smaller identically designed sign offered free home-brewed coffee.

Zander led me away from the noisy crowd toward a softly lit back corner booth. Almost as soon as we sat down, a waitress wearing a poodle skirt from a bygone era came to take our drink requests. I ordered a lemonade; Zander asked for a coke. After she left, I took a better look at my surroundings. The black and white tiled floor was spotlessly clean, and the gold-framed fifties photographs cast a polished gleam against the walls. The waiters, with their white t-shirts, jeans and slicked back hairstyles matched the ladies in the style of that time. Despite the chatter of the restaurant, I sensed an underlying calm, an order I couldn't pinpoint. Even here, in the midst of people enjoying themselves, unstated rules permeated the atmosphere. I shivered.

"Hey, are you cold?" Zander asked. "Do you want my jacket?"

"No. I'm fine, thanks," I said hastily turning my attention to the menu. "So, what's good here?"

"I usually get a burger and fries. They have the best burgers in town."

I looked up; he was staring at me in the same intense way as before. Almost as if he wanted me to say something.

I chose to ignore it.

I shut my menu. "Great, I'll have that."

Relief flooded through me as the waitress returned with our drinks—solving the problem of having to answer any awkward questions in public.

"Here's your beverages," she said placing the cold misty cups in front of us. "Are you both ready to order?"

"Yes, that would be great," Zander replied. We'll both have the deluxe cheeseburger and a side of fries."

The waitress pulled out her small tablet and tapped a few times, no doubt inputting our order, then gave Zander a robotic smile. Her body language revealed she'd done this a lot and she hated it. "Got it. Be back with your order in just a few minutes."

He thanked her and waited until she disappeared before he leaned in close across the booth. "So, you never told me where you're from."

My mouth went dry, and I took a sip of lemonade, biding my time. *Geez, this guy never gave up.* Maybe I'd better give him an answer, so he'd finally put it to bed. "I'm from here. Same as you. I'm surprised I haven't seen you around before."

Lies. Lies. Lies.

Necessary lies. But there was something about him that tugged at my heartstrings. I didn't want to deceive him.

Zander's eyes clouded over with concern. "Well, I guess it was lucky you happened to come by the library then."

I breathed an audible sigh of relief. "Yes, it was," I said lamely.

"Hey, I never told you how wonderful you look tonight."

My face flamed red. I didn't want to admit it but I'd gone to great pains with my appearance this evening. Even trying out the curling iron wand thing left in my room. I'd taken ages trying to decide what to wear, and in the end picked out a knitted knee-length cobalt blue dress, and some calf high black boots. It wasn't exactly my style, but it was in my closet so I thought I'd try it.

"Sorry, I've embarrassed you again," Zander said. "I seem to be good at that. Let's change the subject. Tell me some things you like to do for fun."

My mind scrambled. This seriously had to be the most uncomfortable conversation I'd ever experienced. This was certainly not how I envisioned the evening going.

I tapped my fingers on the table trying to come up with a halfway decent answer.

One. Two. Three...

Had I done anything just for fun? I didn't think so. Everything fun seemed frivolous when every day had been a fight for survival. Even this strange dinner date with Zander appeared unimportant after all I'd endured in Wi Nova. "Why don't you tell me what *you* do for fun?" I said, reflecting the question back to him. I was desperate to get the spotlight off me.

He smiled. "Fair enough. Let's see. Hmmm... Well, I love growing plants; I only have a small garden now, but hope to have a bigger one in the future. But some designs are off-limits, so I have to make sure I adhere to the guidelines. I also tinker a lot. I like to figure out how things work."

I leaned in, eager to ask him why the parks and gardens all looked the same but stopped when the waitress returned with two burgers and a large steaming hot basket of fries.

It occurred to me her interruption had probably saved my behind. I'd almost given myself away. Hadn't I told Zander I was a local, like him? That meant I would already know why the parks and gardens were so symmetrical.

Real smooth Luna. Real smooth.

Better for me to stick to the shadows and keep under the radar. Conversation apparently was not my strong suit. Any more *faux pas* and somebody would start snooping into my background. Hadn't Zander warned me they were always watching? But that was strange too, why would he warn me? I bit my lip, analyzing the situation. The lack of control unnerved me; at least on Wı Nova, my life had been somewhat my own. That is, until my charming mother sold me out for a superior existence. I immediately dismissed the image of that awful day and refocused my attention on the task at hand.

I smiled at Zander before setting to work on my food. It looked delicious. One thing was certain—my taste buds had never been happier. My mouth watered in anticipation for the crisp fries and juicy burger about to invade my senses. I took a bite of the enormous sandwich. "Oh my God," I exclaimed. "This burger is to die for."

Zander laughed. "I presume you like the food here then."

"Like it? I love it," I gushed. "We have to come back here." Oops. Stuck my foot in it again. It sounded as if I wanted him to take me on a second date. I could kick myself. Why had I said that? But fortunately, Zander had started to tuck into his own meal and hadn't noticed my comment. Another lucky save.

We continued on eating in silence, with me living just this side of heaven. Never had I tasted anything this good. After we'd devoured every last crumb, our conversation turned to surface topics, like birthdays, and complaints about teachers and school.

Eventually, Zander suggested we take a walk through town. We left the restaurant and headed down Main Street, passing the library, post office, and grocery store, finally reaching the outskirts of the borough. We stopped at a picture-perfect pond, the village lights reflecting their silvery mooned image on the water's surface. We were quiet for a time, drinking in the tranquil peace of the evening.

Zander reached over and took my hand in his. I gazed up at him, and an unfamiliar feeling of pure happiness flooded through me—but I caught myself—the last thing I needed was to become involved with Zander. I quickly steeled my features.

No one could be trusted in this place.

No one.

Zander looked at me, and for a moment, I thought for sure he was going to kiss me. Instead, he took me in his arms and hugged me. I wanted to pull away. How dare he assume I desired a hug from him? After all, I hardly knew the guy. Who did he think he was? I was just about to stomp down on his foot when he whispered something barely audible into my ear.

"I have memories that don't belong to this place too, Luna."

CHAPTER 16

I yanked myself out of his grasp and glared at him. "What the hell are you doing?"

"Luna, keep your voice down," he said in a low tone.

I whipped my head around to see who else might be listening. But all I was able to make out were the shadows of the lampposts on the sidewalk, and the sound of the wind rustling the leaves in the trees. We were alone.

I stepped toward him and shoved my finger into his chest in warning. "Look Zander, I don't really know you, but I'm not stupid. Did you think one dinner would have me spilling my guts? For what? Just so you can run back to your cronies, or whoever set this up, and blab all the info you learned about me?"

My voice rose to a high crescendo, and I saw Zander take a nervous glance around, his brows furrowed with worry before his eyes locked with mine.

"I'm not spying on you; you have to believe me." His tone was so low I barely made out the words.

"I want to go home," I said, turning on my heels and starting off at a brisk pace. At the corner of my periphery, I saw Zander throw his hands in the air, exasperated, before jogging after me.

"Luna, wait. Please."

I spun once more to face him. "Forget it, Zander. Sorry to be such a disappointment to you, but I'm not as gullible as you assume."

The concern etched on Zander's face was evident, but no way would he play me for a fool.

It had been a stupid ploy all along, so I would let my guard down. Like that would ever happen. I pursed my lips in fury. What the hell kind of game was he playing? Saying nothing more, I hoofed it down the street towards home. The more distance between Zander and me the better.

I had been such an idiot. I might have been arrested. And how had he learned about my memories? He wouldn't know unless he was in cahoots with someone. Or perhaps he was possessed by some kind of psychic ability. How the hell was I supposed to know? My mind raced, trying to come to grips with Zander's unseen knowledge.

"Luna!"

"Stay away from me, Zander. I mean it," I yelled, refusing to slow down. I swung around the corner at full speed, nearly colliding with the hedge. Fortunately, he didn't follow me. Still, I refused to stop running until I reached my front porch. I ran my fingers through my tangled hair, attempting to compose myself. I wanted to appear presentable before I entered the house. The last thing I needed was for Mom and Dad to ask questions. I waited until my breath returned to normal then turned the handle to open the door. Time to face the music.

I found them seated around the coffee table in the living room, immersed in a game of checkers. Dad looked up when he heard me enter.

"You're back! How was your date?" He grinned giving me a quick wink.

I stood there like a statue, struggling to find the right words to say.

"Well go on then," Mom encouraged. "Don't leave us in suspense."

"We ended up at Bob's diner, the food was great," I said lamely.

"And?" she prodded.

I shrugged. "And nothing. We ate, and then he walked me home. He seemed nice and all, but he's not my type."

"Aw, that's too bad," Dad said, sounding not the least bit sad.

I pretended to yawn. "Well, I'm off to bed, I'm tired. Goodnight." I turned to leave before I got interrogated any further.

"Goodnight," Mom said.

"Sweet dreams, Luna Bell," Dad murmured distractedly, his attention already refocused on his next move on the checkerboard.

Once safely in my room, I squeezed my eyes shut and attempted to make sense of this horrible nightmare. Too tired to think, I gave up and got ready for bed. As I put on my pajamas, I spotted my phone amongst the stolen ones still on the dresser. I wasn't used to carrying it around and forgot to bring it with me today.

I made a mental note to return the other phones in the morning. The last thing I needed was to be caught with someone else's cell. I picked them up to put in my backpack when I noticed a red light flashing from inside my phone.

Curious, I examined it more closely, peering at the bottom of the unit to get a better glimpse of the interior. There was definitely some type of mini gadget in there. Palms sweating, I grabbed a long hairpin from the dresser and wedged it into the phone. It produced a brief clicking sound and broke apart, revealing the inner workings. I studied it carefully. Sure enough, barely visible amongst the other parts was a tiny black box flashing a small red light. Instantly, I understood this had to be a tracker. My stomach clenched. Zander had warned me they were always watching. Yes, he may have been lying. But it made sense. Perhaps this was one way they could keep such a "controlled" environment.

I frowned, confused. Why would Zander warn me about them if he just wanted to trap me? It didn't add up.

Not wanting anyone to realize what I'd discovered, I left the tracker in place and closed it up. I looked at the other phones and noted they all emitted the same red light as mine.

The devices here in P8 seemed primitive for the time. They had the limited capabilities of an old-fashioned flip phone; you could text and call people, but that's where the technology ended. On W1 Nova, I'd seen the rich with high-tech gadgets that did everything from playing music to ordering food—a luxury afforded only those with the highest social standing.

My mind switched back to the problem at hand. Did the government know I went out with Zander tonight?

But I failed to bring my phone. Did that mean they concluded I'd never left my room? And what if Zander had carried his with him?

I sighed, shoving the cell phones into my bag before throwing myself down on the bed.

For the first time, I admitted to myself I was in over my head.

If I trusted the wrong person, I could end up dead.

I realized that if I wanted to escape alive, I was going to need some help.

But who could I trust? And where did I go from here?

I didn't have the answers.

CHAPTER 17

I'd just finished first period English and was about to head to my next class when a cold hand clamped down on my arm.

"Please come with me," a voice said in an ominous tone.

I looked up to find my teacher, Miss Preston, staring at me, her lips turned down in sour disapproval. I sat frozen to the spot for a minute, not daring to move. What had I done?

"Miss Redwood, is there a problem?" she asked when I didn't budge.

I jerked my arm free and rubbed it. "Where are we going?" I demanded, not willing to go anywhere without an explanation.

Miss Preston stiffened and straightened up as if to exert more authority. Her coiffed brown bob didn't budge an inch, solid as a football helmet, as she tilted her head sideways to analyze me. Her old-fashioned black suit, with its white, button-down shirt had been done up to her neck, suggesting she was an uptight character. However, if you looked past her bluff, the strain on her narrow face was clear and shouldn't have shown up on someone so young. She was actually rather pretty with her ebony skin and big tawny eyes. Pity she ruined it with the scornful expression that played across her features the majority of the time.

"Are you always this difficult, Luna?" she asked, shaking me from my thoughts.

I refused to answer, and she nodded her head curtly. "Just as I suspected. But at this juncture, that is neither here nor there." She pointed to the door. "After you, Miss Redwood. The principal would like to see you in his office."

"But I didn't do anything."

"I am not your judge. It's between you and Mr. Rhodes. Now come. We don't want to keep him waiting."

Not knowing what else to do, I stood and followed the prim, straight-laced teacher down the hall. The smell of pine cleaning products and macaroni and cheese cooking in the cafeteria melded together in a disgusting concoction. My stomach lurched, and I began to count to calm myself, certain if I didn't relax, the principal would hear my heart pounding through my chest for sure.

By the time we reached the principal's office, I had discovered there were exactly a hundred steps between here and Miss Preston's classroom, but it hadn't improved my anxiety one iota.

Miss Preston knocked on the big wood door housing a gold plaque that read, *Principal.* "Mr. Rhodes?" she called. "I have Miss Redwood here to see you."

"Ah yes. Please come in," a male voice responded.

I'd never actually met the principal; however, I'd seen him at a few school events and assemblies. He didn't fit the perfect mold of P8. I was still trying to figure him out. He seemed a tad flawed for this pristine universe.

I followed Miss Preston into a small office. A cheap plywood desk consumed most of the area, and apart from a rickety little bookshelf tucked in the corner, the sterile room held not much else. I burrowed a little deeper into my sweatshirt, trying to ward off the chill.

"Please, Luna, sit," the portly man said gesturing to the folding chair in front of his desk. His mustache twitched furiously, like it had taken on a life of its own, and made him appear nervous. But that couldn't be right. Must be just a weird tic.

I put my backpack on the floor and slid into the hard seat. I shifted, trying to get comfortable. "Look, Mr. Rhodes, I don't understand what this is about. I haven't done anything wrong."

Mr. Rhodes raised a bushy eyebrow, then turned to Miss Preston. "That will be all Sarah, thank you for bringing Luna. You'd better go prepare for your next class."

"Yes, of course," she replied, blushing right down to her roots.

Miss Preston seemed pretty near afraid of him.

I sized him up. I'd definitely dealt with worse. His cheeks were red, as if he was overheated just by sitting there. A too-tight beige jacket strained against a large paunch that hung over his belt like jelly. His tie, loose against a rumpled white shirt, required a good wash, and I almost waited for the bursting buttons to pop off.

His beady brown eyes bored into me in reprimand. "Now, Miss Redwood, shall we get down to business? I must say I was surprised to find that you may have taken part in such deviant behavior. You've been doing so well recently."

I leaned forward, gripping the edge of his desk. "I don't know what you're on about, so let's just cut to the chase."

I was pushing my luck talking to him like that, especially since politeness appeared to be the key ingredient in keeping P8 running smoothly. But I was sick of all these games. And he caught me at a bad time. Last night, my brain kept repeating Zander's words over and over, preventing me from sleeping. *I have memories that don't belong to this place too, Luna.*

And the trackers were an entire other problem. Tired and still a little nauseous, I wasn't in the mood for this interrogation.

"I dislike your tone, Luna. Watch it. You're already skating on thin ice," Mr. Rhodes said, his voice drifting back to me. "Some cell phones were reported stolen and I was given an anonymous tip that you may have had something to do with it. I thought I would give you the benefit of the doubt and hear what you have to say on the matter. Though I will disclose that more than one person came forward, naming you as the culprit."

He paused as he gauged my reaction. Though my pulse roared in my ears, I didn't allow him to see my fear. I'd conned people all my life—and I needed to now. Nobody would ever have to discover the truth.

I leaned back in my hard chair, and hid my trembling hands in my hoodie pocket, grateful I put it on over my uniform that morning. Showing signs of trepidation would never do.

I took a deep breath and turned on my acting skills, preparing myself to play the part of an innocent victim.

I shook my head at Mr. Rhodes as if confused. "I'm sorry, I have no idea what you're talking about. Whose phones were stolen?"

The principal stared at me speculatively. "We both know whose phones we are talking about. It's all over the school."

I lifted my chin. "I'm sure I don't."

Mr. Rhodes raised a chipped mug of steaming coffee to his lips. The words #1 principal were written on the front. It took everything in me not to roll my eyes. I mean come on, this guy's manipulation techniques were classic old school. He obviously didn't appreciate who he was dealing with.

He tried creating an uncomfortable silence, hoping I would start chattering to fill the quiet. Fat chance. I could wait forever.

When he saw I wouldn't budge, he put his cup down and started shuffling some papers on his desk. "Well then, it seems we have come to an impasse, doesn't it?"

I stayed silent and crossed my arms.

He sighed and looked up at me. "We have reason to believe you stole the phones from your friends, Luna. There is a rumor around school that you have had..." He paused, dramatically pressing down his ugly mustache. "A falling out."

I detected a hint of sympathy in his voice and I immediately pounced. *Find their weakness.* Isn't that what Mama had always taught me? My blood boiled just thinking about that woman. It was her fault I was stuck in this God-forsaken place. I caught myself before I did anything rash, and willed myself to shut it down. There was no damn way she would ruin my life. I could fix this. It was time to implement phase two.

I pinched myself under my sweater, twisting skin so hard tears sprang to my eyes. It wasn't difficult, my eyes were already watery from lack of sleep. "I didn't do it Mr. Rhodes. I swear I would never do anything to hurt my friends." A single tear slid down my cheek as I gazed at him forlornly.

"Don't cry, child, here," he said picking up his small box of tissues. I sniffled and took one, wiping away the tears forming in my eyes.

"Thank you," I murmured.

"Now tell me about this feud with your classmates."

My lips trembled a little before speaking. "They've changed." God, I'd forgotten how easily drama came to me; if my situation hadn't been so precarious this almost could have been fun.

"From what I'm hearing, you're the one who's changed, Luna."

The little breakfast Mom forced me to eat this morning whirled around in the pit of my stomach. I gulped. *Come on Luna. You can do this.*

I sat up straighter. "No that's not it. They are the ones that are different. They aren't kind like they used to be." *Bingo,* I thought smiling to myself. Kindness was currency in this place.

Mr. Rhodes rubbed his chin. "Well, as you are aware Luna, we don't tolerate insubordination at this establishment. However, I can't fault you for not wanting to hang out with unkind individuals. It hasn't escaped our notice that your companions were involved in an altercation with a young man a few days ago on school grounds. Still, I find it hard to fathom a teenage girl would dump her friends so quickly."

I let the tears spill freely now, as I prepared for my well timed semi-truth. "When I saw how they bullied that boy, I decided I wouldn't hang out with them anymore. I've been so stressed out about it I chose not to add to my problems by associating with them." I released a small sob and placed a hand over my mouth as if to stifle my cries. Time for the grand finale.

"I have a lot going on at home, sir. It's been hard."

The principal sat up straighter, his jowls almost quivering with curiosity. "What do you mean? If you are troubled by anything, you can always talk to me about it."

The taste in the air of fresh pencil shavings and stale coffee left my mouth feeling metallic. This dude was so full of it.

I pushed all that aside and waited a beat. Timing was everything.

"I have to decide what college to go to and there is a lot of pressure on me. I need perfect grades to get into a good school and I don't want to disappoint anyone."

Mr. Rhodes visibly relaxed. "Ah well, that's normal. It's an important time in your life. All you can do is your best."

"I swear to you, Mr. Rhodes, I didn't steal those phones. I may not be talking to my friends but I wouldn't risk my future on such a silly prank."

He reached for a pad on his desk and scribbled something on it. "Here's a pass to explain your tardiness to class. I am going to trust you are telling me the truth, Miss Redwood. And I better not hear any more troubling rumors about you. Or there will be consequences."

Not even daring to breathe, I stood up and took the slip of paper he offered and tucked it into my pants pocket. I picked up my backpack and faced him. "I'm sorry they lost their cell phones sir, but it wasn't me. I hope you find whoever is responsible."

"Yes, well so do I. Thank you for your assistance. You better get to class now."

I nodded and turned to leave the room as fast as humanly possible. As soon as I reached the hallway, I paused and breathed a sigh of relief.

I'd done it. And the phones had been in my backpack, directly under his nose during the entire conversation. I decided right then and there to return them A.S.A.P before my so-called friends requested a raid on my locker or something.

⚜

By the time the bell rang for lunch I'd worked myself into a real temper. The government tracking my every move made me want to scream in exasperation. How dare they ruin my life? And with them constantly watching me, how the devil would I ever escape this place?

First things first. I had to get rid of these phones. I felt like they were burning a hole in my bag. But before I did that—a little recon was necessary.

I entered the crowded cafeteria, and the yummy smells bombarded my senses. My stomach growled. Now the interrogation from the principal was over, the all-too familiar hunger pangs gnawed at my belly. No big deal. I'd dealt with a lot worse. This confrontation, however, couldn't wait.

I found my friends at their usual table by the window, their plates laden high with food. My mouth watered at the sight of it, but I concentrated on my mission. I lifted my head up higher, hoping to instill some much-needed confidence in myself. *Quick and painless. Just get in and get out Luna.*

They all stopped talking when they saw me approach. All my cool evaporated, and I found myself turning every shade of crimson as what I wanted to say blurted from my lips in a tumbled rush.

"Look, I don't know who took your phones, but it certainly wasn't me. So I would appreciate it if you quit spreading lies. Especially to the principal." I stuck my nose in the air, desperately trying to give off an air of authority.

Mara tossed her blonde curls back and stared at me in disgust. "Luna, we're sure it was you, just admit it. First, you refuse to be friends because you think you're better than every-one, and then to make it worse, you steal our stuff. I bet you ratted us out to the principal over that stupid kid, too. Seems like something you would do. You get whatever you deserve."

I thought of the kind girl I'd met on the P8 platform, compared to now. What had this warped place done to her? All the anger I had held onto evaporated. I'd been selfish. My memories hadn't been erased. But poor Mara had no choice in the matter. Pity for her welled up inside me.

Orion puffed up his chest and squinted at me. "Look at you —guilt plastered all over your stupid face. Go find someone else to bug, Luna."

Jonah, who'd sat quietly up to this point, raked a hand through his thick, dark curls and smirked. "Man, I can't believe you put up with her as long as you did Orion; this girl's a fricking freak. Who would have guessed a book nerd could be so dumb?" He threw back his head and laughed.

I leaned forward over the table, my voice low. "I don't know what game you're playing, but I'm not interested. Leave me out of it. I didn't take the phones."

The lies flowed off my tongue effortlessly. The instinct to survive was strong. They didn't understand how far I would go.

Mara spoke up. "Why don't you leave? This isn't getting you anywhere." I glimpsed a pleading in her eyes, a spark of human-ity. I hoped that maybe somewhere in there, the Mara of W1 still existed.

It hit me then, this wasn't just about me. I owed it to everyone to get the facts. Something strange was happening to all the people of this place. I hoisted my backpack over my shoulders. It seemed heavier with the contraband inside. Mara was right, I needed to get out of here.

"Fine. Don't listen," I said to the group, and turned on my heels and left.

As I walked away, I imagined their faces if they learned the truth. Were they aware everything they said and did was monitored?

After leaving the crowded cafeteria, I slipped unseen down to the corridor of lockers that lined the hallway leading to the double-doored exit. I looked around. The coast was clear. Most of the teachers would be in the teacher's lounge, having lunch. I'd done some recon work earlier and figured out where Jonah and Mara's lockers were. Since I already had a memory of Orion's, I hit up his first, twisting my hair pin into the lock. It opened effortlessly, nothing I couldn't handle. I'd picked locks and snuck around my whole life. That was why I was so shocked when I heard a voice behind me—just as I was about to make the drop.

"Luna, would you like to explain to me what you are doing in someone else's locker?"

CHAPTER 18

I slammed the locker shut and whirled around to find a short, muscular man in a brown tweed coat peering at me through round owlish glasses. He stood so near that his obnoxiously strong cologne invaded my senses.

I stepped back, leaning against the lockers. I needed some breathing room. His pale face appeared waxen under the artificial lights, and his mouth curled up in a sneer of contempt, revealing perfectly polished white teeth. He moved closer. This guy wasn't even pretending to keep up the pretense of the P8 kindness policy. Maybe once you were considered a criminal all that went out the window and they treated you like garbage. Either way, it was bad news for me.

How had I forgotten about the hall monitors? It seemed thoroughly obvious to me now that he was staring me down. It was the student teacher's job to roam the hallways on breaks and after school. I could've kicked myself. What a stupid mistake— one I would normally never make. I'd completely miscalculated. I licked my dry lips. What the hell should I do? The old me would never have been caught in such a predicament. But to be fair I was at a disadvantage here, and it was too late for regrets.

I needed a plan and fast.

I analyzed the man before me, schooling my features to hide my fear. Time to test my acting skills again. I smiled apologetically. "Oh, this locker?" I rolled my eyes and pointed to Orion's locker where I'd almost stashed his phone moments before. "I know, right? I had a total brain spasm. I thought this was mine. Weird, isn't it? I clearly didn't have breakfast this morning." I leaned against the rows of lockers and crossed my arms like it was no big deal.

The teacher observed me for a moment, his bushy caterpillar eyebrows wiggling together. "We're both aware that's not a plausible answer, Miss Redwood. You'd better come with me."

I swallowed hard. How did he know my name? I'd never seen this man before. The hairs on my arm prickled. Something fishy was going on. He reached out and grabbed onto my elbow. "Ouch," I yelped. But my protests were useless. He ignored me and proceeded to drag me down to the principal's office.

Shit.

I dug my heels in, but it did nothing to stop him, he was too strong.

"You're hurting me," I gasped, trying to pull away from his grip.

"It's no matter where you're going," he snarled in my ear. "Now get in there." He gave me one last shove, propelling me through the door into Mr. Rhodes' office for the second time that day. Mr. Rhodes sat behind his desk, his beady eyes assessing me as I practically fell into the room. He wiped at his profusely sweating brow with a handkerchief and motioned me to take a chair.

"Have a seat, Miss Redwood."

I hesitated but the hall monitor clamped hold of my shoulder, pushing me down. I winced under the pressure.

"I found her snooping in someone's locker out in the hall," the obnoxious man growled. "I decided to bring her in here so you can take care of her."

His sneer made me shudder.

"Thank you for your assistance, Burt. It is no longer required. I can take it from here."

Burt seemed a bit put out, his bottom lip folding into a pout. I bet I was his first hall conquest. The sick bastard wanted to watch me go down in flames.

I gave him a stare that could cut glass and waited for him to leave. Burt didn't budge.

"Now," the principal bellowed, slamming his hand down on the desk.

The normally chilled room practically rippled with heat as the two men faced off, but in the end, Mr. Rhodes won out and Burt scuttled off, his tail between his legs.

Mr. Rhodes pulled himself to his feet and crossed to the door, flinging it closed with a resounding thud. Then, without a word returned to his seat.

My fingers trembled as I twisted them together in my lap waiting him out. Another game.

I stared at him in challenge, daring him to speak. A strange expression passed over his face, almost smug, but not quite.

What was he playing at?

After what seemed an eternity, he leaned back casually against the chair and crossed his feet at the ankles, placing his hands on his extended belly as if he had all the time in the world. Unfortunately for him, the sweat pooling on his forehead gave him away. "So, Luna. Would you like to tell me what all this is about?"

"I don't understand what you mean," I said, my tongue thick and wooden in my mouth. Burt hadn't called me out about the phones. All he'd seen was me opening another person's locker. Did the principal know? Were they watching my every move? Why hadn't I been more careful? I'd been so intent on staying under the radar with my parents and getting rid of those trackers I never stopped to speculate the school might be booby trapped.

I gritted my teeth. My Mom and Dad in this dimension had

made me soft. Complacent in their love. I vowed it wouldn't happen again.

Mr. Rhodes leaned in closer. "Oh, but you do, Luna. Let's not play games, all right? Neither of us has the patience for that." I noticed for the first time the sandwich at the side of his desk. He pulled a piece of greasy bacon from the middle and stuffed it in his mouth, leaving a residue of oil dribbling down his chin.

I tried not to appear disgusted as he wiped off his face and licked his fingers clean. "You and I both realize I have you over a barrel, Miss Redwood. What you have done cannot be ignored. And as such I should do my duty and report this to the government agency." He leaned forward and just for a moment, I detected some kindness in his eyes. But it was just as quickly gone, replaced with a steely determination. "But I'm not going to."

The rosiness in his cheeks deepened as he stood and came around to perch on the front of the desk, mere inches from me. His voice rumbled deep in his throat, and his fingers twitched. What the hell? Why wasn't he going to report me? There had to be a catch.

"What's going on?" I demanded, trying to get a read on Mr. Rhodes. His face remained impassive, his gaze never wavering from my face. "It's obvious now that you are the one that stole the phones. Why else would you be hanging out at Orion's locker? Hmmm?"

"How did you know—" I cut off realizing I'd just implicated myself. Damn it all to hell.

"Yes, I do know Miss Redwood. I understand more than you think. I might consider helping you if you're honest with me. But if not...well...." He was silent then waiting for me to speak. Finally, after a beat, I couldn't take it anymore. He already knew it was me, anyway. I could see no clear way out of this office or my predicament. But I could still play the game.

I leaned in, my palms spread-eagled on the desk. "Fine. I did it. I stole those phones. But it was only because I lost my friends." I turned the tears on in earnest, this had to work.

I continued, between big gulping sobs. "Please, I'll do whatever you want if you give me a second chance. I promise I won't do anything like that again. I swear," I pleaded, my voice now barely above a whisper.

Mr. Rhodes stared at me intently, as if gauging my integrity. I sensed a weakening and hastily carried on with my story. "They've completely changed Mr. Rhodes; they turned on me. They didn't want to follow the rules. I just tried to teach them a lesson about not hurting people, because that goes against everything P8 believes in—and what I believe in." I placed a hand over my heart for emphasis.

He stood and grabbed the handkerchief he'd left on the desk and dabbed at his sweaty face. A flash of what appeared to be pain crossed his features at my words, before he eased his portly frame into the chair and leaned back; it moaned under the weight.

"Luna, Burt, I mean Mr. Cole, saw you out there with the phones. And you directly violated P8's code of ethics. I am supposed to report it."

"But I just confessed! I can make it right. I'll apologize to my friends. Anything."

Mr. Rhodes lips pursed as if making up his mind about something, then spoke. His voice hushed in warning. "No, you won't. You are going to do exactly as I direct. You will make no attempt to return the phones. Is that understood?"

He waited until I nodded before continuing. "You will drop them off at the lost and found. ASAP. As you are aware, it's a federal offense to be in possession of another's phone, and you will get rid of them, if you know what's good for you."

I stared at him, mouth agape.

"You can close your mouth at any point, Luna. You don't want flies to get in do you?"

His small attempt at humor did nothing to quell the tight grip of unease that threatened to take my breath away.

"The bell is about to ring. Have I made myself perfectly clear?"

I managed to squeak out. "Why would you—"

Mr. Rhodes put up his hand to silence me.

"I want no questions. Just do as I say. And tell no one we had this conversation."

The principal's strange behavior had made me forget to keep up my act. I quickly put my chosen persona back into place.

Why on God's green earth was he doing this for me?

"Miss Redwood? Did you hear what I said? It's very important this remains confidential."

I opened my mouth to say something but his eyes flashed a warning. So, I simply nodded.

"Good."

I stood up hands clasped. I would say whatever was necessary to leave. "You won't regret this, Mr. Rhodes. I promise."

Mr. Rhodes stood taking a step toward me. "Now, wait a minute. You're not getting off the hook yet. Just because I'm not reporting you to the government doesn't mean you get off scot free. You'll have detention for a month. And if anyone asks about it, just say you were tardy for class too many times."

"But what about the hall monitor? He saw me—" I pointed toward the door indicating where I'd been caught. Mr. Rhodes didn't let me finish.

"Let me worry about Mr. Cole. He's my responsibility and reports to me. You need to take care of yourself and focus on staying out of trouble. But, before you go, there is one other thing I need to warm you about..." He paused, scratching at his chin, avoiding my gaze, before continuing. "I will need to contact your parents about your detention. I'm sorry, but it's necessary. And a rule that I won't break."

My head shot up, "What? Do we have to do that? What

happened to keeping things confidential? Can't we just keep it between us?"

In one quick stride, he bridged the gap between us. His cheeks exploding into a new rash of red splotches. "Certainly not, young lady. I have already bent the rules enough for you today. Understand, Luna. This is the end of the line. Your parents will be informed of your tardiness. Now go to class."

He stared at me intently as he opened the door. Like he had no choice and I needed to play along. Still I chose to pitch my plea one last time. I didn't want my parents thinking I dug myself further into trouble. Even though technically I had.

"But sir, if you would only—"

He cut me off. "Our business is concluded, Miss Redwood. There will be no more discussion."

Reluctantly, I turned to leave, but his voice stopped me. "And Luna?"

I glanced back over my shoulder and stared at him full on.

"I'm all for second chances, but if you burn me on this, you'll live to regret it."

I shuddered inwardly and nodded. The air had gone suddenly cold, and I hastily made my exit. The stolen phones weighed heavy in my bag. One thing Mr. Rhodes was right about—I had to get rid of them. And fast. I remembered seeing the lost and found box next to the secretary's desk so I made a beeline for her. Mrs. Dalton was stationed right by the office doors to greet visitors and any students that came in to meet with the principal or vice principal. As I turned the corner, I could see she was alone, and no students sat in the chairs that lined the wall. I tried to be discreet and sidled up close, hovering next to the lost and found box. I could see miscellaneous clothes; a red sweater, a cast off sneaker and a couple of headbands, but not much else.

"Can I help you, Luna?"

I jumped at the sound of my name and spun to see Mrs. Dalton a hairsbreadth from me. She was wearing a khaki colored suit, white blouse and pearl earrings at her ears. She donned the same colors as the students and I was beginning to realize that this must be a mandatory requirement for all personnel. She smiled at me kindly. Everyone at school loved Mrs. D. She didn't have any children of her own and she often said the students were her kids.

When I didn't respond she put a small hand on my arm. "I'm sorry to startle you. Did you lose something? Perhaps I can help you find it."

"Uh. No. Actually I came to drop something off. I found them outside," I said lamely. "Someone must have left them on accident."

Mrs. D's brow furrowed in confusion. "Found what, dear?"

My hands fumbled, but finally I was able to open my bag and pulled out the three phones. They burned like fire in my palm.

Mrs. Dalton put a hand to her heart. "Oh my. What a very expensive item to lose. I bet whoever owns them are sick with worry. We should try to find their owners. I'm not sure if they would be safe in the box. I can keep them at my desk and see if anyone comes in looking. It's a shame we don't have the names of the rightful owners," she mused.

Guilt edged at my consciousness. I had to make sure these phones went back to the right people. There had to be a way.

"Look, Mrs. Dalton. I know who they belong to. Let's just say I figured it out. But if you promise not to tell them where they came from. Or rather whom. I'll give you the names."

Mrs. Dalton looked at me blankly for a minute then smiled, as if finally, all the pieces came together for her. *Oh God, don't let her have figured this out.*

"How sweet of you, Luna. Not wanting any of the credit for such a wonderful gesture. But are you sure you don't want them to know who you are? I'm sure they'd love to thank you."

"No!" I said with too much vehemence. Putting out both my hands as if that would stop her.

Mrs. Dalton's eyes widened in surprise. "Well, all right, if you feel that strongly about it. I won't say anything to them."

I breathed a sigh of relief. "Okay. Great. It's just I hate being the center of attention for any reason."

Mrs. Dalton gave my shoulder a squeeze. "I can understand that. I don't really like it myself." She offered me a kind smile and patiently waited for me to give her the information.

"Right. Okay. The names. Here goes. The black phone belongs to Orion Duncan, the pink one to Mara Masters, and the last phone is Jonah Edward's."

Mrs. Dalton's eyebrows furrowed in concentration for a minute before speaking. I swore she could hear my heart pounding right out of my chest. "Luna, I pretty much know everyone at this school and I don't recognize those names. They aren't new students, are they?"

I pressed my lips shut not daring to answer. Was this a trick question? I mean, Mrs. D. seemed harmless enough. But what if she wasn't? My palms began to sweat and I felt the itch to get out of here. But forced myself to stay. What would running accomplish? It would only make me look as guilty as hell.

"I know!" Mrs. Dalton exclaimed, jolting me out of my panic. "Let's check the database. I'm sure they will be on the student list."

I watched as she moved to her desk and slipped into the chair. She stared expectantly at the screen as she tapped some keys on her tablet, but after a few more swipes of the keyboard she looked up, frowning.

"They're not on the list of attendees. I have no record of those students ever attending this school. Are you sure you got the names right?"

I pulled my backpack higher up on my shoulder trying to look innocent. "I don't know. Maybe I got it wrong. I guess that's what happens when you try to do your own sleuthing." I laughed a little as if it was a bit of a joke.

Mrs. Dalton smiled but there was an air of suspicion

clouding her features. "I know you were doing what you thought was right, dear. But you really should leave the finding of the owners to the school. You know how much privacy is valued, not only in this institution, but in P8, too."

I almost laughed out loud at that. Privacy? She had to be joking. But instead I managed to get it together and said, "Of course. You're right. I wasn't thinking."

"That's okay. Just don't let it happen again. Now, I'm going to pop these into my desk and we'll see if we can't find the real owners. All right?"

I could see a crack in her veneer of happiness as she took the phones from my waiting palm. She was suspicious of me. And I needed to get out of here. Fast. Before she asked me any more questions.

"Thanks Mrs. Dalton," I said. Not waiting for a reply I hurried out of the office area.

My mind scrambled, where had my so-called friends gone? I had just seen them in the cafeteria. Why had they been erased from the school system?

What was going on?

৩৯৪৩

When I got home later that day Mom and Dad were both in the living room waiting for me, their faces somber. Dad sat in his favorite chair, while Mom paced up and down behind him, wringing her hands.

"Luna!" Mom stopped pacing when she saw me. "Sit down. Your father and I wish to speak to you."

I sank down onto the sofa, Mom followed suit. Dad leaned forward in his chair. "We heard what happened in school, Luna Bell. And I have to say we are very disappointed in your actions."

Despite knowing that these two strangers weren't my parents, I nevertheless felt a sinking dread fill the pit of my stomach. Somehow, even in this crazy situation, I still didn't want to disappoint them. I inhaled deeply; now wasn't the time to get philosophical. I had a job to do.

"It's not what you think, Dad."

"Oh good, so you have a reasonable explanation for being late to class multiple times resulting in your detention, have you?"

"Well..." I scrambled to think of a plausible confession and blurted the first thing that came to me. "It was Orion, Jonah's, and Mara's fault Dad. They kept me from class because Orion decided he couldn't live without me. How lame is that? And he used the other two to try to pressure me—" I stopped myself. *Oh God. What had I done?* The principal had distinctly said to only state I was late. And not to mention the phones. I suppose technically I hadn't disclosed anything about the phones—just the owners' names. Maybe I could salvage this. But Dad interrupted me before I could.

"Who is Orion? Or Jonah and Mara for that matter? Are these new friends of yours? And do I need to meet this Orion fellow? Why can't he live without you?" Dad's voice rose with every word. I turned to Mom for help. Obviously, Dad was so steamed he couldn't remember straight. But Mom looked blank as well.

I hesitated. Then my curiosity won out. Risky as it was, I had to know. "Orion was my boyfriend, Dad. We broke up. Don't you remember? And Jonah and Mara have been my friends forever."

Mom and Dad crossed their arms as if in a united front, both scowling. "We're concerned that you feel the need to lie to us like this," Dad said, his voice dripping with disappointment.

"I'm not lying," I exclaimed, exasperated.

"We know all your friends. And certainly boyfriends. We are your parents, after all," Mom interjected. "What are you hiding from us?"

"Nothing. I swear."

"Lying and not making good use of your time goes against the very principles we stand for in P8, Luna Bell. You are worrying your mother and I." Dad's voice cracked. Mom turned away, covering her mouth. But not before I saw tears in her eyes.

That's when it hit me. They seriously had forgotten about my friends. My boyfriend even. I could see it now. The completely blank stares were proof.

I swallowed hard against the bile rising up in my throat. *Why didn't they remember them? What the hell was happening?*

There was a reason that the principal didn't want me to return those phones. What if there was something bigger than I could ever imagine behind all this?

But what?

None of it made sense. Was it possible that Orion, Jonah and Mara were sent to another universe like me? But wouldn't someone know that?

"Don't you have anything to say?" Mom whispered. She'd turned back and was staring at me with such pain in her expression, it deepened the lines in her face, as if she had aged overnight. I had to do something about this. If nothing else I had to calm my parents down before they did something rash.

Like call the authorities.

I looked down at my shoes, trying to think up the most plausible lie. Then went for it. Not daring to meet their gaze. This had to work. "Okay. You're right I made those people up because I didn't have a good excuse about being late. It just sort of happened. I didn't want you to be disappointed in me, I guess," I said.

Mom clasped my hand, warm and comforting. "You should have come to us with this, we would've helped you manage your time before it got to this point."

"I know," I mumbled.

Dad's voice sounded gruff. "You know better, Luna."

"I'm so sorry. Really. I promise it won't happen again."

Mom squeezed my hand, then released it. "I believe you, because I know you're a good girl. But still there are always consequences for your actions. Even as adults we have to stick to the rules."

"What your mom is trying to say is, you're grounded for a month. And along with your detention, you will come straight home from school every day, and do your homework. No socializing."

"Dad," I whined jumping to my feet. "Can't I at least go to the library? I really have to do some research for school."

He gazed up at me, puzzled. "There is nothing you would need the library for. School provides all the necessary materials, they make sure of that. Besides, we told you before, we don't want you there so often. So no, you can't go to the library. I'm sorry. And never lie to us again. Or your punishment will last even longer. Now, I suggest you go to your room."

Dad's voice sounded tired, and I daren't push him any further. What a fool I'd been to mention Orion and the others to them. But how could I have known they wouldn't know who they were? Without a word, I turned on my heels and started for my room. As soon as I reached my bedroom, I dropped my backpack on my bed, making sure my phone was still secure in the front pocket. I breathed a sigh of relief. Good, it was there. I didn't want to bring it with me; leaving it would be proof that I never left this house tonight. I crossed to the window and jiggled the latch.

I was going to the library to see Zander. If I got caught, so be it. I'd had enough of this fake life. I needed to find out why all of a sudden my parents didn't remember my ex-boyfriend or my friends. According to my memories Orion had even eaten dinner over here before—and why weren't they registered with the school anymore?

Whatever was happening. It couldn't be good.

I pushed up the window and let the cool wind brush against my flushed cheeks, then stuck out my hand and grabbed at the trellis attached to the house. It was quite a stretch, but I managed to get a good grip by standing on my tiptoes.

I had climbed my way out of plenty of tricky situations before; this should be a piece of cake.

I threw one leg out and then the other, stretching myself to the max until I felt the latticework under my feet. However, when I started to move downward, the pressure of my weight made the thin bamboo buckle. Damn it. If I didn't leap now, I would crash to the ground and then I would be caught for sure.

Taking a deep breath, I jumped.

CHAPTER 19

A blur of motion exploded around me as the ground rushed up, but I was quick and agile. I landed on my feet with the grace of a ballerina and grinned. At least some things never changed. My gloating was short lived however, as I caught a glimpse of movement out of the corner of my eye. It looked as if a shape had detached itself from the shadows. I whirled around, ready to leap, my heart in my throat.

I frowned in annoyance when I saw it was only the neighbor's cat.

Still cautious, I took another look around and then closed my eyes tightly, listening. The only sounds I heard were the wind rustling through the leaves of the trees, and somewhere in the distance, the hoot of an owl echoed on the night air. I breathed a sigh of relief. No one had seen me. Fortunately, Mom was in the kitchen making dinner, and Dad was probably in his office grading some papers. That meant I had about an hour or so before anyone discovered I was missing.

My sneakers tread soundlessly as I took off down the street, speeding quickly toward the library before it closed. I didn't prefer going behind my parents back, but it couldn't be helped. Not only were the phones with their weird trackers an issue—

but the absurd outer image of perfection in this town creeped me out. And what was with the underlying fear of all the adults? I tried to stay away from it all, but the more I tried, the further I was drawn into the madness—as if somehow, I didn't have a choice in the matter.

It only took me about five minutes to reach the library. Winded from running, I waited until my breath returned to normal. When I felt under control, I grabbed the heavy brass door handle and gave it a tug, stepping into the warm confines of the building. The air stilled, and I could almost hear a whispered hush fall over the large expanse as if the books held an energy all their own. I picked up a small movement to my right and quickly turned to investigate.

The outline of a tall man silhouetted against the dimly lit stacks caught my attention. I strained to get a glimpse of his face, but to no avail, the dark shadows kept him well hidden from view. Uncertain what to do next, I stood there frozen like a statue.

As if sensing my dilemma, the man suddenly turned and headed towards me, stepping into the light.

Zander.

I released my breath and lay a hand over my chest. God, I thought he'd been a government official or something. Still, it was disconcerting, the way he'd stayed in the shadows like some sort of stalker. Shaking my head, I wondered what his endgame was. No, I shouldn't speculate, at least, not right now. Zander was the only one I could even semi-trust to answer my questions.

We stared at each other for a moment across the room. Finally, Zander placed a finger to his lips and motioned me over. I cast a last glance around but didn't see anyone, so I shrugged and headed towards him.

Zander led me down an aisle of texts toward the back of the library. He stopped at a big oak door labeled *Private-Personnel Only*. He gave me a reassuring smile, then ushered me inside. We stepped into what appeared to be a modest office. A simple desk consumed the center of the room, and in the corner to the right sat a black filing cabinet. Two piles of records were stacked precariously on a wooden table, looking as if they might topple over at any moment. It seemed surprisingly at odds with P8's usual perfection. The walls were bare, save for a small picture hanging lopsided near the window with an image of an unpretentious shabby wood cabin buried in snow. It reminded me of home and my heart lurched a little. I squeezed my eyes shut, allowing the memories of Nova to burn out. When I finally opened them, I found Zander standing close to me, barely an inch between us. I didn't move, unsure of his intentions. All my brain registered was the heady aroma of soap and books emanating from him.

"You believe me, don't you?" Zander whispered in my ear, jolting me back to the present problem.

"I'm not sure I can trust you. But I have no other choice," I hissed; my voice barely audible.

"What made you return?" his breath fanned my cheek, and subsequently I came to my senses and retreated creating more of a gap between us.

I stared him square in the face, but suddenly hesitated. Something in his eyes told me he was holding back. Finally, without thinking, I blurted, "Do you know about the cell phones?"

He placed a hand over my mouth to shush me. Once he was sure I'd stay silent, he slowly pulled his phone out of his pocket. He pointed at it, then went to the small little desk and removed a pad from the drawer. He frantically began to scribble something down. When he finished, he held it up for me to see. There in his neat, concise penmanship, he'd written a warning.

IT'S NOT JUST A TRACKER. IT'S A LISTENING DEVICE, TOO.

I nodded, indicating I understood as a profound hollowness filled me. I didn't want to believe it, but somewhere deep down, I recognized the truth when I saw it. I swallowed hard. Being here was a risk, talking to him was a risk. Damn, *everything* was a risk.

Zander cleared his throat. "Yeah, the cell phones are great, aren't they? It's best to get the latest models for all the technological advances."

Would whoever was listening to us have noticed the slight pause before he'd answered me? My heart thrummed.

"You're lucky. My parents won't let me get one of the new ones yet. They're so lame," I prayed I sounded normal, that nobody would pick up on the slim edge in my voice. I shoved my hands into my back pockets, trying to calm down.

Zander put the paper back on the desk and wrote again, then lifted it up for me to read. It was a time and date. *MEET ME TOMORROW. AT THE GAZEBO IN THE PARK. 5 P.M.*

I nodded, sucking in my breath to hide my trepidation.

"Yeah, parents can be a real drag sometimes, but don't worry, one day, you'll be able to have the fanciest phone you want," Zander said, stuffing the paper into my palm. He motioned towards the door and mouthed, "*go.*"

His command brought me out of my funk. I had to act normal, or I would never get out of this place alive.

"I hope you're right. Anyway, I better head out, I promised Mom I'd be home for dinner," I replied brightly. "Thanks for the homework help."

He grinned at me, relief flooding his face. "Sure, no problem. I'll walk you out."

And with that, my fate was sealed.

CHAPTER 20

The following afternoon, I gazed out of the classroom window into the school courtyard with longing. I thought about all the things that might go wrong tonight. I tapped my pencil on the desk, hoping the counting would help keep me from worrying.

One. Two. Three. Four. Five...

"Detention is not the place for dreaming, Miss Redwood. Why don't you get started on that calculus homework in front of you?"

I turned to see Mrs. Lennor staring at me disapprovingly as she continued to pace around the room like a caged bobcat.

"Sorry," I murmured burying my face behind my tablet.

All the teachers took rotation on who chaperoned the detention hour. This month, it was Mrs. Lennor's turn. But what made me most uneasy was the fact I'd never seen this teacher before. Not even in my planted memories.

With one eye still on my tablet, I used the other to look at Mrs. Lennor more closely. She appeared to be in her mid-fifties, with dyed brown hair chopped short to her chin. She wore the standard P8 white blouse and blazer. And around her neck, a very large diamond shaped gold pendant stood out almost gaudily against her otherwise prim appearance. But it was the symbol etched on the surface that really jumped out at me. It was so unusual—an outline of a tree, its roots spread out in an unlikely fashion. I wanted to ask her about it, but I'm sure she would have considered it another excuse not to do my work. Still, I felt some kind of pull to it. How strange. I cast all my attention back to my work, trying to avoid whatever weird juju was coming from the teacher.

Satisfied I was doing as I was told, Mrs. Lennor returned to her desk and carried on with grading papers. But every few minutes she would look up, her attention focused solely on me as if the other kids in here—and there were at least a dozen—were of no consequence to her.

I sank down lower in my chair, trying to focus on my math homework. I didn't want to draw attention to myself.

I had a hunch this teacher had been assigned this post specifically for me—that is, if she was a teacher at all. I wouldn't put anything past this place. I frowned. Maybe I was getting paranoid. Still, I couldn't shake the bad feeling deep in my bones. And I'd learned never to question that.

Finally, the hour was up, and everyone reached for their bags, eager to escape. But before we were able to leave, Mrs. Lennor held up her hands to stop us.

"A reminder about curfew, students! No wandering around on a school night past ten p.m., unless you wish to be detained and sent to juvenile camp. For those whose parents haven't informed you, it's a rehab center correcting deviant behavior in young adults. The rules are clear. Please obey them." Mrs. Lennor stared pointedly at me, then turned her attention back on the group. "All right, you're dismissed."

I flew out of there before Mrs. Lennor found another reason to detain me.

I didn't have much intel on this juvenile camp, besides what she'd just told us. I had no memories to draw from. Maybe it was something new. But any way you looked at it, it sounded scary. The last thing I needed was a rehab stint. I would never be able to hide my secret in that place. And what would they do to me when they discovered I was a fraud? Was it possible that's where Orion and the others had vanished to? I shuddered at the thought.

❦

It seemed like an eternity waiting for five o'clock to roll around. I'd arrived at the park early and found a seat on one of the red park benches, placed at eerie, ninety-degree angles all over the area. They, like the trees, had a symmetrical, ordered pattern that I didn't understand. This bench was right near the gazebo, so Zander couldn't miss me.

I shivered and wrapped my jacket closer. It had turned colder since my arrival in P8, but the saplings hadn't changed color or lost their leaves as they did in W1 Nova, instead, they stayed the same bright, bottled green. I wondered if I'd ever get accustomed to this strange phenomenon. The only semi-normal thing in the place was the dried grass under my feet which had become crunchy from the frosty temperatures.

As I waited for Zander, I watched people come and go through the gate. A fence bordered the park, so there was only one way in or out. Red splashes of color dotted the black spires where the spikes and the arches met in the design. If you stared at it long enough, it made you a bit dizzy. I decided to pass the time by counting every spike. It helped soothe my nerves.

Finally, at five o'clock sharp, Zander entered the gate. He looked good, I'd give him that. He wore a stylish black overcoat paired with shiny boots. The coat had remained unbuttoned, revealing a green dress shirt neatly tucked into dark pants.

I began to feel a bit underdressed in my violet sweater and jeans. I'd been so eager to get here I rushed out the door, not bothering much with my appearance. Well, technically, I'd climbed out the window while Mom was busy making dinner. I was still grounded, after all. Fortunately, Dad had been running errands. Even my hair, swept up into a simple ponytail—screamed neat, but hardly glamorous. Clearly, I should have tried harder. I pulled my blue jacket tightly closed in an attempt to cover up my casual attire.

Zander gave me a broad smile as he approached me. "Hi, Luna. It's good to see you," he said, coming up and wrapping me in a bear hug. Shocked, my body turned to stone as his arms folded around me. "You left your phone at home, right?" he breathed quietly into my ear.

"Of course. I'm not an idiot. Now get off me!" I pushed him but he didn't budge, continuing to clinch me in a vice grip.

"Luna, hold on a minute," he whispered. "We have to keep our story straight. If anybody asks, we're on a date. Got it? We don't want anyone to question our being together."

I sized him up, uncertain. I supposed I should make an effort to relax, especially under the circumstances. He smiled at me a little, joking. "That means if this is going to work, you have to stop looking at me with death lasers."

He let me go, and my face flamed all shades of red as I found myself swept into the depths of those crystal blue eyes. What was it about him that made me feel so flustered and awkward, but simultaneously safe and secure?

I turned away from his intense gaze, my mouth as dry as the desert. *Get it together, Luna. You're acting nuts. The crazy government has warped any normal perspective you may have had. Now play the part Zander asks and fix this!*

Annoyed with myself for losing my cool and shoving him aside, I decided I needed to make it right. Before I could talk myself out of it, I placed my hands on each side of Zander's face and kissed him.

"Nice to see you, too," I whispered.

Zander placed a finger under my chin, lifting my gaze to his, searching my expression. Looking or hoping for some kind of meaning—despite the fact he'd just told me it was all for show.

And honestly, I wasn't sure what he found there. Either way, it scared the crap out of me.

Zander reached out to grasp my hand, pulling me a little closer. An unexpected surge of joy took over. And it seemed like my body had betrayed me.

My rational mind screamed; *Don't trust this boy. Get the information you need and move on.*

I cleared my throat and lifted my head. Anything between the two of us would be a recipe for disaster.

He led me to the far side of the grounds. All the while, thoughts swirled around my brain like angry seagulls. Not a soul milled about on such a chilly afternoon, and we walked the periphery in silence. Finally, Zander settled on a park bench set back in a quiet nook overlooking one of the uniform gardens, which I now realized upon closer inspection, was filled with fake flowers. I supposed anything dead ruined the appearance of perfection, it also went against P8's guidelines. Even the blossoms were at the mercy of these crazy rules.

Zander patted the space next to him. "I don't bite."

I rolled my eyes and sat down beside him. I leaned over and whispered in his ear. "Just so we're clear, I had to sneak out of the house to come here tonight. Getting caught is not an option. We can't be long."

Zander picked up my hand, letting it rest in his. I wanted to pull away, but we had a role to play, didn't we? Yes, that was it. It had nothing to do with the weird butterflies in the pit of my stomach.

"I understand. I'll try to explain as quickly as I can. Firstly, let me ease your fears a little. This is a safe space. I checked it out earlier today. Plus, I left my phone at the library. As far as anyone knows, that's where I am."

"And I'm at home doing my homework." I added with a sigh. "Well, at least that part is realistic. Between detention and being grounded that should be my only option."

Zander's smile was gentle as he tucked a stray strand of my

dark locks behind my ear. "It will get better Luna. I'm working on something big. I simply need a bit more time."

I pushed his arm down and stared at him. "What do you mean working on something big? Zander Barringer, how do you know about me?"

Zander turned away, his eyes glistening. "I had a friend once, his name was Billie. He told me the same thing I've just revealed to you now. That he was taking on a huge project. And that he'd uncovered secrets that would change everything. We were supposed to meet up in this very park so he could tell me all about it. He never showed." Zander looked down then, intertwining his fingers with mine.

"What happened?" I whispered.

"It wasn't like Billie not to show, he was a stickler about being punctual, so I searched for him, but never found him. Later, I learned he'd been seized by the authorities."

I gasped. "Where is he now?"

"Well, that's the thing Luna. I think he might have been erased."

I shivered but not from the cold. "Was he murdered?" I choked out hoarsely.

"Not exactly. At least, I don't believe so. When I discovered the government had taken him, it was clear they would never let me visit. So I decided to go home, come up with a plan and return in the morning." Zander paused as he relived the memory, the past haunting his still features. But after a moment, he straightened his shoulders and continued, "By the next day, nobody even remembered him. I asked my parents if they'd seen Billie, and they informed me they had no idea who he was. But Luna, that made no sense, because he always hung out at my house. That's when I realized I was too late. I failed to help my friend when he needed me most."

His voice cracked with emotion and I shot up from the bench and began to pace. "So you're telling me that your friend disappeared and everyone is acting like he never existed?" My tone rose to a fever pitch and Zander glanced nervously around. "Sit down, you're causing a scene. We're supposed to be on a date, remember?"

I stared at him blankly, trying to process his words for a minute.

Nobody even remembered him.

My stomach churned, as my mind connected the dots. Nobody seemed to remember Orion, Mara or Jonah either. Was it possible that they had literally been...erased? No. It couldn't be. I swallowed hard and looked to Zander, who was now tugging at my sleeve, urging me to sit.

I needed to understand more. But I had to stuff all my questions down and act the part. Zander was right. I sank back down next to him, and he immediately wrapped an arm around my shoulders. Probably in an effort to make light of my little outburst. After all, neither of us knew for sure if anyone saw me. Snuggling closer, I did my best to help cover my mistake.

Zander appeared wistful for a second, but hastily looked away when he caught me staring at him. I noted his grip on me had tightened and I wondered what it meant.

He continued his story, voice low. "When he disappeared, I started questioning things. Something weird was going on. Nobody up and vanishes, remembered by no one. I realized at that point there were multiple layers of deception happening here. And someone was lying about everything."

I interjected, "Is that how you figured out that the phones were being used to track people? And listen in on their conversations?"

"No, that came a few months later. Another friend from school, Dafina, began acting strange one day, not like herself. I confronted her about it, and she told me it was nothing. But the flicker of despair on her face was undeniable, pleading with me for help. I decided I would find out what was going on. I didn't want to lose anyone else. I noticed she started to receive calls at odd times; I never heard what was spoken, but I sensed whoever called was checking up on her. At that point, her other friends, including me, started to get phone calls too. They said they were an investigative branch of the government, and they'd read reports about disruptive behavior from Dafina. They had a few questions they wanted to ask me. The interrogation included weird queries—such as, had I spent time with her recently, and if so, had she said or done anything that might be construed as unusual? The day after I got my first phone call inquiring about her, Dafina went missing, and I woke up with two sets of memories. I remember another life. One before this one." He peered at me intently. "I suspect you are experiencing the same thing."

I dodged the question. "So what about Dafina? Did you ever find out what happened to her?"

Zander sighed and picked at an invisible thread on his coat. "No. But I have a pretty good theory."

I covered his hand with mine to stop his fidgeting. He glanced at me, his blue eyes shadowed by the memory of his lost friends. "Tell me your theory."

"I can't. Not until I'm sure. It's too dangerous, Luna. The less you know the better."

I collapsed back against the bench, frustrated. "I think it's too late for that, Zander. Because you're right, I do have two sets of memories." The words tumbled out of my mouth before I even realized I'd said them—announcing even that much terrified me. Should I trust him? What if all this had been some concocted propaganda to get me to talk? No, I doubted it. Reading people was my specialty. These incidents with his friends were real, his loss and sorrow were tangible. There was grief there you couldn't fake. Besides, I was starting to grapple with the reality that my own friends had disappeared. But it still didn't explain how he'd learned about me. I couldn't tell him just yet about Orion and the others. Not till I was sure. My heart ached not being able to tell someone. The weight of the implications threatened to bury me.

Zander took hold of my shoulders and stared me straight in

the eyes. "Be careful, Luna. The government officials have already been to your house, which means you are on their radar. That's how I guessed you were like me. Plus, you were asking way too many questions. Probably why the law got on your tail in the first place."

I opened my mouth to speak; something didn't add up. Zander had singled me out long before those officials had shown up at my door. My gut told me he'd known about me all along. But why was he being so evasive?

Zander continued before I had a chance to say anything. "You have to trust me. I know what I'm talking about. I've been on their radar before, too. And after Dafina—" his voice cracked a little. "Well, it all clicked into place. I started thinking about how the authorities always seemed to identify the perfect moment to make contact. She would become panicked, almost hysterical about something—more than was normal—and suddenly they would call to check in on her. And every time that happened, her paranoia grew. The day I asked Dafina what had her so scared, I received a phone call. When she disappeared, I examined my cell and discovered the tracker. I immediately realized that's how they were doing it. But Luna, we have no way of identifying if there are other devices. They're bound to have spies everywhere. You must be on alert at all times. I scoured the park on several occasions before we met. So, I'm fairly sure it's safe to speak freely. But just because we don't have our phones, we can't get complacent."

"Okay, what are we supposed to do, then?" I asked. "We have to figure out what's going on. We are being manipulated. And I for one, want to get out of this godforsaken place."

"We took a big risk meeting today." Zander said. "It's taken me a while, but the government officials finally trust me again. I accepted a job at the library after I graduated high school last year and am taking college courses via correspondence. I've been keeping my head down, so they'd stop looking. As soon as they did, I started working on my project. But Luna, it's not the same for you. You have a huge bullseye on your back. We can't jeopardize this, and shouldn't talk again for a while. We must lie low. I will contact you when I have a breakthrough. I'm close. I promise it won't be forever."

I stiffened. "I'm not stupid. It's clear there is so much you're not telling me. I don't care about the danger. Tell me what you're working on. Maybe I can help."

Zander shook his head. "No. They will figure us out in a heartbeat. It's better I do this alone. Nobody pays attention to me anymore. I promise I will find a way out of this for us. I give you my word. Now come on, I should get you home."

He stood, indicating he was done talking. The cold wind he'd been blocking with his body hit me head-on, just as Zander's information had. I wanted to demand he tell me more. But the truth was, he was right. If I started to help him in whatever he was doing, the government would start watching him again. And God knows what the consequences for Zander would be if he got caught. Hell, he'd taken a risk even meeting me today.

I reluctantly stood and took his hand and we headed toward home. We were quiet, both of us aware that outside our safe little area in the park, we could quite easily be watched.

Since I'd snuck out of the bedroom window, Zander and I stopped at the corner a few blocks away, so I could walk the rest of the trip alone—hopefully to creep back into the house unnoticed. I turned to go, but he pulled me into a hug and whispered, "It's all going to be okay. Don't worry."

Before I could catch my breath, Zander drew away a little to look at me. "Luna," he said hoarsely, "just this once I..." he trailed off, his fingers slowly tracing the edge of my jawline. "I want to—" something inside him surrendered before he finished his thought. He brought my face near to his, so close our noses nearly collided. Then he kissed me, his mouth soft and warm on mine. I wanted to stay lost in the fiery heat created between us and forget about all the problems that plagued me. But before I realized it, he'd disappeared, leaving me standing alone on the street, with the cold wind biting at my flushed cheeks. I touched my fingers to my lips, trying to preserve the tingling excitement that had arisen deep inside me, sparking a strange sensation I'd never felt before.

Zander had demanded nothing from me. I'd admitted to him I also had the memories of my previous existence, but I gave him little else. Nevertheless, he was willing to place his life on the line. He wanted to get us both out of this mess.

My eyes misted over when I thought about how sweet and kind he'd been. I swiped furiously at my tears. Now was not the time to become sentimental. I must never allow my emotions to override my good sense.

I still knew very little about Zander Barringer and it would behoove me to be cautious.

Trust no one had always been my motto. And it had gotten me this far. I wasn't about to change that. Especially not over a single stupid kiss. It meant nothing.

With resolve in my step, I headed towards the house, preparing to fit back into the role of the perfect daughter. I hesitated, pausing on the street under the shadows of the lamplight, glancing over my shoulder one last time, to reassure myself no one was following me.

No one was there—but a sinking dread somewhere deep down inside me simmered just the same—as I thought about my hopes for the future.

I couldn't control the huge area of my heart that desperately hoped Zander was the real deal. I loved the idea that the two of us together could escape this artificial place, and I would no longer have to play the part of a stranger.

Still, I'd learned long ago that hope was a luxury, one I couldn't afford.

Had anything in my life ever been that easy?

I didn't allow myself to answer that question as I took the last few blocks home.

CHAPTER 21

When detention ended for the day, I had to say I felt relieved. Mrs. Lennor, acting even more creepy than usual, had stared me down for the entire hour. Sweat dripped down between my shoulder blades as I did my best to pretend I hadn't noticed her intense scrutiny. I feigned giving my full attention to my Biology homework. But her eyes boring into my head distracted me so I couldn't focus on the words on my tablet, explaining the intricate workings of a cell.

When she finally dismissed us, I crammed my belongings into my backpack and made a beeline for the door—which unfortunately was becoming a necessary habit. I flew down the hall, eager to run as far away from Mrs. Lennor as possible. But I stopped short just outside the school exit, realizing I would never get the answers I wanted by being a coward. What if Mrs. Lennor was a spy? Zander said anything was probable. She certainly didn't seem like any teacher I'd ever met. And I refused to stand around and do zilch while I waited for Zander to get in touch. He needed my help. If we worked separately, nothing could be connected back to him. He had no clue how skilled I was at being sneaky. Nobody would discover I'd snooped. Besides, we had to discern fact from fiction. And fast.

I stuffed my hands deeper into my jacket pockets, trying to protect them against the cold wind that was making them tingle. I glanced around, searching for somewhere to lie low. An adjacent parking lot lay beyond the periphery of the school where a small brick wall bordered the area. I could sit, remaining hidden, behind a smattering of trees near the back of the property, with a perfect vantage point of the school exit. I would be able to see when Mrs. Lennor left and follow her.

Taking one more swift glance about, I hurried across the street. Just as I'd settled down in my spot under a tree, the door to the school opened, and Mrs. Lennor appeared, donned in a beige wool coat. Apparently, she disliked hanging around after her detention duties. Unlike the other teachers, she didn't carry a briefcase full of papers, only a small black bag that hung over her shoulder.

She seemed a bit jittery, her hands trembling as she put on her sunglasses and buttoned her coat to ward off the chill. She darted a glance over her shoulder, spooked, then, seeing no one, pulled her bag against her chest as if protecting the contents. Setting off at a speedy trot, she quickly moved down the street, her low-heeled pumps clacking lightly on the bordered sidewalk. I popped up from my perch and waited a beat, wanting some space between us. Quiet as a mouse, I trailed her as she disappeared around the bend, away from the high school.

My curiosity peaked as I wound my way down the main thoroughfare, dodging out of her line of vision every time she paused to scan her surroundings. What had her so nervous? In the classroom she was a force to be reckoned with, out here in the open she seemed almost feeble.

A bit of homesickness washed over me. Shadowing people brought back memories of W1 Nova. Stealing money credits or food was pretty much an everyday occurrence for me back home.

Fortunately, this time my belly was full, and I had warm

clothes to wear—but it had been a steep price to pay. Tracking Mrs. Lennor, I felt more like the old me, taking action again. Whatever the outcome—I was doing something. I'd hardly allowed myself to think of my little sister Trinity since I left W1, afraid it would be my undoing. But today her tiny face swam in front of my eyes, and I inhaled sharply, an agonizing pain piercing my chest. I wondered what had become of her and my other siblings. Had Mama's trade of her oldest daughter been worth it? I hoped by some measure they had a better life, even if I wasn't part of it. The sting of that possible truth slashed knives through my heart. I allowed the pain to spur me on. The government might be able to track me, and listen to what I say, but they couldn't read my mind. I would cling to my memories and my thoughts. They were mine. And I wouldn't let anyone take them from me.

I picked up my pace, matching Mrs. Lennor as she turned the corner and headed out of the main city center, toward the outskirts of town. I never had much opportunity to venture outside the area since I'd arrived in P8. I cast a cautious glance in both directions. Even on the outskirts, the trees looked indistinguishable from one another. Laid out in the same strange way I'd seen in the park—except here there were a lot more of them. The pristine sidewalk under my sneakered feet appeared so clean you could almost eat off it, a stark contrast to my previous existence. Up ahead, I spotted a small cluster of brick buildings. Four to be exact, standing like lone giants in a sea of perfectly clipped green grass. Identical in size and shape, they created a sort of tetrad square in the midst of this otherwise empty space. If I didn't know any better, I would say we had landed in the middle of the countryside, and the inhabitants of these structures were the only humans around.

As I came closer to the buildings, I realized the grass appeared greener than in town, the air a bit warmer. But how was that possible? We hadn't walked that significant a distance.

Now that I thought about it, I never heard any mention of the outside of town at all. It seemed strange no one said anything about these tall, erect buildings so out of place in their surroundings.

I followed Mrs. Lennor as far as I dared; there was nowhere to hide once you left the main road—as the woods opposite the clearing were too hard to reach without being seen from this vantage point. She made her way up beyond the gates to the central entrance of the first multistory high rise. I watched as she slipped past the wrought iron fortress and trudged up the walkway until she reached the front door of the about facing building. She paused only seconds, before twisting the doorknob and entering.

She'd been here before.

Her mannerisms indicated she knew exactly where to go. After she disappeared completely from view, I dared creep closer, squinting to see the lettering on the side of the structure. "Dillinger Research Center," I whispered aloud. "Why did you come to the research center, Mrs. Lennor? What game are you playing?"

I turned to head back. I'd explore later, after I hatched a plan and identified exactly what kind of place the Dillinger Research Center was. Besides, my parents would be home any time and would expect me to be there. I didn't need any more trouble.

※

That night, after dinner, while Mom and Dad relaxed by the fire, I broached the question burning in my mind, as casually as possible.

"So I overheard one of the kids at school talking about Dillinger Research Center," I said, picking at the cotton thread of the cushion I held in my lap.

"Oh, yeah?" Dad turned away from the blaze to study me.

"That's a bit strange. What did they say about it?" He took a sip of his tea.

I shrugged, pretending I couldn't care less. "Something about how it lay on the outskirts of town, and was most likely haunted. It got me thinking, I can't remember going to see it."

"That's because there's no reason for you to go there. You have everything you need right here in town. The only people there are the technicians that conduct the scientific studies. I'm surprised you believe such stories, especially coming from teenagers." Dad gave me a pointed stare, as if to include me in that grouping. Obviously, I wasn't high on his trust list. Not that I blamed him.

Mom's eyes narrowed. "You wouldn't sneak over there on your own, would you Luna? You know that's frowned upon. They are doing very important work; we shouldn't disturb them."

I waved a hand away. "Why would I want to go to a boring research center? Don't worry Mom, I have no interest in it. Haunted or not."

As cool as a cucumber, I casually yawned, and stretched my legs out on the couch. She visibly relaxed. Good thing she couldn't see inside my mind, running at full throttle. If only scientists worked at this locale, what had Mrs. Lennor been doing there? And why was it off limits? I'd been around my parents long enough to perceive when they were lying. They didn't want me anywhere close to that research facility. I had a suspicion that if the authorities caught me near that place there would be hell to pay.

I let out a breath, glad I'd left my phone at home today. It allowed me to do as I pleased. Of course, there was always the danger of someone following me. But it was a risk worth taking if I ever wanted to escape this plastic hellhole.

I was startled by the sound of the doorbell ringing through the house. My heart almost leapt out of my chest.

Only one person would come calling at this time of night. I gripped the armrest so hard my knuckles turned white.

Dad got up and went to answer the door.

From my spot on the couch I heard a deep, baritone voice echo down the hall, and shivers ran down my spine.

I recognized that voice.

"Good evening, Mr. Redwood. Agent Morrow. I'm afraid we have a problem."

CHAPTER 22

I sucked in my breath, not daring to move. This was it. This had to be the end. My mind ticked over. They must have seen me go out to the old research center. I'd been too cocky. Why had I believed I could outmaneuver them?

I wasn't in Nova anymore.

My throat constricted with fear as I forced myself to stand, trying to appear confident—as Dad looking haggard and tired, led Agent Morrow into the living room. The agent was exactly as I remembered him, in a crisp white uniform straightened to perfection, and unmoving gelled hair. His mouth twisted into an ugly scowl as he regarded me with disdain.

"Everyone, you remember Agent Morrow. He came to visit us during the routine visits."

Mom inclined her head, nodding a greeting. "It's good to see you again, Agent," she said in her best diplomatic voice.

Despite the horrid situation, I choked back a laugh. That was the biggest lie I'd ever heard. Mom's expression spoke volumes about how she really felt. She definitely shouldn't be a professional liar anytime soon.

"Yes, well, I'm not here under happy circumstances I'm

afraid, Mrs. Redwood. I'm sorry to report there's been a glitch in our system. I apologize for the inconvenience but I will need to look at all the phones in the household."

I frowned, crossing my arms. I'm sure he loved the so-called inconvenience. The sick bastard.

Dad cleared his throat, his body rigid. I wasn't used to seeing Dad so rattled. He was really nervous about this. "What kind of glitch?" he asked.

"It's nothing to concern yourself with, sir," Agent Morrow spouted, standing as erect as a toy soldier. "Simply allow me to examine your equipment and I'll be on my way."

My pulse roared in my ears. Why did he care about the phones? Mine still lay in the drawer where I'd left it since Zander confirmed my worst fear about the tracking devices imbedded inside. I didn't dare throw it away; they would realize I was on to them immediately. But perhaps the lack of movement triggered warning bells back at their headquarters. I swore under my breath. I should have moved it around once in a while.

I'd been such an idiot.

"Luna. Luna. Earth to Luna?" Dad said waving his hand in front of me.

"Oh. Uh. Sorry, Dad. What did you say?"

"Can you get the agent my phone? It's on my desk."

"Bring your own phone as well, Miss Redwood," Morrow interjected, his tone tight. The lines in his face pinched as his ferrety eyes regarded me.

I nodded and hustled out of the den. I grabbed Dad's from his office, then took the stairs, two at a time, racing to my room. I yanked free the dresser drawer and pulled out my phone. I turned it over, and with shaking hands, examined it carefully to ensure nothing looked out of place. I had, after all, busted it open only days before.

I breathed a sigh of relief when I saw it appeared completely untouched. I had done an excellent job of putting it back together.

Dread filled me as I slowly headed downstairs. Just thinking about handing them over gave me the willies. Thoughts scrambled in my mind, each one more terrifying than the last. What if somehow, he perceived I'd tampered with it? What would he do? Before I entered the living room, I steeled myself for the worst and plastered on a fake smile.

"Here you are," I said breezily entering the room.

Agent Morrow was already seated in the corner. The soft lamplight illuminated his dour profile as he examined Mom's phone, which must have been nearby.

He quickly put it to one side when he saw me, and met me in the middle of the room, snatching the phones from my grasp. "Thank you, Luna, perhaps next time you could be a bit more prompt."

Hearing him use my first name set my teeth on edge. His tone made it clear—this was personal. He had a big grievance against me.

Agent Morrow took a precursory glance at both devices, before returning to his spot in the corner, a smug smile plastered on his face. He pulled a small square tool from his bag, its gold surface glittered in the light, and I noticed it had inner wiring looped inside, like netting. He attached it to the outside of Dad's phone with a loud snap and I gave an involuntary jerk. With that accomplished, he grabbed his tablet and hit a few buttons. The cell lit up like a Christmas tree. The little gadget whirred and hummed for a few more minutes before coming to rest quietly in the officer's hand.

Satisfied, he made a note in his tablet and picked up my hot pink, candy-striped covered phone. This was P8 Luna's ghastly sense of style. Could it be any more cliché? I sneered inwardly, unsure why I was so mad. After all, hadn't I been the one to ruin previous Luna's perfect life? I wondered if some version of me had really experienced this reality before. I shook my head; no point in dwelling on questions I had no way of getting answers for. I focused my concentration on the agent. What the devil did the pesky man want?

Morrow lingered over my phone. He slowly ran his forefinger up and down, as if searching for something. This continued on for a good minute before he finally slipped off its case and attached the golden tool. He hit some buttons again on his tablet. But this time nothing happened.

No light. No buzzing. Only interminable silence.

His eyes lit up with excitement and he shifted to grab another gadget from his pocket. But this one was smaller, the shape of a metal pen with a digital blue screen. I watched closely as he inserted it into the phone. The screen lit up with words, but I was too far away to read what it said. He quickly yanked the unit out, his expression stony. I wanted to scream. What did it mean?

He tried the device on my parent's units. No message.

I bit my tongue so hard I tasted blood. But I kept my face neutral. He would never have the satisfaction of knowing the fear that threatened to overwhelm me.

I swallowed nervously as Agent Morrow rose, pocketed his machine and collected up the phones.

He dangled my phone between his fingertips and turned to us, his nasty eyes fixated on me. "Would anyone care to explain why this device has been tampered with?"

For a second, a deadly hush fell on the room. I stood frozen, not daring to breathe. Had I damaged it? Zander never mentioned what to do in a situation like this.

I struggled to come up with a plan, fortunately, Dad stepped forward and addressed the agent. "It's my fault, sir. Luna dropped her phone, and I tried to fix it for her. She needed it for school."

"If that is the case, Mr. Redwood, you violated federal code seventy-eight for failing to notify us of a malfunctioning mobile."

Dad shuffled his feet. "No, well, uh... you see... technically, it wasn't broken, she just dropped it. And instead of troubling you all with it, I patched it up a bit."

"I'm sorry Mr. Redwood, but that type of reasoning simply doesn't hold up. You are directed to report any and all phone problems to the authorities. I will have to take you in for further questioning."

I leapt in front of Dad. There was no way he was going down for this. This was my fight.

"No, you can't!" I exclaimed shrilly. "Listen to me, Agent. It's not his fau—"

Mom gripped my arm so hard I thought it would break. "What Luna is trying to say, is... isn't there some other way?"

Agent Morrow frowned. "No. I'm afraid not." He turned away dismissively and packed up his things, including our phones.

What an ass.

I yanked my arm from Mom's grip and raced after Morrow as he escorted Dad from the room.

"You mind your mother, Luna Bell," Dad said, locking pleading eyes on me. "I'll get this all settled and be back before you know it. I promise." He bent to give me a peck on the cheek, and then looked at Mom, who had come up behind me.

"I'll return soon, sweetheart," Dad promised. "Take care of each other, I love you." He blew Mom a kiss as Agent Morrow pushed him out the door.

I gripped the windowsill so tightly I thought it might break. "Where are they taking him?" I asked sniffling.

"Probably to the government facility for questioning."

I cleared my throat, swallowing back the tears. I had done this. This was all my fault. "What's going to happen to him?" The question hung heavy in the air between us, and Mom took a beat to reply.

She walked over to the window, hand covering her mouth, watching the red taillights fade into the distance. "I don't know,

Luna. But it can't be good," she whispered as she stared out at the receding car.

Every piece of me wanted to chase that vehicle down and bring Dad home. But I knew it was useless to try.

Oh God. What was I going to do?

CHAPTER 23

Twenty-four hours later, Dad still hadn't returned. Neither had the phones the agent had taken. I feared Dad wouldn't be able to contact us. But then again, this hardly seemed the kind of place to show leniency and allow him to call. I paced the floor like a caged lion. Mom had kept me in lockdown all day, worried I would make some valiant attempt to save Dad.

She wasn't wrong.

I'd remained semi-calm, despite my urges to kick down the door and go talk to Zander. He told me not to contact him until he had solutions, but right now he was the only one that might have some clue what happened to Dad.

As the sun began to set in the west, Mom finally let her guard down and stopped watching me like a hawk. Together, we made fried chicken and green beans for dinner, which I forced myself to eat so she wouldn't get suspicious. Normally, I would give my right hand for such a meal, but guilt gnawed at my stomach and it took everything in me to clean my plate. After we'd eaten, we retired to the living room.

Mom sat down with some sewing and I opened my history book, pretending to study. The clock on the mantel ticked loudly. I found myself counting the beats to pass the seconds and calm my jangled nerves. By the time I reached one hundred, the sun had long set, and the stress of everything had taken its toll on Mom. I watched as her eyelids drooped and she nodded off, her hands falling limply in her lap.

I waited another five minutes or so to make sure she was well and truly asleep before tiptoeing out of the room, grabbing my jacket and shoes on the way. With a gentle tug, I opened the door. Once out, I pulled on my sneakers and took off at full speed, racing toward the library, praying it was still open.

When I reached the now-familiar spot, I put my hands on my knees, trying to catch my breath. When I looked up again, Zander was already outside, locking the front entrance.

Just in case he was being watched, I crouched behind the bushes and waited for him to reach the sidewalk. As soon as he was within range, I jumped up and grabbed his arm, pulling him back behind the tall shrubbery with me.

"What the hell!"

"Shhh...it's me," I whispered against his ear. We were alarmingly close, I felt the pounding of his heart against me and I shifted uncomfortably, not liking my physical response to his nearness. Now was not the time to be thinking about Zander that way. I stepped back to allow myself some space, grateful for the darkness that hid my reddened cheeks.

"Zander, they took my dad," I hissed, desperately trying to regroup. Only his silhouette, reflected against the moonlight, remained visible so I couldn't gauge his reaction in the dark shadows.

"When?" he breathed, his voice laced with concern.

"Last night. This is the first chance I've had to get away and tell you. Mom's had me under lock and key. I know you said not to see each other for a while, but I wasn't sure what else—"

Zander placed a finger to my lips and shook his head.

"Do you have your phone?" I whispered, alarmed.

"No. But you shouldn't be here. They're probably following

you, wondering what you're up to. If they took your dad, I'd bet good money you're under surveillance."

The low timbre of his voice ran so deep I could barely hear his words. I closed my eyes and leaned in, breathing in the heady fragrance of cinnamon and books. I wanted to forget the nightmare of my father's arrest.

"Luna?"

I started, eyes flashing open. "Sorry. I was just thinking," I lied. "It's a little late to be worried about us meeting since I'm already here. Might as well make this worthwhile, right?" When he didn't answer I forged on. "Do you suppose we can get him out?"

Zander seemed to be fighting some kind of inner war, but suddenly seemed to make a last minute decision. He grabbed me by the shoulders. "Tell me everything that happened from the beginning, leave nothing out."

I relayed to him what had taken place in the last twenty-four hours, including sneaking out of the house.

Zander slumped, dropping his hands. "It's worse than I realized. So, they took your phones for tampering offenses?"

I nodded. "That's what it seemed like."

"I hate to say it, Luna, but there is no way to get your dad out without being caught. Tampering with phones is a criminal offense around here."

I flashed my eyes angrily at him. "But it wasn't Dad's fault. He was covering for me. We need to do something."

"The best thing you can do for him is to go home and wait. The less trouble you cause, the better it is for him. I just hope you weren't followed tonight. You will be useless to the man if you end up in custody, too."

When he saw my dismay, he wrapped an arm around me. "We have to believe everything is going to be okay. I'm glad you care about him so much. Even after knowing the truth."

I shrugged. "Yeah well, he's been good to me. And I owe him, considering it's my—"

Zander suddenly shushed me, his gaze sweeping up and down the street. The sound of laughter echoed in the night air.

He took a deep breath. "You better go, Luna. The longer we hide here, the more dangerous it is. These bushes aren't exactly Fort Knox."

I stuck up my nose. "This was the best I could do under short notice."

"I didn't mean it like that. I just want you to be safe." He tucked a wayward strand of my hair behind my ear and offered me a small, sad smile. "I wish things were different, and I could walk you home, but it's too risky. We need to keep your father out of as much danger as possible."

I nodded. I knew he was right. I shivered and wrapped my coat tighter around myself. "Okay. But promise me the minute there's a breakthrough you'll let me know. I don't have my phone anymore though."

"Don't worry, I'll find a means to contact you. Now go."

I turned away, unable to say goodbye, concerned this would be the last time I would see him. And my heart did a funny little lurch at the prospect.

I pushed all that aside and made my way back home. I walked at a normal pace, not wanting to draw any attention to myself. Though in hindsight that was probably what I should've done in the first place. Still, I was comforted by the fact I would have missed Zander if I hadn't run. He'd already been locking up when I arrived, and I had no idea where he even lived.

Head down, I slowly took the steps up to my front porch, but I stopped suddenly stifling a scream, as a shadowy figure loomed in the doorway.

My heart froze.

They'd found me.

CHAPTER 24

My brain screamed at me to run. My chest heaved as I tried to gasp in air. I couldn't move.

Dared not.

What if Mom was inside, hurt? I couldn't just leave her there, despite my body's immediate need to plunge into survival mode.

The face still hidden in shadow meant I needed to get closer. But before I could move, whoever it was pushed off the door-frame. Heading straight for me.

"Luna? Where have you been? I've been worried sick. I woke up, and you weren't there."

I put a hand over my heart. "Oh my God. Mom. You scared me. I thought you were an agent or something."

"Get in the house before someone sees you," Mom said, pulling me inside.

"No one saw me. I was careful. I just needed some air," I replied indignantly as she shut the door abruptly behind us.

She whirled on me. "What were you doing, wandering around at night?" She looked at her watch in dismay. "And this close to curfew? You know you're not allowed out on the street past ten."

I frowned. Was it really that late? Having to keep track of

time was as annoying as hell. Why did this place have so many rules? All I wanted to do was save Dad, a man who had been kind to me. Did I have to hit a wall at *every* turn?

Mom must have seen the frustration on my face because instead of yelling at me again she said, "Come on then, let's discuss this over a nice cup of warm milk. I expect we both need to unwind before bed."

Not knowing what else to do, I trailed her into the kitchen. I watched as she bustled around, putting the pot on the stove, poured the milk, and placed a sprinkling of cinnamon into the swirling white liquid. The sweet fragrance of the spice filled the air, as she continued to stir, and I relaxed a little following her movements. She placed the hot drink into two big mugs and set them down on the table, before seating herself opposite me.

I wrapped my hands around the warm cup and gazed at the creamy froth, doing anything to avoid facing the woman I called mother. I knew what I would find there. Fear. Disappointment. Worry. All the things I had no idea how to handle—as my previous Mom hadn't given a flip about me.

We sat quietly, just sipping our drinks and listening to the ticking of the clock. Every click of the second hand sounded like torture to my ears. For a brief instant, I wondered what happened to Dad. Had they hurt him? Did they find out anything by taking my phone? The questions tumbled about my mind in a frenzied confusion.

I'd been so lost in thought, I started when Mom pushed back her chair and rose from the table.

"There's nothing that can't wait until the morning, Luna. Let's get some sleep."

I sighed, about to get up myself, when she suddenly turned from the sink to face me.

"I would rather not sleep alone tonight." Unshed tears filled her eyes as she silently pleaded with me. I quickly stood and pulled her into a hug.

"I'll stay with you, Mom. Remember, you are never alone."

Mom patted my hand, lips trembling. "You're such a good girl."

My chest tightened. If only she knew what I was planning.

I squeezed my eyes shut for a second, trying to get my bearings.

She's not your real mother Luna, get a grip, I chastened myself.

Mom moved to the door and turned out the light, and together we headed upstairs to bed. As I lay down next to Mom, I realized how much I had missed having another warm body sleeping beside me. My entire life I'd shared a mattress on the floor with my siblings. Sure, they may have kicked me now and again, but it seemed strange without them here. Especially Trinity. I allowed myself the luxury of my memories—the warmth of her body against mine as she slept, listening to her breath go in and out in a perfect rhythm, and the soft brush of her hair on my cheek. I let the words of the lullaby I used to sing to Trinity before she went to sleep wash over me. It was short, and something I'd never admit to writing to anyone. But here in the darkness, I allowed myself this one concession, every syllable soothing my tattered soul. The government could not read my mind, here lay a safe space all my own. They could never take that from me. I would make sure of that.

Wait for me deep in the meadow
Through the purple flowered fields of home
Back to where it all began
I will find you no matter where you roam
Lay your head down
Close your eyes
Listen to the sweet dreams of tomorrow
Where its safe and warm
And hunger is a memory
I am forever your protector
My sister. My heart.

Mom reached over and gripped my hand, pulling me out of the past and back to stark reality. I shifted my head on the pillow to face her and said the only thing I could—and it was the truth.

"I miss Dad." *And Trinity*, I wanted to say. But that was for another place and time.

Mom brushed the hair off my forehead. "Me too, sweetheart. We will have to say a prayer tonight that wherever he is, he's okay and will return to us."

I nodded, not daring to speak against the lump that had formed in my throat.

"Luna, no matter what happens, I'll always be here for you. I won't let anything happen to you."

I pressed her hand to my face. "I know, Mom."

At that moment, I realized I'd never felt closer to a parent in my entire life. My real mother hadn't cared about me. Yet, somehow, this woman—a stranger—filled a hole in my heart I didn't even realize existed.

I stayed awake a long time, considering what her reaction would be if she learned I wanted to get away from this place. It would break her. But eventually exhaustion won out, and I fell into a restless, guilt-ridden slumber.

❦

The following morning, my father still hadn't come home. I paced up and down the living room, wracking my brain for a plan. There had to be something I could do. Zander's warning rang hollow in my head. They'd held my dad hostage for this long, maybe even torturing him. I refused to stand by and do nothing. Especially when he'd taken the fall for me.

"Sit down, Luna, you'll wear a hole in the carpet. Goodness, I wish it wasn't Saturday, at least then you would have school to keep your mind off things."

I looked up to find Mom standing in the doorway, dressed in her red wool coat, a small black purse hanging from her wrist.

"I'm heading out for some bread and a few other items. I need to get out of this house. Would you like to come?"

I sank down on the couch. "No. I want to stay here in case there's any word."

Mom bustled over and kissed my cheek. "All right, love. I won't take long. Keep the doors locked." Her shoulders slumped, disappointed that I wasn't going with her, but it couldn't be helped.

I'd finally hit on an idea.

I walked Mom over to the entryway, shutting the door and turning the bolt behind her. Then I lifted the sheer curtain and waved. She nodded approvingly then got in her car and took off down the road.

I watched until she was completely out of sight, then raced upstairs to change. I quickly pulled a black sweater over my head and put on some equally dark pants. I turned to the mirror and swept my hair back into a sleek ponytail.

I didn't have the address for the main government building but I had a hunch it was one of those other buildings I'd seen near the Dillinger Research Center. It didn't take a brain surgeon to figure out that's where they were keeping Dad. I bet that was the reason they discouraged visitors.

I took a deep breath, gazing at myself in the mirror—that would have to do. I turned and raced downstairs knowing there was little time. My fingers shook as I tried to tie the laces on my sneakers; I prayed I wasn't about to make things worse. That done, I stood up and headed toward the kitchen drawer for a pen.

I scribbled a quick note to Mom, telling her I'd gone for a walk to clear my head—despite the fact I was sure she wouldn't believe it—especially after how freaked she'd been last night. But by the time she received this message I would probably already be there.

It only took about ten minutes on foot to reach the spot where I'd followed Mrs. Lennor. I stayed in the shadows for a minute, examining the small cluster of brick buildings before me. From here, they all looked identical in size and shape; it was impossible to tell which one might be the main facility. Sweat formed on my brow and I wiped it away. The air seemed even warmer than it had last time. Back at the house, the wind always had a bite to it, but here the breeze was warm and I was suffocating in this thick sweater I'd put on earlier.

I skirted the perimeter of the facilities, still fascinated by the texture of the ultra green grass under my feet. I moved soundlessly until I reached the outskirts of the complex. There was a guard at the front entrance, dressed in a get up similar to Agent Morrow's. His crisp white uniform stood in stark contrast to the almost artificial hues of the surrounding area. Two blue stripes ran across his jacket at the top of his shoulders and I wondered if they signified anything important.

At close range, it was clear the building he guarded was the very one I sought. The grand archway was a bit fancier than the other three, made of what appeared to be sparkling crystals flecked with gold. The surface glinted in the bright sunshine, almost blinding me. The crest above the door displayed large eagle wings, underneath read the words, P8 Government Headquarters. Philadelphia.

Bingo.

Even as I stood there, I saw there was no way I would be able to gain entrance to this place unless I went through the front gate. They'd built it like a fortress, with very few windows and doors.

I sucked in a breath and with firm resolve, headed straight toward the guard, head held high.

He seemed startled by my appearance, making me aware that he didn't receive many visitors—at least not ones he failed to recognize. But he quickly regained his composure and puffed up his chest like a peacock, standing even more erect.

"Name," he barked gruffly.

"Luna Redwood. I'm here to—"

He put a hand up to silence me. "Identification Card."

"I don't have one. I'm just trying to get information about my father. If you would just—"

"I'm sorry that's not possible without an Entry ID card."

Damn. Damn. Damn.

The man scrutinized my face like he'd find something hidden there.

"Please. I'm not leaving until I get answers about my dad. His name is Martin Redwood." My voice rose, shrill and tense with emotion. But I tried to keep it civil. After all, he had the keys to this place.

I glanced down at the badge on his lapel that identified him as Davies. "Officer Davies, I'm not looking for trouble, I promise. Just information."

He stood stock still for a second, eyes unblinking. Probably hoping if he didn't budge, I would magically disappear into the ether and make his job a million times easier.

He had no idea who he was dealing with.

"Why don't you move along? This is no place for a young girl." His eyes narrowed in challenge, as he waved his hand in a tight gesture back toward town.

I bunched my fists to my side, doing my best to control my temper. "I told you, I'm not leaving until I get some answers," I said through clenched teeth.

The officer smirked, enjoying this little tête-à-tête. "Fine. Have it your way."

He lifted his hand and pressed a small device that I hadn't noticed before, concealed in his ear. "Agent Mills? Yeah, this is Davies. We have a situation at the entrance."

I couldn't hear Mills' reply but judging by the big Cheshire cat grin on Davies' face, it probably wasn't great. "Yes, sir. Copy that."

He pushed his finger to the button and clicked off.

My heart pounded as I wiped my sweaty palms against my legs. This Mills guy would either arrest me, or give me some answers. I stood there, torn between a yearning to flee or staying and hopefully getting some good news.

My feet decided for me. They wouldn't budge. My father, practically a stranger, had risked everything to cover for me. I would not run like a coward.

"So who is Mills?" I blurted out to Davies. "Does he have information about my father? Is he going to let me in to see him?"

Davies laughed so hard it crackled in the air like lightning, startling me. "You'll be lucky if he doesn't kick you out on your ass."

My mouth fell open in disbelief. P8 did not use words like *ass*. Wasn't this guy worried he would get caught? Perhaps the policies were different out here in no-man's-land.

Before I could respond to Davies, a massive man, at least six-foot four, loomed over both of us. His long shadow darkened the steps of the building, and I shuddered. His taut, ebony skin reflected warmly in the morning sun, his features hard and chiseled. His shaved head appeared almost polished, but it was his intense eyes that locked onto mine that held me spellbound.

"What seems to be the problem, Officer Davies?"

"This girl wants information about her father, Martin Redwood. Won't take no for an answer." He gestured with his chin toward me as though I was no more than an insignificant fly.

I bit my tongue; I didn't dare say anything I might regret. I needed this information.

"What's your name girl?" Agent Mills barked.

I held his stare. "I'm Luna Redwood and I'm not going anywhere until I find out about my father."

Agent Mills squinted at me and skirted so close I smelled his bitter aftershave. He clenched a toothpick between his teeth, rolling it back and forth over his tongue, not saying a word. He slowly pulled it out and sneered, "We don't take kindly to ultimatums around here, missy. Watch yourself."

I pressed my lips together until he stepped away. I wouldn't give him the satisfaction of witnessing my trepidation, despite the fact I was shaking like a leaf inside.

Agent Mills leaned against the brick façade, as if he had all the time in the world. "Now surely I don't have any information about your daddy. But what I can tell you is— and consider this a warnin'—if you want to be smart and help your old man? You will turn right 'round, head home, and never set foot on these premises again. Because if I find out you've been snooping here in things that are rightly none of your business, well that ain't goin' to sit pretty for dear old dad, is it?" He smirked and waited for me to back off and leave.

That wouldn't be happening, no way would I go without getting what I came for.

"I thought you didn't have any news on my father," I spit out.

"Lies you tell, sweet child. Lies you tell."

His honeyed southern accent dripped with the threat. He obviously wasn't a local. I wondered where he originated from and what his purpose was for being here, certain he knew the whereabouts of Dad. He must have or he wouldn't be acting this way. For Dad's sake, I needed to leave and plan a different approach, think things through a little more.

I swallowed hard and pushed back the tears that pricked my eyes.

Never show your weakness.

I straightened to my full height, though it wasn't much against this giant. "I'm not threatened by you. I'll find out about my dad somehow. But for now, today, I will do as you ask and leave. But it's not for you."

Officer Davies, who'd merely been a bystander up to this point, stepped forward and looked down his nose in contempt. "Well go on then, get, before I arrest you for trespassing. And no more attempts to find your father. It'll only lead to trouble. Now scram!"

He yelled the last part and this time I jetted, running fast toward the safety of the trees. I didn't stop until I made it back home.

I had a sinking feeling my temper and stubborn pride may have stirred up an angry hornet's nest and worsened conditions for Dad. But that seemed like the least of my problems. The fact they refused to release any information about him when they clearly knew who he was, had me more worried than before. What were they doing to him? Why wouldn't they let his family visit? So many things didn't add up. There had to be something I could do. I climbed the steps to the house, still breathing heavily from my run, and sat on the porch swing trying to calm myself.

Think. Luna. Think.

But no matter how I tried, I thought of only one person I could turn to.

Zander.

And it annoyed the crap out of me. The only person I wanted to rely on was myself.

❦

Once again, I stood lurking in the shadows outside the library, praying Zander would appear soon. Only this time I'd given myself a wider berth—hiding behind some trees across the street. This was a dangerous game. Why had I never pressed him about where he lived? I felt like such an idiot. Out here, I was exposed. What if Zander wasn't even working today? It was close to noon, so if he was here, he should be taking his lunch break anytime now. Perhaps he'd purposely not disclosed his address, so I wouldn't come looking for him. After all, he told me to stay away.

I waited what seemed like an eternity, but after about ten minutes I saw some movement coming from the entrance. I tensed when I saw the door open, ready to duck and hide. I breathed a sigh of relief when Zander appeared. He wore a button-down blue shirt and dark jeans. I couldn't help but appreciate his fine form. I gave a prayer of thanks he was here today. I stared at him, silently pleading with him to notice me. It must have worked, because he looked around cautiously and then spotted me standing across the street.

His jaw dropped slightly in surprise and I realized he never expected I would make the same mistake twice.

Crap.

He frowned, but came over all the same.

I'd never seen that expression on his face before—shock, anger, and frustration all mixed together. And hidden under all that emotion there was a hint of good old-fashioned fear.

When he reached me, he rubbed the back of his neck and took a deep breath before speaking to me. "Luna, you can't be here," he whispered desperately. "It's too dangerous. What were you thinking?"

"Zander, I appreciate that, but this is an emergency." I placed a hand on his arm, pressing harder than I intended.

He gently extracted himself from my grip. The anger I'd seen only moments ago slowly dissipated, as if our contact shifted something inside him.

"They're always watching. Don't you remember?" he sounded like a broken record. But his voice had become soft, his blue eyes revealing tenderness—or maybe I just imagined it. I shook my head. It had to be all in my mind. With everything going on, I was starting to crack. Zander definitely wasn't interested in me. That kiss we'd shared before had been a fluke. An adrenaline rush from the danger we were facing and the secret we carried together. If anything, he was probably still mad as hell I'd come out here again. How many times had he told me to stay away, and I'd ignored him?

Besides, did I really want him to like me in that way? I needed to get back home to my family. And I wasn't a hundred percent sure I could trust him. But he was my only hope at the moment.

"Luna?" Zander's pleading brought me back to my senses.

I cleared my throat and ran my sweaty hands down my black jeans, trying to get a grip. "Of course I remember, but I had to see you," I whispered. "Listen Zander. I went to the government building outside of town. They wouldn't let me visit Dad or give me any information. What do I do?"

Zander put his fingers up to his temples and closed his eyes for a minute, attempting to collect himself. Finally, he opened them, weariness etched in his face. "Why did you go there? We talked about this."

"I couldn't stay away. After they had him for twenty-four hours I had to—"

"Stop talking, Luna," he pleaded begging me not to say too much.

Was it really possible that we were being observed? We seemed so alone out here. I hoped to God it hadn't come to that.

He stepped closer, his hot breath on my cheek. My whole body flushed with pleasure. "I don't know what to do or how to help your father. Going to that building was a bad idea. Just like being here is. This may have far-reaching consequences you know nothing about. Please. Go home. Wait. Act as if everything is normal. Go to school, do your homework, be a teenager. Don't send them any more red flags. Got it?"

I didn't argue. I only nodded, realizing that Zander had confirmed my worst fear. I had made things a million times worse for the man I had known for only a short period as my father. I moved to step back but before I did, Zander took my hand and squeezed it—as if he sensed the guilt swallowing me whole and wanted to comfort me. Even that small gesture ran a risk of implicating us both.

But nothing could placate me. I'd messed things up big time.

"I better go," I whispered shattering the silence and pulling away. No need to put Zander in any more danger.

"See you soon, Luna. I promise." He was scrutinizing me, almost as if he was willing me to read his mind and decipher its contents.

However, all my senses picked up on were the sound of the birds tweeting in the perfect trees and the awareness of my heart pounding in my chest. I turned away and walked up the street toward the house. I didn't dare glance over my shoulder. But the sensation of Zander's gaze at my back never left me until I hung a right at the corner and disappeared out of sight.

When I got home, Mom was in a panic. She flung open the door before I even reached it and launched herself into my arms.

"Thank God you're okay! I was worried sick something had happened to you."

"I wrote you a note," I said muffled against Mom's shoulder.

"But you were gone so long." She pulled back to look at me.

I shrugged. "I had a lot on my mind."

"I realize this thing with Dad is hard. But you can't just disappear and leave a note. We have to stick together. Be a team."

If she learned what I'd done, how much of a team would she want to be then? I mean, it's not like I was her flesh and blood or anything. Not that it meant much. Mama couldn't wait to sell me down the river for a better life. Of course, Mama wasn't blood either, but she'd been the only mother I'd ever known...until now. W1 Nova believed in matching children with their societal equivalent. Nobody knew their biological parents. The files became sealed forever once the baby was placed in their permanent home. But still, she was my Mama. And she was a part of me whether she wanted to be or not.

I tried to use the rage that welled up inside, but instead, it swallowed me whole and turned to despair.

"You must be hungry. Let's go eat. I've made us some lunch. Chicken salad, your favorite."

I plastered on a fake smile for her sake. "Sounds great, I'm starving." The truth was, I wanted to barf, but she didn't need to know that.

Mom beamed and looped her hand through my arm, leading me into the house toward the kitchen. We were about halfway through our meal when there was a rap at the door. My head snapped up at the sound, as did Mom's, her face white as a sheet.

I clutched at the napkin in my lap like a lifeline. Adrenaline poured into my veins, wondering who could be on the other side of that door.

I jumped to my feet, pulse pounding in my ears, unable to wait any longer. I had to know. "I'll answer it Mom, you just finish your salad."

"No, sweetheart. Let me get it. It may be important."

With shaking legs, she made for the door and I followed, not daring to leave her alone. Mom looked through the peephole. Her hands shook as she gripped the doorframe and gasped, clutching the wood to remain steady.

"What," I whispered. "Who is it?"

She whirled around to face me, eyes wide. "It's an officer."

CHAPTER 25

"Ma'am, my name is Officer Five. On behalf of the P8 government I have a message for you pertaining to Mr. Martin Redwood," the man said in a monotone voice. "Please sign for the registered document." He outstretched his hand, revealing a small tablet, awaiting a signature. I swore his arm made a faint whirring sound, barely detectable to the human ear. The fellow standing in our doorway was no one I recognized. Only his uniform seemed familiar, similar in design to the others I'd seen, except this outfit was black instead of pure white with some simple silver detailing at the corners of his lapels. Yet, there was something off about this guy. Something I couldn't place. I stared at him for a moment and then the truth hit me like a wall. I gripped the doorknob and swallowed hard against the lump in my throat.

They hadn't even bothered to send a real person to do their dirty work.

This was a robot.

I'd heard in passing about the robot delivery systems. But thought little about them until now. Minions, programmed to bring unwanted messages, the kind that the actual officers didn't want to deliver themselves. Anything not to create a scene. It made me think of the small girl, Ever Hopkins, at the W1 transfer station, who wasn't even considered important enough to receive assistance from an actual human being for her trip to P8. That was a bad omen unto itself.

I took in the automated machine. He looked very lifelike and almost passed for a human. I understood why at first glance someone might miss he was an android. However, on further inspection, I noticed his amber eyes were glassy, with black swirling rings in the background of his irises, showing he ran by a processor, not a real ticking heart. In other words—not mortal.

Mom signed the small tablet with a shaking finger and the robot produced a registered letter from inside his uniformed pocket and gave it to her. The letter bore an old-fashioned wax seal representing the government crest. Speechless, Mom fingered the bold red indents.

Almost as if on a timer, the mechanical man bowed his head awkwardly and said, "Delivery complete. Officer Five signing off. Have a good day." He then made a 180-degree turn and started marching off like a broken little toy soldier, returning to the unmarked vehicle idling in our driveway.

Mom, not waiting for him to leave, slammed the door shut, leaning heavily against it. We both knew it would have been pointless to ask a robot questions about Dad. The only information we would probably receive was in that envelope clutched in Mom's hand. Every bone in my body told me it wasn't good news.

Mom lifted the envelope and tried to tear at the seal, but her hands were still shaking so badly she failed to get a grip on it.

Without saying a word, I took the letter from her and met her fearful eyes. She nodded silently in assent, tears already sliding down her cheeks.

I ripped it open, the noise slashing like a knife into the silence of the entryway. I cleared my throat, searching for my voice to read the awful words on the page.

We regret to inform you that Mr. Martin Redwood took his own life in barrack headquarters while awaiting questioning. We are sorry for your loss. His body will be housed here at the government main building until suitable funeral arrangements can be made.

Sincerely,
The office of P8

I pressed my lips together to prevent myself from screaming out loud. What a bunch of crap! There was no way Dad took his own life. He would never have done it. But I was certain of one thing.

My father had been murdered in cold blood.

This place was hiding much more than I realized.

My mother let out a small cry, akin to a wounded bird, and slid to the floor, her body wracked with sobs as she buried her head between her knees. I knelt down and rubbed her back, unsure how to comfort her, my own grief palpable.

"It's not true," I whispered. "Dad would never do this."

Mom said nothing, only continued to weep. I held her close, both of us encased in sorrow. Perhaps it was best I spoke no more about it. The last thing I needed was to put Mom in danger, too.

Guilt surged through me so powerfully I suffocated under its weight. Dad wouldn't be dead if it hadn't been for me. Somebody died because of me. That's not how it was supposed to go. I couldn't find the tears. They were bottled up inside, with no way to get out.

Perhaps I didn't deserve the release that crying brought. I'd lost the only father I ever knew because of my own stupidity.

After about five minutes, Mom's sobs quieted. She lifted her head, exposing her tear-stained cheeks. She cupped my face in her hands. "I'm the one who should comfort you, Luna. I'm sorry."

The love in my mother's eyes almost became my undoing. I

didn't deserve any compassion. "It's okay, Mom. We'll get through this together," I managed to choke out.

She said nothing else for a moment, only nodded and released me from her grip, wiping the tears from her cheeks. "Your father wouldn't wish us to be sad. He would want us to go on with our lives," Mom whispered, squeezing my hand.

She never asked why I didn't cry, and I loved her even more for that. She stood up and brushed herself off. "First things first. We'll clean up our lunch mess and then set about with some funeral arrangements." Her voice cracked on the last part and she covered her mouth before rushing off to the kitchen to tidy up. There was no way either of us would finish our meal anyway.

I sat on the floor, listening to the clang of the dishes in the sink, trying to get my bearings. What now? I'd messed everything up and had no idea where to go next. I didn't dare visit Zander again. I would probably end up with more blood on my hands. But what of my father? What really happened? Did they torture him? Perhaps he finally gave in and told them it had been me that tampered with the phones. I wouldn't blame him if he did.

Despite the hollowed out burn that erupted in my stomach, I stood to go help Mom. The one thing I could do was be here for my P8 Mother. She seemed to be the only person who ever loved me.

My heart lurched. Well, apart from my father anyway.

I knew that his death meant the beginning of something new. Something horrifically new. And it terrified me to turn the page and discover what that might be.

Mom and I spent the afternoon catering to well-meaning friends that called or stopped by to offer their condolences, but also to get the updated gossip about what exactly went down. Word spread fast around town as soon as the funeral director was noti-fied. No secrets in this place.

Despite all that had happened, I couldn't help but see the stark contrast between my two worlds. Here, everyone offered aid in one form or another, while back home you could sell a child, no problem, with few questions asked.

But I suppose everything has its price. This world held a whole closet full of skeletons. And I learned the hard way, they were quite capable of murder. Anything to keep the peace. As absurd as that sounded.

Around six p.m., Mom and I, thinking we'd seen the last of the well-wishers, collapsed on the couch, when suddenly the doorbell rang. We'd eaten nothing all afternoon, neither of us having much of an appetite, but I'd made us both some hot tea.

Mom put down her cup on the coffee table. "I suppose I should see who that is," she said wearily.

"No, Mom. Let me get it. You relax. I'll be back."

"Whoever it is tell them thank you for me, all right? But honestly, I hope it's not another food offering. Not that I'm not grateful, but we've run out of space in the kitchen."

Mom wasn't wrong. What started out as a small collection of people bringing meals had escalated to the point where every available surface now held a covered dish. None of the guests stayed, simply gave their condolences and then tried to get the scoop as to what happened, since Mom had been so tight-lipped on the phone.

I gave Mom a short smile. "Don't worry, I'll find a place for it." I patted her hand and rose from the couch, disappearing into the main hall to answer the door.

The bell rang again.

"Okay, okay. I'm coming. Hold your horses," I muttered.

I yanked open the door and I gaped in surprise when I discovered who was standing outside.

"Zander."

"Hey, Luna."

His eyes appeared gold under the yellow porch light, his silhouette shadowed by the already encroaching darkness. But I saw a determination in his face. He wasn't here for a social call. Zander wouldn't have shown up anywhere near me unless it was important. My heart gave a little leap. Did I dare believe he'd made a breakthrough? My excitement dampened almost immediately as I thought of leaving my distraught Mother.

"I'm so sorry to hear of your father's passing. I wanted to stop by and give you this."

He reached inside his jacket and procured a pocket-size black book. "Here, take it. It has always brought me comfort in my times of need."

I took the small worn volume with shaking hands, wondering what he could possibly give me that would improve this situation. I looked at the cover. Embossed into the dark leather, was gold lettering revealing the title of the book. I glanced up at him, surprised.

"It's a bible."

Zander gave me a small smile. "Yes, it is. Before you go to bed tonight, look up Proverbs 3:27. I think it will help you."

I frowned at him, puzzled. Something about how he said it, like it was more than just a bible passage. What did he want to tell me? I searched his face looking for clues, but found nothing. His features remained schooled. His eyes, however, almost pleaded for me to understand.

Not knowing what else to do, I simply nodded and said, "Thank you, it was nice of you to stop by."

"No problem. Again, I'm sorry for your loss. See you around."

Without another word, he placed his hands in his jacket pockets and turned to leave. When he reached the end of the driveway, he looked back at me one last time and waved. But his gaze burned a hole into the bible I still clasped in my hands.

He didn't want me to forget.

I returned the wave, letting him know I understood, and he disappeared down the street.

I shut the door, heart pounding. I squeezed my eyes closed and leaned against the wall for support. I had so many unanswered questions. Things that should not be spoken of here. I wanted to yell at Zander to come back but of course, that was out of the question.

I shifted and remembered the bible, clutched in my hands.

"Luna? Who was that? Is everything all right?" Mom called from the other room. I jumped at the sound of her voice, almost forgetting she was waiting for me to return.

I took a deep breath. "Everything's fine, Mom. Just a well-wisher with a casserole. I'm going to put it in the fridge. Be back in a minute."

Another lie. There were so many.

Still, what choice did I have? I needed to read that passage. It might be a clue. And I refused to wait a second longer to find out.

I raced into the kitchen and sat down at the table. I flipped through the volume with ease. Back on Wı Nova, Mama insisted we keep a bible around the house. She thought it made us look classier, though I suspect she herself never looked at it. But it had been the only book we owned, and I'd taught myself to read and write with the tome. I'd recite the passages again and again, repeating the sounds until I understood what they meant. Now, I effortlessly thumbed through the familiar text until I found Proverbs three.

My heart stopped. Tucked into the tiny corner of the binding was a small folded piece of paper.

Zander had a message for me and he'd used the bible to deliver it.

With trembling fingers, I reached for the note and read the contents.

CHAPTER 26

I studied the words in Zander's small, neat print.

10 p.m. DRC.

I'd seen that abbreviation before. I wracked my brain, trying to remember where. Then I realized there was only one place that fit those initials.

The Dillinger Research Center.

Why did Zander want me to meet him there? I bit my lip, struggling to make the connection between my father, Zander, and the research center.

Had Zander discovered something? I crunched the small scrap of paper into my palm. I'd been so excited to see Zander at the door. But what if this was a booby trap? I still had no proof I could trust him. I had to face facts. My father mysteriously died *after* I told Zander about confronting the guard and Agent Mills.

My initial thought had been I shouldn't have gone. But Dad may have already been dead when I arrived. Maybe this was all a setup to make me believe he'd been alive this entire time. But why would they care about that?

Zander might be the reason my father got taken in the first place.

My mind churned, looking for the trick, the lie, any kind of betrayal. But nothing clicked. Something inside told me Zander was telling the truth. If this was a hoax, he had me fooled, and I didn't believe I was that gullible. At least the old me wasn't.

Mom shuffled into the kitchen, her slippers scuffling on the tile floor, jerking me back to the present moment. "Luna? Is everything all right? You've been in here a long time."

I jumped up out of the chair, hastily stuffing the small wad of paper into my pocket.

"Sorry, Mom. I was thinking about making some tea. Would you like some?"

Mom's brow furrowed, concerned. "Are you sure you're okay? You just made us some. It's sitting on the coffee table in the living room, remember? In fact, I only came in to tell you it was getting cold."

I squirmed under her scrutiny. "Yeah," I stammered. "I uh... went to reheat the water to warm it up."

Mom put her own half-finished cup on the table and placed her arm around my shoulders, hugging me close. "Come sit down. You don't have to be strong for me. It's okay to let go."

The gentle touch of this woman I barely knew, who'd been more of a mother to me than my Mama had ever been, was my undoing. I collapsed into the vacant chair and sobbed, great gulping tears onto her offered shoulder.

I didn't just cry over the loss of my P8 father, a good man, but for everything that happened since I left home. I cried for my sister, who I missed so horribly it ached, and I cried for the young girl willing to do anything to save her family. I would never be that girl again. The truth I'd been carrying weighed like a giant brick in my heart.

This much emotion was deemed improper in this strange new universe I found myself in. Nobody here tolerated an unstable human being. It led to trouble. Mom realized it was breaking the rules, but here behind these walls, she let me cry.

When I had no more tears left, she pulled out a handkerchief and wiped my cheeks. "There now. It's good to release it all."

Her voice hitched as she spoke and she brought her hand to cup my face. She searched my eyes, looking for something. She was paler than usual, and her blonde hair lay mussed and flat against her head in a manner I'd never thought she'd allow. Her fingers shook a little against my cheek, but her tone was deadly serious. "You can't tell anyone we cried this way, Luna. Promise me. A few tears is fine, but sobbing like this is forbidden. We can break the rules this once, but we must keep this between us girls."

I frowned. "Why is it so forbidden?" I hiccupped, still trying to control my ragged breathing.

It was Mom's turn to be confused. "What a silly question. The laws over expression are quite clear. Too much emotion leads to unwise choices. They are required to maintain order."

I opened my mouth to retort that it seemed barbaric, but one look into my mother's drawn face and I realized I shouldn't worry her any further. Black rings shadowed her eyes, swollen from crying.

I patted her hand. "Why don't we call it a day? It's only seven, but I'm exhausted. And it looks like you could use some rest."

She looked torn, still worried about me questioning emotional outbursts. But her exhaustion won out. "Perhaps you're right."

She got up slowly, as if it pained her to move and headed toward the stairs. "Goodnight, Luna. I love you."

"I love you too, Mom."

And somewhere deep inside I realized that I meant it.

Which made what I had to do tonight that much harder.

A few hours later, I lay in bed wide awake, waiting, listening to the tick of the clock in the hall, its smooth rhythm soothing my troubled mind. Finally, at nine-thirty, I got up and tugged on black jeans and a shirt. Dark colors were always best for not being detected at night.

I was relieved to get up and have somewhere to go, away from the suffocating silence of this house. All I kept hearing in my head was Mama's voice.

Never let them see your weakness.

I pulled my hair into a tight ponytail and gazed at myself in the vanity mirror, giving myself a talking to. "You will never cry in front of anyone ever again, Luna Redwood," I whispered, face stern. "You had a momentary lapse, but never make that mistake again."

I stared at my reflection, eyes glinting, hard as steel.

Never again.

Satisfied, I turned away and noticed the bible Zander had given me, resting on the vanity where I'd left it. I picked it up, running my fingers over the embossed words that read, *Holy Bible,* lettered in gold on the cover. I'd been in such a hurry to read Zander's note, I never looked at the verse he'd mentioned. What if it meant something? Before I changed my mind, I flicked to Proverbs 3:27. "Do not withhold good from those to whom it is due, when it is in your power to act."

I slumped back against the chair, thinking. What was that supposed to mean? Did Zander want me to appreciate that what we'd been trying to do was "good" and I shouldn't have guilt about it? One thing I agreed with—I had the power to act. I would do everything within my control to change this situation —even if it killed me.

With a renewed determination, I stood up and grabbed my coat off the chair before heading out the door.

I had a job to do.

It was time to meet Zander and uncover the truth, once and for all.

The Dillinger Research Center loomed large against the dark sky, creating shadows on the perfectly manicured lawn. I shivered despite my warm fleece jacket. I noticed for the first time that the center stood a bit aloof from the other clustered buildings where I'd tried to get in to see my Dad. It seemed they wished to isolate it and set it apart. A few trees scattered around the perimeter, gave it an asymmetrical feel, contrary to the usual tidiness of P8. It appeared they were haphazardly placed on purpose, in an effort to hide something. I looked harder, trying to penetrate through the inky darkness. The center had no outside lights, like the main buildings. Apparently, nobody wanted to draw attention to the place.

I edged in closer and could just make out some kind of brick wall fortification around the perimeter. Was that to ensure people didn't get out? Or for the sole purpose of warding off the general public from entering?

Why hadn't it occurred to me to look for my father here? It was almost as if an invisible cloak shielded my mind, preventing me from searching out other possibilities last time I came. I had been so focused on the main building everything else faded away. And to make matters worse—the center was just precisely far enough away from the other construction that it was literally out of sight. Had they made this strange design to trick the eye? To allow you to see only what they wanted? I'd definitely seen all four structures before. But my eyes naturally gravitated to the ornate brightness of the first building, the others, dull and plain, recessed into the shadows.

Before I determined anything else about the Dillinger center, a hand clamped down hard on my shoulder. I instantly spun around and swung my leg out bringing whoever had been behind me to the ground. It wasn't the first time I'd used that move. When you were a thief, you learned a few tricks of the trade. It gave you those necessary minutes to escape.

"Luna, it's me," Zander hissed. "Let up."

I took my foot off his chest, but didn't help him up. "You

shouldn't sneak up on people like that Zander. It can get you killed."

"Duly noted," he muttered, getting up and brushing the dirt off himself. The light of the moon fell on his blonde hair as he raked his fingers through it, sending a leaf fluttering onto the grass. The idiot should have worn a hat. At least he had the common sense to wear black.

"Why don't you explain what's going on? From my point of view, this all seems pretty suspicious. First, I confide in you about what happened with Dad. The next minute, he's dead."

Even the words on my tongue, tasted metallic.

He sighed. "Are we back to this? I thought you trusted me now."

I glared at him. "I'm not stupid. Facts are facts. You're turning me in, aren't you? Is this some kind of sick trap to get me?"

"Of course it's not. I care—" Zander stopped talking as soon as he saw the stony expression on my face.

"He was the only father I ever knew. How could you do this to me?" My voice rang high and shrill, but I caught myself and stuffed my emotions back down. Being weak would never do. I'd already made that mistake once tonight. Standing here in the dark with an almost stranger forced me to recognize it had been ridiculous to think Zander had the answers to everything. What a fool I'd been. This place had a strange effect on me and I'd let my guard down. And it cost me my dad.

Zander cast a quick glance around before taking a step closer, honing in on me. I started to move aside, but he grabbed my hand to stop me and I saw the determination etched in his eyes. There was also something else I'd never seen in him before. Deep anger. Not the annoyed irritation I experienced when I'd shown up at the library, and he asked me to stay away. This was far reaching—and went beyond me. His ghosts from the past haunted him.

"Listen to me. You have this all wrong."

"Oh, do I? Then why is my father dead?"

Zander spoke so quietly I almost didn't hear it. "Is he really gone, though?"

I snapped my hand back. "Don't even joke about stuff like that, Zander Barringer, or I'll lay you out again."

He shook his head. "We're wasting time. There's a reason I called you out here tonight. Let me show you something, and then you can make your own decision about me."

I narrowed my eyes, trying to gage him. I might be walking into a trap. But what choice did I have?

I crossed my arms, and nodded, afraid if I spoke it would expose how rattled I felt.

Zander put a finger to his lips and led me by the hand away from the shelter of the trees, toward the Dillinger Research Center. From this distance, I made out the profile of a very large insignia on the side of the structure. The same I'd seen on the main building a few days ago. Only this symbol was much larger, the eagle wings expanse stretched from one end to the other. They wanted to make sure everyone understood who owned this construction.

I considered it a warning.

My hand grew sweaty clasped in Zander's grip, and my heart raced. We were exposed out here in the open. A mixture of fear and excitement tore through me.

The outskirts of the city lay quiet and pristine—but deadly undercurrents rippled below the surface. The closer we got, the more I perceived its pull. But I had no time to analyze it because we'd already reached the six-foot fortress wall. Made with a mix of silver and brick, it had a braided trim, patterned with the number eight, repeated all the way along the outer edge. It was a strange design, and if I wasn't so freaked that Zander planned to breach the edifice, I might have been more curious.

"Zander are you insane?" I hissed through gritted teeth.

He didn't turn around, only kept moving.

I tried pulling my hand back to stop him. But he held tight, and I didn't have the strength to fight him without the element of surprise on my side.

He spun on his heel and gave me a silent look that told me to be patient. He didn't dare speak so close to these white stone walls. I reluctantly fell into step behind him. I wasn't used to following orders, but I forced myself forward.

Was this the beginning of the end?

CHAPTER 27

Zander bypassed the front gate and made a beeline for the north side of the building, shrouded in darkness. He pointed to a small blinking red light, hidden in the top corner under the eaves and motioned for me to crouch down behind the wall, out of its line of vision. On hands and knees, we crawled over the noticeably warm ground to a section of the barricade that seemed a bit out of place compared to the rest. This area of the wall appeared more tattered, the cement edges worn away leaving an inconsistency in the pristine brick pattern. It wasn't an obvious flaw, something only a trained eye would detect.

Zander squatted down in the direct spot where I noticed the oddity. Slowly, and carefully, he began to pull bricks from the facade, creating a hole wide enough for us to shimmy through. He waved me forward, pointing to the opening. I understood exactly what he wanted me to do, but I hesitated.

What if there were guards on the other side of that barrier?

Still, I recognized if I desired answers, I'd have to take a few risks, so I bent down and poked my head through the gap to survey my surroundings. We were near the back door, which appeared almost as large as the front entrance. I saw the electronic keypad that allowed access, along with a hefty padlock from the dark ages added for good measure—but there was no guard anywhere in sight. The camera Zander had shown me earlier pointed toward the front of the building, and there were no security cameras on this end.

Cocky idiots. They didn't believe they required any surveillance—that was the good news. But unfortunately, the bad news was the door had been grated with heavy steel. I didn't see how Zander could get through it. Especially not without setting off the security alarms. A small jab from Zander at my back, warned me I needed to hurry. I sucked in a breath and stepped through, Zander at my heels. In an instant, he'd replaced the bricks in the wall and leapt to his feet, racing over to the rear door, coming to a screeching halt at the steps. It was then I realized he wasn't aiming for the entryway.

He intended to breach a window.

Not a bad idea. I probably would have done the same. I watched as Zander pulled a thin, microscopic piece of metal from his pocket and wedged it between the frame and the latch. A soft click penetrated the silence and I held my breath, certain the security system would screech any second, alerting the guards to an invasion. But nothing happened.

As if hearing the thoughts in my head, Zander whispered, "It's a special metal, undetectable to computer scans. It won't even register the unlocked latch. The metal fools the computer program into believing it's still locked." He grinned at me, his white teeth practically glowing in the moonlight.

I crossed my arms and gave him my best withering stare. "And this is supposed to impress me?"

His grin grew wider. "I'd like to think so."

He turned back to search through the backpack at his feet, procuring a small, flat tool, just large enough to wedge between the frame and the sash. He pushed it into place; the window slid up with ease.

I wondered how many times he'd done this. His movements, fluid and sure, indicated he was familiar with the process. Not to mention that the window must have been oiled beforehand, otherwise it would have squeaked. He'd planned this out, right down to the letter. As someone who prided herself on being sneaky, I had to admit I *was* impressed. But I would never tell him that. His head would swell so big it would burst.

Zander nudged me forward, pointing to the opening. "It's time to go inside. I'll give you a boost up," he whispered. He cupped his hands together and lowered them for me to step onto so I could leverage myself through the window.

I hesitated, if this was a trap, the authorities would be waiting to arrest me on the other side—pinning me with charges of forced entry. I mean, it looked dark but maybe that was all part of the plan, to have the element of surprise. A piece of me wanted to refuse, but curiosity won out. I could always run if need be. I'd done it before. Most of all, I needed answers and my intuition told me this might be the best way.

So instead of protesting, I carefully placed my foot in his open palms and jumped. My fingers gripped the ledge, as Zander's strong hands grabbed my waist and lifted to help pull me over the sill. I frowned, irritated that I'd required help—even more annoying was the fact that I enjoyed the sensation of his touch as he encircled my middle.

Careful, Luna. Remember what we talked about. Trust no one.

Once inside, I quickly sprang to my feet to make way for Zander, who followed right behind me, smooth and agile as a cat.

I looked around. Obviously, the room didn't get much use. I noticed some buckets filled with mops leaning against the wall; I surmised we'd ended up in some kind of utility storeroom. Zander pointed to the small door in front of us and motioned me to follow him. We crept out into a long hall, the antiseptic smells from nearby laboratories hitting me full in the face. Zander knew where to go, his footsteps silent and sure. The hallway hosted a labyrinth of doors. I remained alert; ready to fight any security guard that might pop out. But no one did. I wasn't positive if it was because of the late hour or because the agents were beyond confident their walls were impenetrable.

Zander's familiarity with this place made me uneasy. When we came to what I figured must be the heart of the building, he flattened like a pancake against the wall. He reached out his arm and shoved me back next to him. I assumed it was because there were security cameras parading this corridor, protecting a high clearance area. There were no windows in this section of the structure, keeping us in the pitch black. It would be difficult for someone to make out our two shadows threading their way along the core of the Dillinger center.

We reached a four-cornered intersection where the wall no longer concealed us. How would we cross the wide expanse without being caught? I inhaled deeply; preparing to run for it, but Zander had other plans.

He grabbed my hand and took a sharp right turn, leading us away from the open area. But I halted mid-step when something glinted in the dark. Zander skidded to a stop but not before almost taking my arm with him.

"What are you doing?" he hissed. "We need to keep going," He turned his head both ways, checking our surroundings, tugging at my sleeve.

"What is that?" I murmured, ignoring his plea and pointing to the gold I'd seen on the wall. I crept up to it and examined it closer. Even in the darkness I could see it was some kind of photograph. I shut out Zander's protests. Every bone in my body told me this was important. But I didn't know why. Quickly, I reached in my boot and extracted a small flashlight, and spun it to the image. Zander didn't make a sound but tried to snuff out my torch, practically tackling me for it. But I was quick and side-stepped him, shining the beam onto the portrait.

My heart caught in my throat. It was Mrs. Lennor.

"Scientist of the month. Elia Watford," I said in a hushed voice, reading the plaque at the bottom of the image. I let the light shine up to the photograph again to be sure. It was definitely Mrs. Lennor. "Scientist? But—"

Before I could do or say anything else. Zander took the flashlight from me and wiped it out. "Not now, Luna. We may not be in line with a camera in this spot, but we are only about ten steps away from one. And those aren't good odds. We're sitting ducks out here. Come on." His voice was coaxing and pleading all at the same time, and I could practically smell his desperation. But all I kept thinking was if Mrs. Lennor was a scientist, why was she masquerading as a teacher? It explained her strange behavior but little else.

Zander grabbed my hand, holding tighter than before. Probably considering me a flight risk. I let him lead me away from the image that had now burned like a brand in my mind. We crept down a few steps into a very long galley; he opened a door and pulled me into another closet. As my eyes adjusted to the dim light, I could see this space was filled with a clutter of complex-looking machines.

I blinked and stared up at the wall of flickering video screens, each one showing different surveillance angles. The massive control panels engulfed the place, casting off colors in contrasting hues. Sweat trickled down my back in the overly warm space as the incessant hum of working machinery resounded loudly in the room, echoing in my ears.

I stepped closer, observing the screens before me that showed vast, stark white rooms filled with a labyrinth of data ports and huge machines. They were silent on screen, but I imagined the roar they had to produce in person. In the center of each room was a circular tower that even now sparked with orange light that danced around and through it, like a spiderweb. The contraption was connected to the floor at its base and was covered in dials and instruments. "What in the hell is it for?" I murmured, more to myself than anyone.

Zander, who must have heard, stepped up behind me. "From what I've been able to gather, the big towers are a power field," he said. "They're used to import all the data from everyone's phones. This is where everything is tracked. I couldn't tell you before; you were being so carefully watched. I had an opportunity at the park, but I just couldn't bring myself to put you in that kind of danger."

I took a shaky intake of breath to try to settle my nerves and my temper. I didn't want any trace of fear to show, even in front of Zander. I bit my lip, trying to calm down. If our roles had been reversed, I wouldn't have told Zander what I'd found, either. His reasoning was lame. But I couldn't blame him for something I'd do myself. Besides, we were here now, with bigger fish to fry. So instead, I asked a question that had been niggling at me. "My parents said they run important experiments here. Is any of that remotely true?"

Zander snorted. "Not that I've seen. Probably more propaganda. This place is a glorified spy center. And their so called 'scientists', are the government minions eager to do any dirty work necessary. One of the first things that tipped me off was how it seemed a bit warmer out here, beyond town. And the ground held more heat. I soon discovered that they needed to dispose of the waste heat produced by the microchips, and the other electronic components they utilize to track us. They use the ground as a heat sink and there's so much of it, it's affecting the temperature of the air. I guess that's what happens when you need enough equipment to keep track of everyone on P8."

I swallowed hard. "I have noticed the extra warmth. Especially tonight, when we were crawling on the ground." I paused, trying to get the words I wanted to say out without my voice cracking. "Zander. By dirty work do you mean like what they did to my dad?" Zander stared at the screen and I could see his jaw working, clenching in frustration. "Yes, Luna. Exactly like your dad. And more." He shook his head briefly, pulling his gaze away from the monitors and handed me back the small flashlight he'd taken from me in the hallway. "I better do what I came in here to do, before anyone sees us."

Zander knelt down to look at some wires under the dashboard and motioned for me to shine my light down on him.

Curious now, I obliged without a fuss. Though honestly, I really wanted to scream at him to tell me why we were really here.

With the help of the small beam of light, Zander pulled a red wire from a thick bundle of cables tucked under the mainframe of the console and disarmed it. It had to be the main security cable.

"What are you doing?" I hissed. Perhaps Zander was an amateur after all. "They'll detect the system is down and come running. Are you completely insane?" I crouched next to him, looking at the damage.

He turned from the equipment to face me, his warm breath on my cheek. My heart skipped a beat—for a minute I forgot where we were—and I stared at him. Sometimes Zander seemed so familiar, and it only added to my confusion. I managed to pull myself together and hastily stood up, eager to create some space between us. The self-imposed pressure I'd put myself under had made me addle-brained. I had placed too much hope in Zander's ability to get me away from this place, and that wouldn't do at all.

Plus, he could be a traitor.

Zander rose and grabbed my arm, which silenced my incessant mental chatter.

"It's okay Luna, I've done this before. I've bypassed the alarm that lets them discern the cameras are down. They can't hear or see us until I bring everything back online. They won't ever learn we were here. We just have to be careful about looking out for guards. Fortunately, there aren't many on night shift. We should be fine." His voice sounded low in his throat, almost a whisper, but I had no trouble hearing him in the small room.

"Tell me why we're here. You seem pretty familiar with this place."

"I've been staking out the research center for months; it's been the main focus of my investigation."

I frowned. "Investigation?"

"Yes. I've been sneaking in and out, trying to find out why everything they do is top secret. That's how I figured out this was the main spy center. I'm sure the answer to uncovering what's happening to me lies somewhere within these walls..." he trailed off, pausing for a minute before looking me in the eye. "I mean, to both of us. I plan to discover why we still have our memories."

I wrapped my arms around myself, trying to contain the bubble of excitement welling up inside me. I needed to be realistic. "What makes you so sure all the answers are here?" I asked.

"Well, I wasn't at first, but then I discovered something I couldn't explain. Come on, follow me. I want to show you."

"Wait!" I grabbed Zander's arm to hold him back. "There's something we have to do before we go."

"What?" Zander stared at me quizzically.

"I need to find out about Mrs. Lennor."

"Mrs. Lennor? Who's that?"

I rolled my eyes. "Don't you pay attention? She's the woman in that picture out there who isn't Mrs. Lennor at all. But an Elia Watford. She was pretending to be my detention teacher when all along she was one of these scientists. I bet you there is a database or something about employees we can access. I'm good at hacking—and we may find some more answers."

I could see Zander warring with himself, his fists clenching. "No, I don't think so, Luna. We can't risk being stuck in here."

I ignored him and yanked down the dataport. My fingers flew over the keyboard, trying to trace any sign of an Elia Watford. I bypassed a security wall and quickly found myself with a pile of files as long as my arm listed on the screen. "Bingo," I whispered.

"Luna, I don't think—"

"Quiet. If you're going to be a baby, then go," I said, not turning away from the screen. "I plan on getting some answers."

I heard a sigh. "Of course I'm not going to leave you here. What are you looking for?"

"I just did a scan of Elia Watford. And I found a bunch of files. I'm just trying to see..."

My voice trailed off and Zander came closer looking over my shoulder. "What did you find?"

"Look at this file. It's called the watch list." With trembling fingers, I tapped the screen and a directory of scientists popped up, along with a catalogue of the names of their assignments. These so-called assignments had to be the citizens of P8.

"My God. This looks like an index of all the people that are under scrutiny right now," Zander breathed. "There are so many names here."

The scientists were recorded in alphabetical order and I scrolled to the W's. Sure enough Elia Watford was there. And right next to it...was my name.

"She was assigned to me? Like I was some kind of experiment? What is this place?" I choked. "I can't do this anymore."

"Hey, look at me."

I managed to turn my eyes away from the comport to meet Zander's. He put a hand on my shoulder. "You can do this. I think I've found a way out. But we need to leave this security room. We're running low on time."

"But you don't understand. Mrs. Lennor could be the reason my father is dead. She's probably the one that figured out I messed with my phone, if she's the one assigned to me."

"Stop it, Luna. You can sit here and feel sorry for yourself or do something about it. Now, are you in?"

I lifted my chin. "I am not feeling sorry for myself."

"Good. Let's go. I need to show you why we're here."

"Fine," I muttered. "But this isn't over."

I turned back and closed out the file, even though I was aching to see who else was on the list. Did Zander have a scientist assigned to him? Did Mom? So many questions whirled in my mind as I erased my computer key strokes, leaving no trace I'd been here at all.

As soon as I was done, Zander took the flashlight from me and turned off the small light, casting the room into darkness. The only sound was Zander's soft breathing echoing my own.

He groped for my hand, once secured in his, he carefully opened the door. He scoured the hall, making sure the coast was clear and then stepped out.

He took me back the way we'd come, only this time there was no reason to hug the wall or lie low. The dark halls and dead cameras gave us new freedom. But we understood the danger all the same, and walked quickly. Zander said there might be guards around, but I'd yet to spot one. Perhaps they were asleep on the job.

We soon found ourselves back where we started. From this side, it looked to be a delivery entrance, but I knew better. Zander pulled the handle, and it swung open easily on its freshly-oiled hinges. The padlock that had appeared so intimidating before, suddenly seemed to have no purpose, like an ornament on a Christmas tree.

They were indeed arrogant fools.

Zander took one last quick glance around to make sure the coast was clear and abruptly pulled me back out into the cool evening air.

"I thought you brought me into the building to show me something," I whispered.

We were both wearing black and blended into the night seamlessly, otherwise we would have been exposed standing out here in the open. As it was, I felt a little uneasy, Zander's blonde waves shone like a beacon in the moonlight. I wished for the second time that day he'd worn a hat. I was grateful the only other visible parts of Zander were his crystal blue eyes. They looked excited now.

"I am. I just needed to shut down the security for our protection. No one can witness what I'm about to reveal to you. We can't be on the live feed. This is huge, Luna." His voice remained quiet but animated.

As my eyes readjusted to the outdoor light, I glanced around. Everything appeared normal. Nothing out of place—the same as before. What could he possibly have to show me? Surely the files we discovered inside held more interest. Seriously, what was his plan? Give me a tour of the blue dumpster over in the corner? Because that was the only thing I saw back here.

Zander must have noticed my dubious expression, but he quickly forged on. "I've been sneaking in and out of this place for the last six months. But it wasn't until you showed up and the government got off my tail and started focusing on you that I made some progress. I conducted my own research without being under anyone's scrutiny. I began coming here every night. Until one day, by accident, I found this."

Zander gripped my hand tighter, and he dragged me towards a non-descript portion of the wall surrounding the building. This was different than the section we'd entered from—perfectly symmetrical, no oddities made it stand out. In fact, if anything, this barrier looked thicker and even more impenetrable. My skin crawled. I felt like a trapped animal.

Zander released my hand and placed his two palms on the high wall. "I think I always knew there was something strange about this partition. There's a warmth here, an energy under my fingertips—then, one day, I saw it."

I frowned. "What do you mean you saw it? It's a wall, Zander. There's nothing special about it," I said. "Is this why you brought me all the way out here? To look at some barricade?"

Zander turned from the divider and gazed at me patiently. "It sounds crazy, I know, but trust me on this." He came up beside me. "I want you to concentrate. Let everything else fall away. Keep your eyes on the perimeter," he said waving his hand in front of it. "Focus."

I wanted to roll my eyes at him and his nonsense, but a gut

instinct told me to go along. I crossed my arms to show I wasn't impressed, but began to zero in on the citadel before us anyway.

It seemed like ages that I stood there, staring at a bunch of brick like an idiot. But then, just when I was about to give up and call Zander an ass, I saw it. An outline, so faint, I barely made it out at first, but then, the more I concentrated, the more was revealed, until finally I became aware of a makeshift door, completely camouflaged within the barrier. I strained harder to study it more clearly.

But before I could make out anything else, I heard footsteps approaching from the door we'd just exited.

Someone was coming.

We'd been found.

CHAPTER 28

Zander pressed a hand to my shoulder and whispered, "Run!"

There was no need to tell me twice. We high-tailed it out of there, not stopping until we reached the front gate. Going back the way we came was pointless—the cameras were still off, thanks to Zander's handiwork. The lamppost ahead burned brightly, so we took a hard left and skirted around it, so as not to be identified, making it to the safety of the trees in the nick of time. Two men emerged from the shadows where we had been standing seconds before.

I didn't dare breathe as I stared at them, certain they'd spotted us—but quickly realized we weren't even on their radar. They leaned casually against the side of the building. One of them laughed into the cool night air, creating puffs of smoke that emanated from his lips and escaped into the darkness.

I grinned. They truly hadn't noticed. They were simply on break. *Thank God.*

I finally let out the breath I didn't realize I'd been holding and leaned back, relieved, only to find myself collapsing against Zander's hard chest. He must have been protectively hovering directly behind me.

I reveled in his warmth; there was a familiarity here between us I couldn't place, overwhelming my senses. What was it about Zander that took me so keenly to the past? It's not like I'd ever known him in W1. I would have remembered him. It occurred to me in that moment I never asked Zander where he was originally from. Before he told me he had memories that didn't belong to this place, I assumed he always lived here. He'd made it seem that way. I'd been so focused on myself I hadn't thought to ask where his memories originated.

"Let's go," Zander whispered in my ear, "We only have about five minutes until the system starts up again. We better get out of here before it does." His voice was gravelly, he was attempting to sound normal, but I knew otherwise. I heard the pounding of his heart against my back. Our close proximity had affected him, too. He reached for my hand and stood, pulling me to my feet alongside him. We didn't speak as we walked through the woods toward home, both of us caught up in our own thoughts. When I finally looked up again, we were already at the edge of the forest clearing; the church steeple loomed in the distance. Suddenly, Zander stopped short, and I almost plowed into him.

He shot out an arm to steady me. "Sorry. I thought this would be a good place to talk, before we get out in the open—in case there are spying eyes. It's late, but you can never be too careful."

"Where are you from?" I blurted. Finally getting out the question that had been plaguing me since we left the research center.

Zander looked at me, puzzled. "What do you mean? I'm from here. This is my home."

I pushed him away and glared. "None of this makes sense. You told me you have memories too. You confided in me. At first, I assumed it was a trap, but now you've shown me this brick wall, and I'm at a loss as to what to believe."

"Hey," Zander stepped closer, taking my hand. "I explained to you what happened to my friends, how they disappeared. That's why I want this. They deserve more than an erased memory. Besides, you haven't exactly revealed any details of your past. I have no idea where you're from, either. I'm pretty sure it's not here."

We stood so close I smelled the faint scent of his cologne. I wanted to open my mouth and tell him everything. But something held me back. I didn't want to risk any betrayal. But wasn't he my only hope?

I looked down at the ground, helpless, unable to speak.

Zander released me. "It's okay. You don't have to answer that. Everyone has secrets they need to keep."

His voice sounded distant, mysterious. What secret did Zander have? Was I reading too much into this? I didn't dare ask him.

He scraped a hand over his harried face, and sat down under a big old maple. Even the trees in the forest here were symmetrical, as if someone had planted them in perfect garden rows. It seemed unnatural.

"You didn't see what I was trying to show you in the wall did you?" his voice sounded defeated, like a little boy lost.

"No, Zander I did. It was the door, right? I wasn't sure if there was anything else there, it took me so long to discover it, and the guards came before I could dig further."

Zander grinned, his white teeth shining in the dark night. His exuberance returning, he jumped up and grabbed my arms in excitement.

"Yes! That's it, the door! I'm so glad you noticed it too. What a relief. We need to open it, determine what's there. We can come back—"

I held out a hand to stop him. "We can't just open it. What if it's a trap? I'm not sure that's such a good idea."

Zander's rubbed his temples. "You can't mean that. Not after everything that's happened. Some risks are worth taking. Aren't you angry that your father is dead? That the government killed him?"

"Of course I'm angry, but have you ever opened that door? It might go anywhere."

"The door's locked, Luna. I hoped we'd figure out how to break in together."

I'd never told Zander about my past. He didn't realize my skill at picking locks, no matter how complex. But I wasn't about to offer my services. At least, not yet.

"What if where that door goes is worse than where we are now?" I asked.

"What if it's not?" Zander retorted. "Maybe just maybe, beyond that hidden door are answers. Haven't you been searching for that ever since you arrived here?"

"I don't know. I just—"

It was Zander's turn to stop me. He took both of my hands in his. "Look Luna, I can't force you to do something you don't want to do. I assumed that after your father's death you would do anything to see what the government is hiding from us. I have a feeling that list we found is only the tip of the iceberg."

My resolve slipped a notch. Perhaps Zander was right. But I'd been burned before. And at least here I had a nice mother. One that actually loved me. But what about my siblings? Little Trinity? Their faces swam before my eyes. Could I walk away from her because I was afraid there was nothing better?

I licked my dry lips and stared into Zander's eyes. "Give me tonight to consider it. Can you do that?"

"Of course," he said hoarsely, his voice chocked full of emotion. "Let's go home." Some of his buoyancy returned, but not to the same level. He hesitated for a beat, before wrapping his arm around my shoulders.

Needing the comfort of another human being—I let him. I allowed myself this one moment of weakness before making such a huge decision. Besides, I didn't have the energy to shrug him off like I normally would. His presence, warm and comforting, wasn't something I was quite ready to let go of.

Near the outskirts of town, we passed by the cemetery where

my father would be buried in a few days. He hadn't been placed in the ground yet, but I still felt his spirit around me. I stopped and gazed at the perfectly aligned gravestones, each one marked with a flawless red rose. Even the poor rose didn't have the privilege of wilting in this strange place. My stomach contracted into a tight ball—understanding the implications of a single flower.

"Zander, why don't you go on ahead of me? I'll see you tomorrow. I want to stay here and think for a little while."

Zander squeezed me tighter for a moment, then released me, peering about wide-eyed, his face muscles twitching nervously. "Are you sure? I hate to leave you out here alone."

"I've been on my own for a long time. I can handle myself, don't worry. Besides, we can't take the risk of being seen together in town. The chances are slim since it's so late, but still. I need to remain here for a few minutes and talk to my father. I realize how crazy it sounds, but..." I let my voice trail off, unsure how to continue.

Zander stuffed his hands in his pockets, his eyes haggard with uncertainty. "That doesn't sound crazy at all. Trust me, I get it. Just stay safe, okay?"

"Thanks. You too. I'll come find you at the library tomorrow. Don't worry, I'll be subtle."

Zander nodded, smiling a little, like he wasn't absolutely sure he believed I could be stealthy. But I didn't call him out on it. I was too bone weary for that.

"Goodnight, Luna."

"'Night, Zander," I said. He turned and walked away, heading toward home. He didn't look back, and I watched him until he faded into a small speck in the distance. Then, finally alone, I shifted my gaze skywards, trying to connect with a father I barely knew. One I cared for just the same. He'd sacrificed everything for me. The sting of hot tears pricked at my eyes; I had been so stupid.

I brushed away a tear with my hand. I mustn't be weak. It wouldn't help at all.

I wrapped my arms tight around me and spoke loudly to the ghostly, silhouetted headstones.

"Thanks, Dad, for being the father I never had. And for protecting me when all the chips were against us," I whispered hoarsely. "I never experienced a Dad's love before you. I want you to know I loved you, too." I put my fingers to my lips and blew a kiss to the wind. I hoped somehow it reached him, wherever he'd gone.

I turned to leave. I knew now what I must do.

CHAPTER 29

The bright sun filtered through the bedroom curtains onto my face. I moaned, turning over and burying my head under the pillows, as the real world came crashing down.

Last night. The decision.

Knowing I wouldn't be able to fall back asleep; I tossed the duvet off and shivered as my feet hit the cold wood floor. I rose on shaky limbs and crossed the room to grab my robe to ward off the chill.

I needed a shower to warm up; that would make me feel better. I padded into the bathroom and allowed myself a few extra minutes, luxuriating under the hot spray of water. Who knew when I would have this luxury again? After we discovered where that door led at the DRC, we could end up anywhere.

After my shower, I selected my wardrobe—all black—which seemed to be my color of choice these days, more out of necessity than anything else. I dressed, adding a warm sweater to ward off the cold. Then I made my way downstairs to find Mom already in the kitchen, flipping pancakes.

"I heard you rustling around up there, so I prepared us some breakfast. Are pancakes okay?" Mom asked.

"Pancakes sound great. Thanks, Mom. But you didn't have to go to all this fuss."

Mom waved her spatula in the air. "Nonsense. Now sit down. They're ready."

I plopped down at the table waiting as mom dished up the steaming hotcakes. Maple syrup and a bowl of sliced strawberries were already on the table and my mouth watered as I inhaled the delicious aromas. This fabulous breakfast was the kind of indulgence I dared not even hope for back on WI. How things had changed.

That's one thing I'd learned from this experience—life was continually shifting and I just had to try to keep up. My life had become a rollercoaster I could never get off.

I glanced over at Dad's empty chair, and my chest grew tight and heavy, as I struggled to absorb the loss. When I'd pulled myself together, I looked to Mom. She was staring at me, her eyes glittering with unshed tears of grief, her food untouched.

She reached over and took my hand that had been fiddling with my fork. "I miss him too, Luna." A deep sadness engulfed her, and I wished with all my heart I could erase it for her.

Instead, I was about to add to her pain. What kind of monster was I? What would she think of me if she knew what Zander and I were up to?

To top it all off, there was the stark truth—I was the reason Dad lay dead in the county morgue. Sure, the government had been the one to pull the trigger, but it never would have happened if it hadn't been for me.

I pushed those thoughts aside; they wouldn't help Mom now. I squeezed her hand and gave her my best smile. Seemingly satisfied, Mom returned to the task of eating. She pierced the fluffy pancake with her fork and gently placed it in her mouth, chewing with concentrated effort. It looked as though she was being force fed dry sawdust instead of yummy pancakes. But I understood how she felt.

We continued our breakfast in silence until I ultimately

snapped and blurted out what had been plaguing me since this whole nightmare unfolded.

"Mom, do you believe Dad killed himself?"

Mom gave a sharp intake of breath, and the cup of orange juice she'd been about to drink from halted in midair. Her face twisted with anguish as she pressed her lips firmly together in a solid white line. Gently and with shaking hands, she returned the glass to the table. She cast her eyes down as she spoke.

"It's not for me to say, Luna. But I believe your father loved life and us." She looked up at me, placing her fists into her lap so I wouldn't see them tremble under the table. She continued on, "All I know for sure is there was nothing in this world that would compel him to choose anything that might endanger you."

I swallowed hard and pushed back the hot tears prickling my eyes, more certain than ever I'd made the right decision. I owed it to Mom to find the answers. The risk be damned.

❧

Several hours later, when Mom had lain down for a nap, I decided it was time to leave. It was better to go without explanations. I'd already left too many notes that led her to worry. A clean break was best.

Earlier that day, I'd pretended everything was normal, I'd played the part of the dutiful daughter and brought hot tea and cookies to her bedroom, never saying a word about my plans. It relieved me, not having to lie. The lies always came too easily to me. At least this time, that particular skill wasn't required.

I grabbed my jacket from the hook on the wall as I left, the small bible Zander had given me just a few short days ago, still tucked in my pocket. It seemed as if an eternity had passed since then.

The crisp air cooled my hot cheeks, and I breathed it in deeply, ridding myself of some palpable tension that had built up in my body, about to swallow me alive.

I counted my breaths... *one, two, three, four, five, six, seven, eight, nine, ten...* repeating the sequence again and again until I reached the library. I gazed up at the now familiar, but intimidating brick building. I waited there a good minute before going inside.

Every time I came here, I knew the risk. Another chance to be nabbed by the authorities. To any outsider looking in, it must have seemed like I had a death wish.

The government was always watching. I believed Zander now. And I was about to make things a million times worse by talking to him, *again*. I counted on my book ruse being enough to fool them.

I mean, seriously, did they have nothing better to do than follow a sixteen-year-old girl around?

I really hoped that wasn't the case. But one thing was for certain, standing out here, looking like an idiot definitely drew unwanted attention. I quickly raced up the stone steps and opened the big, heavy door. The quiet hush inside contrasted mightily with the hustle and bustle of the street outside. It took me a minute to acclimate. The aroma of books soothed my frayed nerves. How I loved that smell. I cast a glance around. As usual, there were few patrons; I saw only one other person lingering by the stacks.

Knowledge was power, and the government liked to discourage their people from coming here. I spotted Zander over by the circulation desk, our eyes locked. He'd probably seen me as soon as I entered.

I walked over to him, pulling the bible he gave me out of the inner pocket of my jacket.

"Hey, Zander. I just stopped by to return this to you. It was really helpful, especially the passage you suggested. So...thanks."

Zander smiled at me. "No problem. Glad it helped."

"I hope you don't mind, but I underlined the section because it moved me so much. I can buy you a new one if it bothers you. Sorry," I grimaced. "I'm not sure what came over me."

GENEVIEVE CROWNSON

Zander waved his hand in a carefree gesture. "No worries, that's fine."

"Look at it first, before you agree," I said. "I put a bookmark in the page." My eyes sought out his, pleading with him to get my underlying message.

Zander provided no sign of understanding, his facial features remained consistently neutral. But I was good at reading people, and the sudden tenseness in his shoulders gave him away. He understood I wanted him to look inside.

"All right, if it will make you feel better," Zander replied in a disinterested voice. Casually, he opened to the page I'd book-marked. I saw him glance at the small paper tucked into the binding where I'd scribbled him one simple note last night.

I'm in.

"This looks perfectly fine. You shouldn't worry. In fact, I kind of like it highlighted." He gave me an encouraging smile. "But before you leave, I have a book I've just finished reading that I expect you will enjoy; it might take your mind off things. Let me go get it." He closed the bible and slipped it into his pants pocket before turning without a second glance in the direction of his office in the rear of the library.

It seemed like an eternity before he returned. I half expected an officer to come and take me away. It felt like my whole body twitched in trepidation—but you'd never know by looking at me. Heart thumping in my chest, I pretended to peruse a nearby shelf of books, running my fingers casually along the spines. My skin grew clammy but my face showed no emotion.

I supposed I needed to thank Mama for my skills in decep-tion. Before she'd shipped me off to this strange new universe, she taught me the art of appearing confident even in the worst situations. So far it had never steered me wrong.

The sound of returning footsteps broke me out of my reverie. I rarely allowed myself to dwell much on Mama, it made me too angry. And anything fueled by anger when trying to be covert led to serious mistakes.

"Here we are then," Zander said beaming at me as he handed me a blue hardback. I read the gold-lettered title on the spine and almost laughed out loud. If nothing else, this would further make this entire exchange believable. Zander was devilishly smart. Maybe I hadn't given him enough credit for being sneaky.

"Really? How is a book on gardening going to help me?" I grinned, like actually smiled for real for the first time in a long while.

Zander looked sheepish. "I figured it would be good to get your hands dirty, and enjoy the fresh air. It always helps me. And if that doesn't float your boat you can just study the pretty pictures of flowers," he smirked.

"Ha.Ha. All right fine. I'll try it."

"Excellent. Now make certain you read the passage on roses, there are some great tips on getting more blooms."

He turned serious again, and I understood the underlying message.

"Sure, I'll get right on that," I replied sarcastically, trying to keep up the charade. All I really wanted to do was rip open the book and find the section on roses where I was almost positive another note waited for me.

We politely said our goodbyes, and I consciously kept my pace slow and assured as I left the library, even though I wished to high-tail it out of there.

The walk back seemed interminably long, but it had been mere minutes on the clock. When I finally reached home, I exhaled a sigh of relief. Mission one accomplished. I checked in on Mom; she was still sleeping, so I softly tiptoed to my room and closed the door. I slipped off my coat and shoes and flopped on the bed, already tearing through the pages, trying to find the right section. I'd decided not to open the book in the street in case it brought undue attention.

Halfway through the text, I found the part on how to plant roses. Tucked in the crease was a tiny slip of stationery.

"Bingo," I whispered. With shaking hands, I plucked the

note from its home and unfolded the paper. Zander's now-familiar script stared back at me. *"Cemetery. Tomorrow. Midnight."*

I groaned. Why so long? I had already prepared myself for leaving. It was going to be a nerve-wracking twenty-four hours.

Still, at least the government hadn't issued Mom and I new phones yet, so they couldn't track me. It made me uncomfortable, though. I wondered about the delay. If they were so intent on observing me, you would assume they would have been on the ball about it. Perhaps Mrs. Lennor a.k.a Elia Watford was tailing me the old fashioned way. I shivered just thinking of it.

Tomorrow would be the day of reckoning.

I would find out the truth, even if it killed me.

CHAPTER 30

The moon lay hidden behind thin grey clouds and wispy streaks of moonlight filtered through the gaps, creating eerie shadows on the grass. The dim light accentuated the low-hanging tree branches that reached out like claws towards the granite grave-stones. I shivered, pulling my arms protectively around me, more from apprehension than cold. Tonight could all blow up in my face.

I was startled out of any further dire thoughts by a sudden sharp gust of wind that ripped my cap from my head. I made a lunge for it, but I was too late, it had disappeared into the black night. Annoyed I hadn't been paying enough attention, I impa-tiently swept back the dark strands that escaped from my pony-tail. I attempted to rein them in by tucking them behind my ear but to no avail. My hair was a wreck, and the hat was gone. Off to a good start.

I looked up and saw that the clouds were moving across the ominous purple sky at a furious clip. The leaves tumbled over my military-style black boots, as a large cloud covered the moon completely, casting me into inky darkness.

"Great," I muttered. "Just what we need, a storm." I cast a

quick glance around. *Where the hell was Zander? He'd better not be late.*

Without a flashlight, I struggled to make out the edge of the woods, mere feet from me. How on earth was I supposed to find him? Maybe if I knew this area and studied it—but there hadn't been enough time for that kind of prep work. A flash of anger shot through me as I thought about how much Zander was in charge of this little farce.

I had considered coming out here on my own. I remembered where the door was, after all. How hard could it be? I didn't need Zander for that. Feeling a bit more in control, I began to formulate a plan. I would head for the DRC via the woods, from there I'd...

I jerked back as a tight hand clamped down on my shoulder.

I whirled around, ready to pounce but a strong arm reached out and blocked me.

"Sshhh, it's only me, Luna," Zander whispered.

I dropped my stance, annoyed.

"What the hell, Zander? I told you never to sneak up on me like that," I hissed. I hastily shook him off. I'd always prided myself on knowing precisely when someone approached or lurked behind me, and it irritated the heck out of me that I hadn't heard him come up. After all, it was how I'd become such a good pickpocket.

"Sorry," Zander said giving me a lopsided grin. "My bad."

I grabbed the flashlight from him and turned it off. "You should only have this on in an emergency," I ground out the words between clenched teeth. "Unless you can't handle the dark," I smirked.

The barb spilled out of my mouth almost like a gag reflex, before I could stop them. But hey, I nearly had control of my situation and then he'd shown up like a bad penny.

"It's just a flashlight. Calm down."

My nostrils flared in anger. *Calm down? Who the heck did he think he was? The boss of me? Wasn't he the one who had acted all paranoid about being seen?*

Since I wasn't sure if we were alone or not, I bit my tongue and stomped toward the woods, not bothering to ask him if he was coming. He could go to hell for all I cared. I wanted to do this my way.

Zander ran after me to catch up. Which didn't take a lot. His strides were much bigger than mine. Sometimes being short was a real pain in the neck.

He touched my arm, and I yanked it back. "Come on, Luna. I'm sorry. I messed up, please forgive me."

I stopped walking; we were at the entrance to the woods now, and I barely made out his silhouette. He wore dark jeans and a black leather jacket that ran tight across his shoulders. It was annoying how good looking he was when he was being a jerk. I took a sharp intake of breath trying to cool down. The thick moisture in the air, now filling my lungs, had created patchy fog, especially around the low-lying sectors of the forest. To anyone with a big imagination, this would seem like a haunted wood. Luckily, I didn't take stock in all that nonsense. It was always best to stick with the facts and deal with what lay smack dab in front of you.

A flash of rare winter lightning zigzagged across the sky illuminating Zander's face, and the remorse etched across his features was apparent.

I breathed out a sigh. I had to let this go. My anger wouldn't solve anything. Besides, I needed to keep my eye on the prize. No matter who I had to bring along. I wasn't going to grovel, but I *may* have overreacted *a little*.

"Fine. I'm sorry too. Okay? Now let's kick some ass."

Zander's white teeth flashed, as he smiled into the darkness. But he instantly sobered and darted a quick glance around. "Come on," he whispered. "We need to get out of sight, we shouldn't talk here." He grabbed my hand and led me into the thick grove of trees. As he pulled me deeper into the woods, I noticed he was wearing a dark hoodie under his jacket that covered most of his hair. At least he'd been smart enough to cover it this time.

We walked along in silence, threading our way through the darkened forest. It took all my attention to navigate through it—especially since I'd dropped Zander's hand almost as soon as he picked it up. I regretted the decision now with the fog closing in, and his long strides making it difficult to keep the pace. If I was being honest with myself, his close proximity and occasional touch made my nerves crackle. Electricity sparked between us, but I didn't want to face that at the present moment.

Nothing could screw this up. Nothing.

Besides, hadn't I just decided he was an annoying tag along? Not to mention a potential pathological liar? I groaned. What was wrong with me?

Two steps ahead, Zander abruptly stopped and at first, I thought he'd overheard me groan. But when I looked up, I saw we were mere feet from the edge of the clearing. I hurried over and came up beside him, hands on my hips, surveying our target. Zander stretched his arm out, warning me not to go any further. I toyed with the idea of making a smart remark but decided against it. Instead, I gazed at the Dillinger Research Center which stood almost like a ghostly mirage, shadowed by the other buildings.

"We have to be careful, Luna," Zander said in a low voice. "I can't get inside to turn off security this time. They figured out someone had tampered with it when we were here before. As a result, they've beefed up security, both physically and on the internal server. The good news is that there's still only one camera near the front of the building. All we have to do is bypass that and make it to the back. Obviously, our chances of getting caught are a lot higher. Are you okay with this?"

He turned his gaze from the structure he'd been staring at to look at me in the semi-darkness.

"How do you know they've beefed up security?" I whispered.

"That's not important right now. All that matters is we make it to that secret door. Are you in?"

I made a mental note to interrogate Zander later—if we ever got out of here alive. For the moment, I just nodded my head in affirmation and Zander settled in to work.

I watched in fascination as he knelt down on the ground and pulled out a small device from his pocket, about half the length of a pen. He pressed down on one end and a tiny blue ring of light appeared at the tip. He pushed another smaller button on the side and a filter the size of a snowflake popped out and magnified the light into an arc in front of us. Curiosity got the better of me and I finally piped up, "What on earth are you doing? What is that thing?"

"You'll see," he whispered. "Watch."

He placed the device in his palm, light facing out, and somehow the cone grew wider and bigger. I gasped when a series of red webbed lines appeared around the buildings.

"Motion detectors," I whispered.

"Bingo," Zander said. "And we have to make sure we don't touch any of them or we will trigger their alarm. No problem, right?" He grinned at me to lighten the mood, but I wasn't having it. I'd done enough breaking in to know it would be suicide to mess with those. I crossed my arms and glared at him.

"Since when did they install motion sensors?" I growled. "You failed to mention that very important piece of information."

"I found them when I did some recon work last night. Once I received the rumors about the increased security, I figured I better go have a look. I'm glad I did." Zander shifted on his knees making more room for me. "Come closer, I want to show you something. It's not as bad as it looks at first glance."

He motioned for me to kneel beside him. I lowered myself down, and he tucked me under his free arm so we were fully lined up with his left hand, holding the device, the gadget still emanating the cone of light. "Won't they be able to see that blue light from the building?" I whispered.

"No," he grinned. "I like to think I have a few tricks up my sleeve. The illumination from this can't be detected through an indoor lens. Especially the tinted windows P8 is famous for. Neat, huh?"

"You're a great one for secrets," I muttered.

Zander ignored my cryptic comment and pointed toward the DRC building.

I tried not to dwell on the fact Zander held me so close I felt his body heat through my jacket. Instead, I focused on his words.

"If you look carefully, there are only four real lines criss-crossing the front expanse of grass. At first glance, it appears like there are many more. It makes me wonder why they needed a mirage for invisible motion sensors." He let out a soft low whistle. "These guys don't mess around. Anyway," he said, "if we stick to the perimeter, we should be fine. I planned a route yesterday. We can crouch down and go to the right side and stay out of the camera's viewpoint. It's the same one we saw hidden under the eaves before." He gestured to the roof.

I brought my gaze up to see the almost concealed camera nestled in the building's ridge, blending in perfectly with the aesthetics, like everything else. "Bastards," I muttered.

Zander continued, ignoring my sentiments. "Once we get to the back of the structure, it's only a matter of figuring out how to open that door."

I smirked at him through the darkness. "I might have an idea for that."

Zander raised his eyebrows in question. "Oh yeah? What is it?"

I stood up from my crouched position and shook out my tingly legs. "You aren't the only one with tricks," I boasted as I reached down and took out what I'd hidden in my left boot earlier that evening. I held out my hand to show him. It's shiny silver circumference shone brightly in my palm.

Zander leaned in to inspect it. "Wow, what is that?"

"I've been working on it all day. I didn't have much to work with, I had to cobble together a few things. But it will suffice. I used some stuff I discovered in Dad's office."

Zander continued to stare at it, confusion clearly showing on his face.

"It's a lock pick," I said, exasperated. God, this kid lived a sheltered life. Didn't everyone know what a lock pick looked like? Granted, mine appeared a bit handmade, but it would do the job. I'd learned a long time ago how to make tools out of practically nothing. I'd acquired some good hauls back on W1 with my inventions.

"This is incredible, Luna. I'm so impressed." He rubbed his thumb along its thin metal ridge and beamed at me proudly. My hackles rose, and I squirmed under his intense stare. Talk about awkward.

"It's not that big a deal. Are we ready?" I asked eager to extract myself from this uncomfortable moment. "Time to get this show on the road."

"Okay. Let's do it."

I nodded pocketing my lock tool, and joined Zander who had already crouched down to the ground. Slowly and with painstaking care, we crawled toward the DRC. Nervous sweat trickled down my back as we neared the security camera, its incessant whirring ringing in my ears. What if it sensed us and swiveled this way? We would be doomed for sure. Adrenaline fueled me to move faster, and I breathed a small sigh of relief as we moved past the surveillance unscathed.

Over the next five minutes, we managed to sidestep every booby-trapped line in our path and finally made it to the rear of the building safely—but we were still in danger. We had to get beyond the wall to access the mysterious door. We couldn't remove the brick and enter in the same manner we had the other day—and for good reason. Zander's handy pen had shown a motion detector right over that exact spot. Almost as if they knew that was how we'd broken in last time.

I cringed, a sour taste in my mouth. Perhaps they'd seen us. But if that was true, why hadn't we been arrested? Or worse, why hadn't they killed us?

Zander yanked on my sleeve, motioning that we needed to climb over the barrier.

Fan-freaking-tabulous.

It wasn't an impossible feat for Zander, who stood at least six feet tall, which I guessed the wall height to be. As for me...well... let's just say it would be a lot trickier. I was strong, that helped— and I could scale it if need be. I looked up at it and gulped. Or maybe not.

I appreciated the fact that Zander considered me capable, or he wouldn't have brought me here. And I was glad that he didn't deem me incompetent. I would have kicked his ass if he'd said I couldn't do it.

Zander placed a hand on my shoulder and stood stock-still, his eyes wide and alert as he checked our surroundings one more time. We both strained our ears, listening for the sound of guards. Nothing. I shook my head at Zander, letting him know I didn't hear anyone. As far as I was able to detect, the coast was clear.

Zander too, must have been satisfied, because he squatted down and crouched into position, cupping his hands together for me to step into so I could launch myself up the barricade. Knowing there wasn't a second to spare, I didn't hesitate. I placed my foot in his offered palms. Once my shoe was firmly in place, he hoisted me up and I grabbed at the flat brick. It was almost impossible to get purchase on the slick surface, but my strong fingertips dug into a small area where the slab had broken, and I got some traction. I pushed my right leg up, letting my boot rest on top, then slid myself up and over the divider, agile as a cat. Zander scrambled after me. Instinctively, I gravitated towards the safety of the periphery.

I'd expected to find the cavalry hiding behind the wall, waiting like silent soldiers to pounce. But the place was devoid of any human presence. I released a breath I didn't know I'd been holding. My eyes darted to the back exit. They had left it completely unattended.

Unease snaked up my spine. It seemed a little too easy. Shouldn't someone have caught us by now?

Zander came up behind me, whispering in my ear. "I'll keep a lookout while you see if you can pick the lock on the gate."

Anticipation coursed through me. I tried to control my excitement and forced myself to take slow, deliberate steps toward where I remembered the location to be. It took a minute for the door to appear, but at least it was quicker than before. I grinned as the shimmery outline of the entry came into view.

Time to unlock this bad boy.

I stealthily crept forward until I was almost on top of the door. Up close, I saw it was more of a golden color, like a gleaming pot of gold. My gaze fell to the bolt mechanism. It didn't look any different from a normal lock. In fact, its silver workings were rather ordinary compared to the gilded trim it was attached to. Honestly, I expected something a little more challenging. What if this was a waste of time? No. I shouldn't let my mind go there. Maybe they just didn't expect anyone on P8 to consider ever breaking and entering. After all, this door was never meant to be seen. That had to be it.

Before I was able to investigate further, footsteps pounded on the promenade. I froze. Soldiers. Headed this way.

I whipped my head around, fully expecting to see an agent coming at me with a gun. But it was Zander. He grabbed my hand and pulled me back into the protective shadow of the east side of the building. I didn't dare breathe as I watched two soldiers talking in the exact spot where I'd been standing only seconds ago.

"What did you see out here, Agent Rorry?"

"Movement, sir. The energy sensor picked up red and yellow colors which indicated something alive down here. Sir. Lieutenant Penn. Sir."

The agent, who must have only been a couple of years older than me, looked green around the gills. A thick sheen of sweat coated his forehead and his pale bloodshot eyes bulged out. His bulbous nose was as bright red as his protruding ears and he wore a white military-grade P8 uniform that lacked the code of colors of more experienced personnel. This was a newbie.

"There's nothing down here, Rorry. I hope you didn't bring me on a wild goose chase," Penn barked.

"No, sir. I'm sure, sir. Perhaps it was an animal."

"Don't contradict me, boy!" the Lieutenant yelled. "Scan the perimeter. Next time, I expect you to double-check all security breaches are valid before you bother me. Hurry up so we can go back inside. That's an order."

Penn puffed out his chest. He towered over Rorry in height and rank. He wore the same white uniform, but the left side of his lapel was covered in medals and colored stripes, indicating he was pretty high up the food chain. One of his medals caught my eye. A gold diamond shape, it stood out from the rest. I strained to see the strange symbol etched into the metal. An outline of a tree, its roots spread out and floating towards the very tip of the pendant. But there was more. Buried inside the roots was something else I had trouble making out from this angle, and I didn't dare move closer in case they spotted me. But it seemed familiar. Where had I seen that before?

The sound of Agent Rorry's voice jolted me out of my musings.

"Yes sir! Right away, sir!" Agent Rorry yelped, his Adam's apple bobbing furiously. I silently prayed for him to hurl his guts. That would be a perfect distraction.

But no such luck.

He was heading right for us.

Zander squeezed my hand so tight I thought my bones might snap. I licked my dry lips. *Think Luna, think.* We needed a disturbance and fast. If I didn't come up with something, we were about thirty seconds away from being caught. And then it would all be over.

I scanned our surroundings, desperate for an idea. We had nothing to work with. Unlike the terrain back home, there was nowhere to blend in. There wasn't a soul here. In fact, I was sure the agent heard my pounding heart. Rory swept his flashlight so near to us he almost clipped the edge of Zander's jacket. I held my breath as the beam moved away, heading in the other direction.

That was close. But fortunately, that one scan of light had given me an idea. On practiced silent toes, I took a step forward and reached down to pick up a large rock I'd seen in the torchlight seconds before. Zander tried to stop me, but I shook him off.

I knew what I was doing. Time to create a diversion.

I felt the jagged edges of the stone underneath my fingertips and gripped it in my palm. "Here goes," I whispered under my breath as I threw the object hard—it arched in the air; flying wide and long before landing with a clatter near the front of the building, far away from us.

The crash sent both men scrambling, and I ducked back to safety just in the nick of time. They bolted past us at breakneck speed, heading toward the noise.

"I told you there was something out here sir," the boy panted excitedly.

"Oh, shut up, you nitwit and start searching for the source of that commotion." He picked up his receiver as he ran. "Code red. I repeat, code red. Lockdown facility and proceed at high alert level ten until I command you to stand down."

The Lieutenant's voice faded away as he sprinted toward my decoy. Zander and I looked at each other, each thinking the same thing. If they put this place on lockdown, we were done for.

"Luna, we have to leave now. We can return later," Zander whispered, his breath hot on my cheek.

"Don't be stupid," I said in a low tone. "It's too late. We only have seconds until they activate code red. And that can't be good. Besides, I didn't come this far to chicken out. Caught or not, at least we'll know one way or the other what they're trying to hide. Come on." It was my turn to drag him along by the hand. I took a quick furtive look around, knowing I probably only had minutes until more guards appeared. But for this moment, we were alone.

"Let's get to the door, while the coast is clear," I instructed Zander.

He wavered uncertainly, but he didn't attempt to pull back. We were both willing to take the risk.

We made a beeline for the glimmering door and crouched down in front of it.

This would be a race against time.

The lock seemed to wink at me, as if daring me to open it. I reached out a shaking hand with a mix of fear and excitement. Adrenaline surged through my veins as my fingertips brushed against the metal surface. Instead of being solid as I expected, it became transparent to the touch, then suddenly disappeared. I stared, mouth agape, unable to comprehend what had just happened.

"Uh...Luna," Zander whispered poking me, "Look." I jerked my head up to see what Zander was pointing at. Where there had once been a door, was now a deep, swirling void. It reminded me of those images I'd seen the government post back home of the galaxy. Except there were no stars, only a blanket of rolling black.

"My God," I whispered.

"It's trying to suck us in," Zander exclaimed, grabbing for me.

I felt it, too. It took our combined strength to remain on solid ground.

"What is this?" Zander said looking at me, as we stepped back to safety.

"I don't know, but everything in me wants to go through it," I said.

"Me too."

"Luna, we have to think about this, we might—"

"I know. You don't have to say it out loud."

We could die jumping into an unknown, this could all be a trap, it could drag us out of P8 forever...there were so many possibilities. But what choice did we have? And what if wherever this ended up led to answers? Could we really walk away from that?

"We have to jump, Zander, there's no choice anymore. They will be here any second. It's either them," I pointed back to where the agent and lieutenant had gone, "or this black void. My money is on the void."

I tried to sound light, but Zander's eyes were serious. The wind around the opening picked up, and I wasn't sure how much longer it would stay accessible. That and the fact we were having trouble staying grounded. It seemed to me the decision had been made for us. A loud clap of thunder boomed, and the ominous sky above us unleashed a torrent of rain, soaking us both.

"Okay," he yelled over the storm's fury. "Let's do this." His eyes locked with mine. "On the count of three?"

I nodded, and he grabbed both my hands, holding them in a vice grip. I squeezed my eyelids shut and started to count. "One, two—"

"Wait!" My eyes flew open, looking to Zander. What was he doing? We were sitting ducks out here.

I opened my mouth to yell at him, but Zander placed a finger to my lips. "I have to do this first," he whispered.

"What?" I screamed, barely able to make out what he was saying over the now howling wind. Suddenly Zander bent down and kissed me. Taken aback, I had no time to go into defense mode. And I found myself tilting my lips up to his, eager for more. My body began to tingle with pleasure as he released my hands and grabbed my hips, gently pulling me closer, deepening the kiss. I didn't want him to stop. There was a longing between us, something achingly familiar. He trembled as he pressed against me. My heart raced, washing away all common sense. There was only Zander and I in this moment. As he leaned in even further, a sudden gust bulldozed into us, and we nearly toppled over, but at the last second Zander tightened his grip and righted us. He smiled impishly at me; eyes bright. "Well now, I guess that's our cue to move on."

Still reeling from the unexpected kiss, I had no words, but remembered our goal. I removed his hands from my waist and held onto them. I looked up at him and nodded, I was ready; however, my body was still a shaking wreck. If we ever made it out of here alive, I would deal with my pesky emotions then.

I was about to start the count again, but boots—more than two sets—pounded the pavement, heading in our direction.

"Jump!" I yelled to Zander.

And together we fell into the dark void.

ABOUT THE AUTHOR

Genevieve Crownson graduated from the College of Charleston with a Bachelors of Science degree. A love of writing led her to pen her debut novel, *The Soul of the Sun*, book one in her highly anticipated trilogy, The Argos Dynasty. She currently lives in beautiful Charleston, SC with her family and beloved four legged friends. You can find her at www.genevievecrownson.com or any of her social media sites @gcrownson.

ALSO BY GENEVIEVE CROWNSON

In the Argos Dynasty Series:

The Soul of the Sun

The Power of Alchemy

Ring of Fire

For free books, behind the scenes sneak peaks, special offers, plus other fun goodies join Genevieve Crownson's mailing list here:

www.genevievecrownson.com

www.ingramcontent.com/pod-product-compliance
Lightning Source LLC
Chambersburg PA
CBHW031725170626
46808CB00005B/1898